RETURN
OF THE MYSTIC GRAY

FROM THE AUTHOR OF
CRATER LAKE

RETURN
OF THE MYSTIC GRAY

FROM THE AUTHOR OF
CRATER LAKE

STEVE WESTOVER

SWEETWATER BOOKS
AN IMPRINT OF CEDAR FORT, INC.
SPRINGVILLE, UTAH

Other books by Steve Westover

Defensive Tactics
Gold Clash
Crater Lake

ISBN 13: 978-1-4621-1187-9

Published by Sweetwater Books, an imprint of Cedar Fort, Inc., 2373 W. 700 S., Springville, UT 84663
Distributed by Cedar Fort, Inc., www.cedarfort.com

LIBRARY OF CONGRESS CATALOGING-IN-PUBLICATION DATA

Westover, Steve, 1974- author.
Return of the Mystic Gray / Steve Westover.
  pages cm
Summary: Ethan, Jordan, Allie, and Brady return to Crater Lake to find their fallen friend, Jacob.
ISBN 978-1-4621-1187-9
1. Adventure stories, American. [1. Adventure and adventurers--Fiction. 2. Supernatural--Fiction. 3. Brothers and sisters--Fiction. 4. Indians of North American--Oregon--Fiction. 5. Crater Lake (Or.)--Fiction.] I. Title.
PZ7.W52712Ret 2013

                                2012050190

Cover design by Angela D. Olsen
Cover design © 2013 by Lyle Mortimer
Edited and typeset by Melissa J. Caldwell

Printed in the United States of America

10 9 8 7 6 5 4 3 2 1

CONTENTS

CONTENTS

CONTENTS

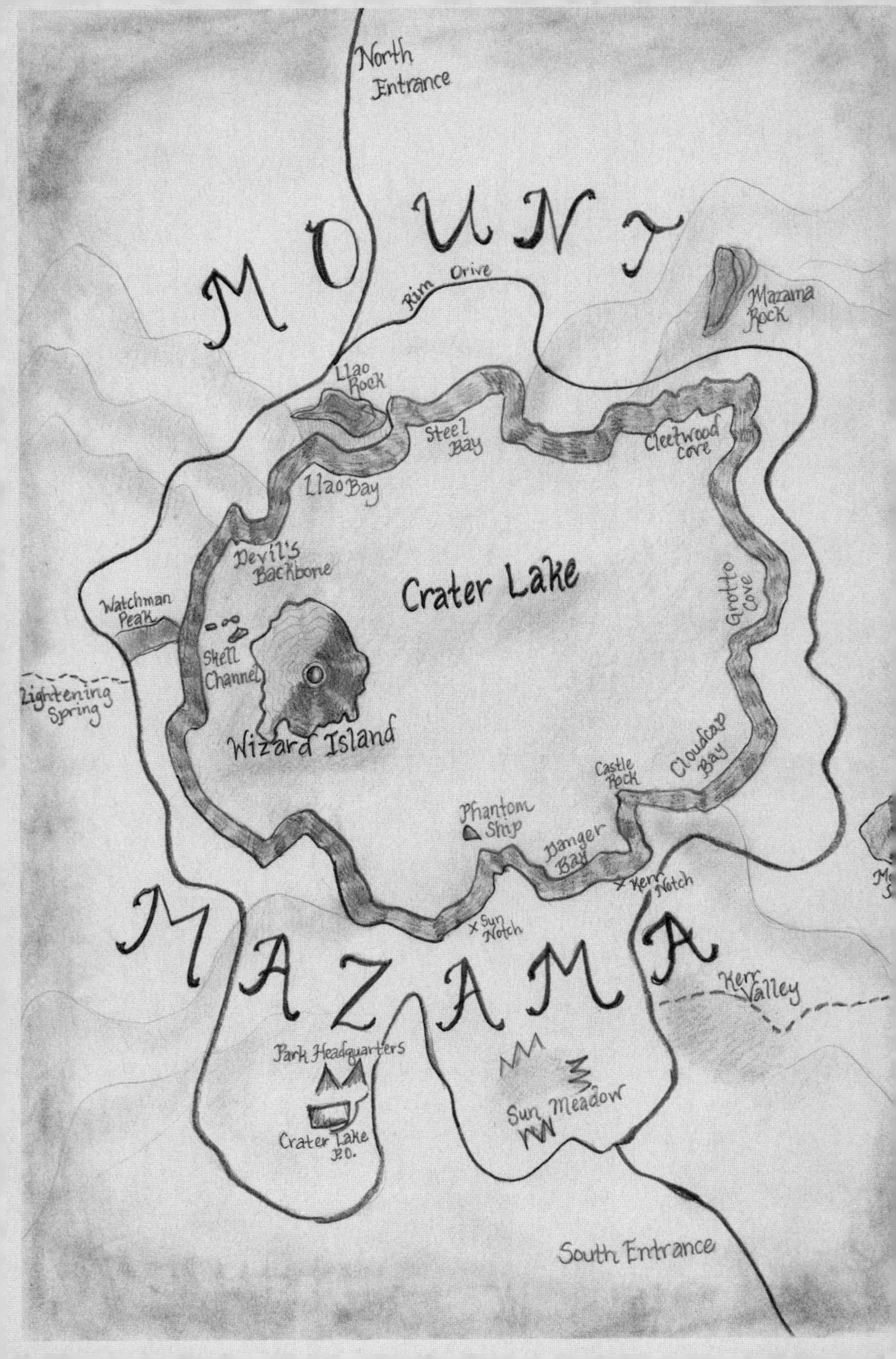
North Entrance
MOUNT
Rim Drive
Mazama Rock
Llao Rock
Steel Bay
Cleetwood Cove
Llao Bay
Devil's Backbone
Crater Lake
Grotto Cove
Watchman Peak
Shell Channel
Lightening Spring
Wizard Island
Castle Rock
Cloudcap Bay
Phantom Ship
Danger Bay
Kerr Notch
Sun Notch
MAZAMA
Kerr Valley
Park Headquarters
Sun Meadow
Crater Lake P.O.
South Entrance

BODYGUARD

ETHAN CLENCHED HIS JAW AND GROUND HIS TEETH AS HE stood in the darkness of Jordan's doorway. His little sister's sheets lay crumpled in the middle of the bed, and her pillow was on the floor. Her bed was empty . . . again.

After returning home from Crater Lake, his sister's nightmares had become a torturous combination of unrelenting and unpredictable torment. His parents lamented Jordan's constant hypochondria and moody behavior, but they didn't know how to help. They did their best to soothe her at first, but the therapist's instructions to "resist her manipulations" had caused them to act distant and uncaring. They thought they were helping, but it just made Ethan mad. No one at home could understand Jordan's suffering after the ordeal at Crater Lake—except him.

He'd been at the Crater Lake Ranger Station with his Uncle Bart when Jordan first saw the necklace of three interlocking round stones; the fiery red, sky blue, and clear glass stones mesmerized him just as they had entranced Jordan. Jordan's visions had started after she placed the ancient necklace over her head, and she hadn't been able to shake them since. At Crater Lake, the visions had guided Jordan to Wizard Island and into the lake to find the "Old Man," but at home they only managed to torment her, and Ethan couldn't determine any sense or purpose. After returning home from Crater Lake and the first nighttime incident when Jordan sleep-drove the four-wheeler around the corral, Ethan was determined to keep his sister locked safely inside her room at night. But he didn't always succeed.

Pulling on his boots, Ethan crept out his sister's window and began his search of the small farm. He traversed the tree-lined pathway to the corral as he followed Jordan's tracks in the frosty grass. Standing at the gate, he peered inside. The gentle lowing of cattle was soothing, but the frigid air caused Ethan to shiver. The sliver of moon provided little light and only added to the blackness of the night. Ethan felt like he was back in the black tunnel beneath Crater Lake.

"Jordan!" he whisper-shouted into the corral.

The only response came from a brown heifer that nuzzled up to the fence, looking for a scratch on the ears. Ignoring the cow, Ethan knelt to examine Jordan's tracks. She had definitely been here. He reached onto the orange, tubular cattle panel with both hands, climbed over, and walked into the pasture, his head swiveling as he searched for his sister. The heifer walked along-side for a few moments until Ethan relented and scratched her head. Seemingly satisfied with the ear rub, the cow peeled away and returned to her watering trough in the corner of the corral.

Passing through an open cattle barn that acted as a gateway to the back pasture, Ethan reached his hand out to touch the towers of square hay bales. Even in the dark, he was impressed with the staggering height and the tremendous amount of work it represented. Stacked against the interior walls of the barn, the hay rose unevenly, three and four bales thick. The silhouette reminded him of the nearby Kansas City skyline. Ethan smiled with satisfaction at the labor of his hands.

Staring into the darkness, Ethan couldn't see Jordan any-where. Only the faint shadows of roaming cattle stirred in the night. But then he heard the dull sound of buckling tin over-head. He stared up at the corrugated tin roof of the barn and then gasped when he detected movement on top. Stepping far-ther away from the barn to get a better view, Ethan strained his eyes. At the apex of the roof near the barn's edge, a figure stood, her feet straddling the steep pitch.

"Jordan, what are you doing up there?" Ethan hollered. The howl of feral dogs in the distance drew his attention away momentarily. But determining there was no danger, he refocused on his sister atop the roof of the barn. "Jordan! Come down, now!" he said. There was still no response.

Running back into the barn, Ethan climbed the stacked bales of hay. The higher he climbed, the more the bales wobbled beneath his feet as he transferred his weight from one stack to the next. Nearing the rafters, Ethan climbed onto the tallest bale of hay, but his foot slipped. He kicked against the stack, sending the hay tumbling two stories to the ground. Dangling from the rafter, Ethan swung his leg and pulled himself up.

He rose to his feet and prepared to walk across the beam like a tightrope acrobat, but then, deciding on a more cautious approach, he turned sideways and began inching his way across the beam while shuffling his hands along the angled truss for balance. Even in the dark, Ethan navigated the rafters with relative ease, stepping from beam to beam. He had navigated the rafters many times, but usually it was for daylight fun, not as part of some midnight excursion to rescue his nutty sister.

At the end of the rafter, Ethan pushed on a swinging door and climbed through to the outside of the barn. Placing his hands on the roof, he found a firm piece of wood siding and stepped on it. Once he found a handgrip, he pulled himself onto the roof. He crawled on all fours, the tin popping beneath him with each movement. Looking ahead, Ethan could see Jordan standing at the edge of the roof, calmly facing the darkened pasture and a thirty-foot drop. The contents of his stomach rumbled like a boiling pot of split pea soup as he thought about her proximity to death.

"Jordan, it's me. Be careful. I'm coming up behind you. Don't freak out or anything," he said evenly as he held out his hands in a calming motion. Jordan turned toward Ethan's voice but didn't acknowledge him. Instead, fear covered her face as she started to pant. "Don't do it, Jordan. Relax. I'm here. Don't move."

She turned back around, bent her knees, and leaned toward the edge of the barn, as if preparing to jump. Then she looked back at Ethan. She held her stomach, gulped, and screamed. "Stay away from me!" She looked over the edge again.

"Jordan, trust me. I'll get you down. Don't jump." Rushing up behind his sister, Ethan reached for her arm but couldn't grab hold. Then, he lunged forward and grabbed Jordan around the waist, pulling her away from the ledge. He placed his hands firmly on Jordan's shoulders as he turned her around to look at her. "Jordan, it's me."

Jordan's eyes opened wide with alarm. They darted from side to side and then up and down. Then she threw her hands around Ethan as she cried, "How did I get here?"

Ethan never bothered asking such questions because the answer was always the same . . . the visions. He shook his head and held her tight against his body as he shifted his feet into a wider stance. The tin buckled beneath him, and he peered over the side of the barn. He wanted to get her down, but she was still too emotional to concentrate on her escape. "It was just another vision, Jordan. Same as always. Everything's going to be just fine." He soothed her the best he could. "You're safe now, Jordan. It's all right." He rubbed her back and then placed his hand on her cold arm. "You're doing good. Everything is fine. Do you remember anything?"

Jordan remained quiet for a moment, and all Ethan could hear was her heavy breathing. He could feel her heart pounding against his chest as he held her close. Then Jordan took a deep breath and found her voice. "I was standing on the cliff above Crater Lake. The water was crystal clear. Blue. It shimmered in the sun. It was so pretty and warm."

"How'd you get there?"

"There was a gray wolf. He chased me. I had nowhere else to

go—" Jordan paused as another soft sob cut her words. "I was going to jump into the water to get away." She wiped her eyes and swallowed as she pulled her head away from Ethan's chest and leaned to look down into the pasture. Her feet shuffled backward, and her voice trembled. "I was going to jump, Ethan. I had to get away."

"From the wolf? Was it close?"

"I can't remember." Jordan's head cocked, and she looked to be deep in thought. "No. The wolf chased me there, but it wasn't the wolf I was afraid of."

"Then what?" Ethan could rarely understand Jordan's visions, and he had no real hopes of understanding this one. But the more he spoke, the calmer she became.

Jordan's weak voice became strong and angry. "It was Chief Llao. He was there. He called for me, but I only heard your voice. He reached for me and his fingers brushed against my arm." Jordan swallowed. "He tried to calm me. He smiled at me. He said, 'Jordan, it's me. Don't freak out or anything.' But I had to get away from him. He scares me."

Chief Llao—I hate that guy. Ethan cringed at the memory of the evil spirit chief who haunted Crater Lake. Then he considered Jordan's words. They were his words. He had said those things as he approached Jordan. The odd mixture of a false reality with real events confused him. "Don't worry about Chief Llao. He's one creepy dude, but he's nowhere near us," Ethan said. He waited for a moment as he studied his sister. "You doing okay? What do you say we get down from here?" he said calmly. He grabbed Jordan's hand to take her to the hatch leading into the barn.

"Wait. There's something else."

"Can you tell me after we get down?" Ethan looked at his sister but relented when it appeared arguing about it would take more time than listening. "What is it?"

Jordan bit her lip and then looked up at Ethan with a smile on her face. "The wolf just sat on the ground behind Chief Llao."

"Yeah, so?"

"When I looked back, the gray wolf was gone, and I saw . . . I saw . . ."

"Jordan, what did you see?"

Jordan grinned again. "I don't know what it means, but I saw Jacob. He was sitting where the wolf had been. He was fiddling with his glasses, and then he waved that goofy, Australian-style cowboy hat at me." Her smile broadened. "It seemed so real. He seemed real. I miss him, Ethan."

Ethan fought away the emotion as he remembered Jacob's death at Crater Lake. "Yeah, me too."

Jordan relaxed, and her breathing slowed. "What do you think the vision means? Do you think Jacob could be alive?" Jordan asked.

Ethan shook his head, wishing it were possible but knowing it wasn't. "Come on. Let's get down from here." Ethan felt the December wind blowing across his bare arms, and he smelled the familiar mixture of chilled cow manure and hay. It was stinky, but it was home. He grabbed his sister's hand as they straddled the steep tin roof.

"I think it means something, Ethan," Jordan said as they walked. "I think Jacob is out there. I think he's alive," she said.

Ethan shook his head. "The visions will fade. Just give it time." He squeezed her hand as he led her to safety.

When they returned to the house, Jordan lay down while Ethan tucked her in bed. Then he gathered a few things from his room. He laid a sleeping bag in front of her window and hung metallic chimes from a hook on the ceiling directly in front of her door. He tied a tripwire around the doorknob, through the chimes, and across the floor in front of Jordan's bed. If another crazy vision tried to lure her from the room, Ethan would be there to protect her. As a final preparation, Ethan set his alarm so he could be out of Jordan's room before his parents awoke. Not that he really needed an alarm. He didn't sleep anymore. Ever.

"Just in case," Ethan whispered. He smiled at his sister and then inched his way into his sleeping bag. "Suspicious parents are bad enough. Worried parents are a nightmare."

Jordan scowled, and a whisper of breath escaped from her lips, but she didn't respond. Ethan shifted in his sleeping bag and adjusted his pillow.

"Ethan, why am I still having these visions? What do they mean?" Jordan asked.

Ethan shrugged. He had no idea.

"I mean, at Crater Lake the visions helped, but I gave the necklace back to Uncle Bart when we left. I gave it back to him, Ethan," she repeated, shaking her head. "Why is this happening to me? Am I going crazy?"

Kneeling next to Jordan's bed, Ethan placed a hand on her head. "Listen, I don't know why this is happening, but you're not crazy. Come on, you need some sleep." Ethan pulled her covers up to her chin.

Lying on the floor, Ethan opened his backpack and pulled out four thick books. He hadn't slept since returning from Crater Lake. It had bothered him at first, but not anymore. Not sleeping gave him more time to read. He read textbooks, scholarly writings about Native American culture and legends, novels, and even encyclopedias. And he remembered everything. Clipping a reading light onto the cover of his book, Ethan began his night-time ritual.

Things would never be the same; Ethan knew that now. He looked up at Jordan as she closed her eyes and adjusted her position. Ethan licked his finger and turned to page one of his first book of the night.

PYROMANIA

ETHAN PLACED HIS BOOKS IN THE BAG, REMOVED THE booby-trap alarm he'd hung in front of Jordan's door, put away his sleeping bag and pillow, showered, dressed, and had breakfast cooked before his mom entered the kitchen. She rubbed her eyes and forced a grin when she noticed the table was set and the food was prepared . . . again. "Morning, Mom," Ethan greeted, barely looking up from his *Conservationist* magazine. His eyes raced up and down the columns, reading and remembering every word. He flipped the page and continued his speed-reading.

His mom fluffed her wild hair as she yawned. "Hmmm. That looks thrilling," she joked, pointing at Ethan's reading material. His gaze paused as he looked up, and then he was off again. He turned the page with an efficient flip.

"You might be surprised." Ethan watched his mom shake her head. She looked doubtful. "For example, did you know that by 1926, wolves had been extirpated from Yellowstone National Park, and in 1966 the gray wolf was one of the first species listed as endangered?" Ethan looked at his mother, hoping for a sign of interest. But her eyes were glazed. He knew that look well.

She muttered only one word. "Extirpated?"

Ethan breathed in slowly as he prepared to explain, but his excitement to share had diminished. "It means local extinction.

They began reintroducing wolves to Yellowstone in 1995, and . . ."

Mom's voice rose to match her eyebrows as she pulled out a chair and sat. "Oh. That's really something. So what's for breakfast?"

She had changed the subject, like always. Ethan sighed and then answered, "My specialty, of course."

"Eggs again?" Jordan whined as she entered the kitchen. Her tight curls bounced as she skipped. She showed no ill effects of her nighttime excursion. "I want pancakes."

Ethan's eyes rose above his magazine. He flipped the page as he stared at his little sister. "Then make them."

Jordan looked at the eggs. Then she looked at the fridge and the stove and decided to sit. Scooping some eggs onto her plate, she made a face as she took her first bite. "I want pancakes."

Ethan smirked and ignored his sister.

The phone rang, but no one at the table budged. Ethan lowered his magazine and looked to the wall, but as usual the cordless was nowhere to be seen. The phone continued to ring, begging for someone to pay attention. But Mom only looked at her watch and grumbled something about the time and how it's rude to call so early. Jordan shoved another bite of eggs into her mouth to escape any expectation that she would need to get up to answer. The harsh rattle of the phone polluted the morning peace until Dad whisked into the room, cinching the knot in his tie. He brushed through some papers on the counter until he uncovered the phone. Looking at the display, he pressed the "Answer" button and immediately handed it to Mom as he bent over to kiss Jordan on the forehead. Grabbing a handful of eggs, he placed it between two plain pieces of bread, grabbed his satchel, and waved to Ethan as he ran out the French doors to work.

"Hello?" Mom said into the receiver. Ethan grinned at the sudden sweetness and alertness in his mother's voice. He watched her brow furrow and a light scowl cover her face. "Sure, of course I remember you." She glanced at her watch again.

"Mom, who is it?" Ethan asked, butting in.

Mom waved his question aside. Standing, she rounded a corner and walked into the other room, but not before Ethan heard her say, "Allie." A smile covered his face as he remembered the cute cheerleader that had shared his Crater Lake adventure last summer. Creeping to the corner between the kitchen and the living room, Ethan leaned against the wall and strained to hear.

"Ethan, that's not very polite," Jordan accused.

"Shhh." He leaned his ear closer to the corner and listened to his mother's half of the conversation, but with Jordan jabbering as an intentional distraction, he only picked up pieces. He heard his mother gasp, and it sounded like she apologized. But then she got defensive, and then she apologized again.

"Ethan, what's she saying? Who's on the phone?" Jordan asked from her seat.

"Be quiet. Mind your own business." Ethan closed his eyes and concentrated as he listened. Then he felt a tickle on his arm. Opening his eyes, he saw Jordan pressed up against him with her curls dangling across his elbow.

Jordan looked at Ethan, grinned, and then spoke loudly. "Mom. Ethan's listening to your call."

Covering his sister's mouth with his hand, Ethan tried to listen but yelped as he felt sharp pressure on his finger. He removed his hand from Jordan's mouth and examined the teeth marks in his skin. "You little . . ." Ethan stopped as his mother strode back into the kitchen with a blank expression. "What is it, Mom? What's wrong?" He followed her back to the table and waited impatiently. His mother took a bite of food and chewed slowly. "Mom?"

"Do you remember Allie?" his mother asked. Jordan's eyes lit up at the mention of her friend, and Ethan instantly started to blush. "That was Allie's mom."

Ethan's loose curls bounced as he shook his head. "So, why is she calling?"

"Their house burned down last night," Mom said stoically. Jordan gasped. "Is Allie okay?"

Mom bit her lip. "Well, no." Ethan's eyes widened with alarm as his mother continued. "She's missing. Allie got out. She climbed through her window and onto the roof, and then slid down the gutter downspout. She gave her mom and dad a hug after they escaped from the house, but then she disappeared."

"Disappeared? What do you mean 'disappeared'?" Ethan asked.

"And they think you know where she is," Mom added. "Ethan, I told Allie's mom you couldn't have any way of knowing where she is. You haven't spoken to Allie in months, right?" Ethan's head lowered as his mother held out her hand. "Let me see your phone."

Jordan stared as Ethan handed over his phone. He watched in silence while his mother scrolled through his contacts list and then did a quick review of his saved texts. "We text sometimes. It's no big deal." Ethan shriveled under his mother's glare. "But I don't know where she is. I promise. I'd tell you if I did. Why wouldn't I?"

Mom's eyes shifted from Ethan to Jordan and back to Ethan again. "Allie's mom thinks you might be trying to protect her. That's why."

"Huh?"

"Mom, that makes no sense. How would keeping Allie's location a secret protect her?" Ethan asked.

"Ethan, they think Allie started the fire, and they think she did it on purpose."

– 3 –

DRAGON BREATH

ALLIE SOBBED, BUT SHE DIDN'T HAVE ANY MORE TEARS. Her eyes had dried out hours ago, sometime between the inferno that engulfed her home and the first rays of desert daylight. Huddled in a large concrete tube near a spillway at the edge of town, she sat with her knees held tight to her chest. Winter nights get cold—even in Vegas. Rubbing the goose bumps on her arms, she shivered as she replayed the night's fiery events in her mind. She didn't mean to do it. She didn't even understand how she had. The flames had erupted from her mouth without warning. No. That can't be true. Something had to have caused it.

Closing her eyes, Allie concentrated on each moment leading up to the fire. She had just changed into her pajamas and threw her clothes on the floor next to her bed. Then what? She thought harder. Next, she had stepped toward her dresser and felt a stab at the center of her bare foot. Looking into the mirror, she clenched her jaw as she tried holding back the profanity. But it felt like a rusty nail had been driven through her foot. She looked at the floor and saw the keys she had stepped on. The pain shot through her foot and up her leg. Her eyes bulged, and then she opened her mouth to let out a pained scream . . . but then it happened.

Instead of sound, flames had shot from her mouth. The blaze rolled along the wall and then up the ceiling until it consumed the entire room. Allie wiped her eyes and shook her head at the memory. "Pure craziness," she muttered.

Holding her legs tighter, Allie thought about Ethan and Jordan, Brady and . . . her head shook again. "Jacob," she whispered. Her thoughts seemed random. As hard as her mind strained, she couldn't trace the connection between the fire at her home and her friends from Crater Lake. Why would she think of them now? Then she thought of the flute and was instantly awash with images of a campfire on the shore of Crater Lake and memories of her battle on Wizard Island blasting zombies with fire and ice. She loved the powers of that flute. She had missed it . . . until now.

A smile crossed her lips for the first time since before her house burned. She thought of the flute that had given her such extraordinary power in defeating the ghouls on Wizard Island: the blinding light, the gusts of wind, the fire, the ice. She didn't have the flute anymore. It now lay somewhere at the bottom of the deepest lake in the United States, but . . . Allie thought for a moment and then scooted out of the concrete pipe and down a slight ramp until she was standing in what felt like a dry concrete river bed. She spun in place, looking at her surroundings. When she was certain no one else was around, she began her experiment.

Allie thought about fire. She tensed her muscles, opened her mouth, and envisioned an explosion of heat blasting outward, but nothing happened. Wondering what went wrong, she stood with her mouth agape until she realized how stupid she must look. She hunched her shoulders and tried again, this time with a minor variation. Lifting her foot, she kicked her toe into the concrete to mimic the pain from stepping on her keys. The pain welled inside her. She held it back and then opened her mouth to scream. Flames poured out and shot toward the tube where she'd spent the night. The flames were bigger than anything she'd seen with the flute, and the sight terrified her. She tried closing her mouth to muffle the scream and quench the flames, but her mouth was locked open, and the blaze continued blasting outward. Allie concentrated. She thought only about the fire and ignored the pain in her foot. After a moment, she closed her mouth and the flames disappeared.

"Whoa!" Allie licked her lips expecting to feel warmth from the blaze that had passed through them, but they were cool. The only residue from the fire was the odd aftertaste of Tabasco deep in the back of her throat. She belched and made a face as the flavor overwhelmed her for a moment.

Glancing down at her purple plaid pajama pants and flip-flops, she knew she needed to change into something warmer. She wanted to go home, but there was no home anymore. Everything was gone—her clothes, pictures, diary, cell phone, computer, everything. And it was her fault.

Allie's shoulders slumped as she thought about her parents. They must hate her. In one moment, she'd destroyed everything they had spent a lifetime building.

Allie climbed the steep concrete slope and stood in the decorative pebbles along the sidewalk. Holding her arms to cut the chill, she walked slowly out of the barren cul-de-sac and looked longingly in the direction of her destroyed home just a couple of short miles away. In a few blocks, she was out of the residential housing area and near a busy street. With a deep breath, she held out her arm and extended her thumb.

At sixteen, her life was just beginning and ending all at once. She could never go back.

4

THE WORST PARENT EVER

We're going to be late for school." Ethan looked at his mother across the coffee table. Instead of signaling her defeat, she leaned back, set the phone on the sofa beside her, and then crossed her arms and legs, ready for a standoff. "Mom, I have a test." They stared at each other, and Ethan crossed his arms to match her resolve. "It's important."

Mom's eyes narrowed. "I want the truth, Ethan. Don't think I won't ground you just because tomorrow's your birthday." She uncrossed her legs and leaned forward with her forearms resting on her knees, her hands clasped together. "I need to know. You got a text from Allie last night. Where. Is. She?"

"Ground me?" Ethan scoffed. He turned away from his mother and toward his little sister. Jordan sat on the love seat beside him, but she didn't appear to be engaged with the conversation. Normally, she found great pleasure any time Ethan got busted. But today she looked straight ahead, staring at a blank spot of wall beneath a family portrait. The emptiness in her eyes was all too familiar to Ethan. "Jordan!" he whispered harshly, hoping to pull her from her trance. She didn't respond.

"You'd better believe it, Ethan," Mom continued. "Grounded: from school, books, any reading material whatsoever. I'll do it," she threatened.

Reaching over to Jordan, Ethan placed his hand on hers.

She blinked slowly. He exhaled and then glared at his mother. His voice took on an edge that instantly raised his mother's eyebrows. "Grounded from school and books? You realize that makes you the worst parent *ever*."

Mom smiled. "I can live with that."

Ethan rolled his neck slowly, eliciting a series of cracks. He took a deep breath and glanced out the window to see if the bus was there. "I can't miss this test. I told you, I don't know where Allie is. That's the truth."

"Fine. Then tell me what this text means." Mom read the text Allie sent last night. "Dagger boy AWOL. Dad n hospital☺"

Ethan shook his head. "I didn't even see that until this morning."

"What's it mean?"

Running a hand through the side of his fluffy hair, Ethan shrugged as he thought about his friend from Crater Lake. In many ways, Brady was just a big bully. But after all they had been through together, Ethan still considered him a friend. "I think it means that Brady ran away again. Maybe his dad got hurt or something. I don't know. He lives in Oregon. I don't really talk to the guy."

"What's that have to do with Allie and the fire?" Mom asked.

"Excellent question!" He paused. "I don't have a clue." Ethan peeked at the time on his phone's display, and then his head lurched up as he heard the squealing brakes from the bus out front. He turned in his seat and stared out the window. He watched with surprise as Jordan stepped calmly into the road in front of the bus and climbed in. Ethan hadn't even noticed she'd left the love seat. She was sneaky that way. He saw her backpack sitting on the floor at the corner of the love seat. "She forgot her bag. Can I take it?" Ethan asked excitedly as he stood. Mom shook her head, and Ethan slumped back into his seat as the bus pulled away from the curb. Holding his neck with his right hand, he looked again at the time on his phone.

"It's troubling," she said.

"What's troubling?"

"That two of your friends ran away yesterday: one after putting his dad in the hospital, and the other after lighting her house on fire."

"Oh yeah. That."

Ethan's phone buzzed and shimmied briefly on the cushion next to his mom. She pretended not to notice, but Ethan could tell it was killing her almost as much as him not to look. Then Ethan leaned to look at the display. The phone buzzed again, and Mom picked it up, but the screen only displayed "unknown caller." The text read, "☺".

Mom smiled. "It looks like that could be our girl. Let's give her a call and find out where she is so her parents can stop worrying."

"Then can I go to school?" Ethan asked. She nodded. "Good. Give me that thing," Ethan said, reaching for his phone. He pressed a couple of buttons and waited as the phone started to ring. Finally, there was an answer on the other end.

The voice was shaky. "Ethan, is that you?"

5

SCHOOL BUS HIJACK

THE HEAVILY ACCENTED VOICE ON THE OTHER END OF THE call was unfamiliar to Ethan, but he responded with assurance. "Yeah, this is Ethan." His mother leaned her ear close to his so she could hear the conversation.

"This is Maria. I have a question about our homework. Can you talk?"

Ethan's eyes scrunched as he concentrated on the voice. His mind raced to recall anyone in any of his classes named Maria, but he couldn't come up with anything. "I can't talk right now. I'm about ready to leave my house. But we can talk when I get to school." He looked at his mother with a disappointed look on his face.

"Okay. I'll talk to you later." The call ended.

Ethan looked at his mother. "Sorry. It wasn't Allie." He waited for a moment as he and his mother both slumped back into the sofa. "Can I go now? If I hurry, I can beat the bus."

The corner of Mom's lips curled down as she nodded. "Get going."

Ethan jumped up and shoved the phone in his pocket. He picked his winter coat off a hook near the door, zipped it up, grabbed his bag, and opened the door. "Don't worry, Mom. I'll let you know if I hear from Allie, and you can check my phone after school."

"Agreed."

***

Ethan chained his bike to the rack at the front of the school and waited just outside the entrance. He watched his breath rise from his mouth like the exhaust from the school buses that began cresting the hill in front of the school. Pulling out his phone, he redialed Maria's number. He held the phone next to his ear inside his hoodie. He heard a click on the other end of the line and waited nervously for someone to speak. When the line remained silent, he began. "Is this Maria?"

"Yes."

Ethan cleared his throat. "Who are you?" He heard a shuffle on the other end of the call, and then he heard the familiar voice of a friend.

"Ethan, it's me—Allie."

Ethan's shoulders rose, and then a relieved plume of breath escaped his mouth. He listened to silence for a moment until he figured out what to say. "Allie, are you okay?" He heard a soft cry on the other end of the phone. Asking his first question unplugged the dam, and his questions gushed out so rapidly that he didn't give Allie time to respond. "Who's Maria? What happened to your house? Did you start the fire? Where are you?" He listened to Allie cry, and then his voice softened as he asked one more question. "Is there anything I can do to help?"

The buses started lining up along the curb, and students trekked into the cold, past Ethan on their way into the middle school. Even in the morning when they'd rather be sleeping, the students had a lot to say. The sound of chattering tweens and teens made it hard for Ethan to hear Allie's voice. He lowered his head and covered his other ear, concentrating on Allie's answers. But the ruckus of unloading students was too loud, and then a twelve-year-old boy knocked into him after being shoved by a friend. Ethan struggled to hear as he kept one eye on the last bus in the line. Then, one answer pierced the middle school rumble.

"I did it, Ethan. I don't know how, but I did it."

Ethan stood, stunned. The noise in front of the school seemed to float above him until it disappeared. He felt a sudden and overwhelming sadness. The power of the emotion enticed him to curl up and hide from the world. It was powerful but didn't seem rational. Ethan held the phone in front of his eyes as if he could detect a lie in it. He couldn't believe Allie would do such a thing, and he didn't know what to say.

Allie continued between sobs. Though he could hear Allie try to explain, Ethan refused to let her excuses enter his brain. The buses in the caravan pulled away, heading next to the grade school around the corner. But the final bus in the caravan, his bus, inched forward and then stopped. He watched for Jordan in the window, but he couldn't see her.

The folding bus door swung open with a crash. Then grade school kids filed down the steps clutching their backpacks as they scurried off with looks of confusion and fear stamped on their faces. Ethan jolted upright and watched the unusual scene. Once all the kids had run from the bus, the driver also exited. Ethan had been riding Ms. Blanchard's bus for years, and he knew her well, but he'd never seen panic in her eyes like he saw now. Ethan scanned the frightened children for his sister, but he couldn't find her. Then the bus door closed, and once again the bus started inching forward. Ethan couldn't imagine what could have caused the kids and bus driver to flee from the bus, and he didn't know who could possibly be driving. "Jordan?"

"Ethan, are you listening to me?" he heard Allie yell into the phone. He looked at the receiver again and then placed it to his ear.

"Allie, something's wrong. I've got to go. I'll call you back." Ethan hung up, shoved the phone into his pocket, and ran through the grade schoolers to get to the bus. Looking through the door window, Ethan could see Jordan standing behind the wheel. She stared straight ahead, dazed in another visionary trance. Ethan gulped. Jordan's visions had made her do plenty of crazy things in the past, but she had never put others at risk.

The danger always seemed content to attack Jordan and Jordan alone, until now. Ethan slammed his fist on the door as he ran alongside the bus, but Jordan didn't flinch. She faced forward with a blank stare. The pounding in Ethan's chest echoed his pounding fist on the bus. He fell behind as the bus picked up speed but continued thumping the yellow metal of the bus until it passed him fully. Then, he kept racing after it. The bus slowed at the stop sign exiting the campus, and Ethan was thrilled that, despite Jordan's entranced hijacking, she seemed to be abiding the traffic laws.

Ethan pumped his legs as fast as he could, and he made up ground as the bus made a sharp turn to the left at the stop sign. Reaching for the back of the bus, Ethan stretched his arm and grabbed the handle on the rear emergency door. The bus accelerated. "JORDAN! STOP THE BUS!" Ethan screamed, but the bus continued to accelerate until his feet couldn't keep up. He could either hang and drag behind like a rag doll, or he could let go and give up, which would likely earn a few bruises and scrapes. Ethan refused to accept those options.

The toes of his shoes scraped along the pavement as his grip on the emergency door handle began to slip. Kicking one leg up onto the bumper, Ethan lifted himself off the road. He lifted his other leg and crouched on the rear bumper as the bus sped along. He was committed and couldn't let go. The toes of Ethan's shoes clung to the bumper as he scooted to the far side of the emergency door. He pressed down on the handle, but it didn't budge.

Ethan pried his hand in between the frosty handle and the door. He looked back at the school, hoping to see some adult give chase. But no such luck. Now, it was simply a matter of waiting to find out where Jordan was going. The bus made a series of sharp zagging turns through town as it sped forward. Ethan hoped someone would come looking for them, but even he couldn't tell where he was any longer. *Are we going back to the house? Or maybe to a fast food joint to pick up a breakfast burrito?* Ethan doubted the last one, but there was no telling. Guessing was pointless because he was *always* wrong when it came to Jordan's visions. Three things were certain: he was stuck on the bus until it stopped, Jordan was really going to get it for this fiasco whether it was her fault or not, and his final destination was bound to be a surprise.

Ethan shivered against the bitter December wind. "I hate surprises."

– 6 –

MYSTERY FLIGHT

ETHAN'S KNUCKLES LOOKED LIKE A BLOCK OF ICE THAT HAD been hit with a hammer. The white skin split and fractured in a web of freezing pain, but he couldn't let go of the door handle. He could hardly wait to get to wherever Jordan was driving. *Anywhere will be fine*, he thought; *no, anywhere with heat*. Burying his face into the elbow of his jacket, he breathed into his arm and enjoyed the momentary warmth that spread across his cheeks and nose. But the heat quickly disappeared, so he exhaled more warm breath that blanketed his face. After what felt like miles, Ethan lifted his head to see where he was, but the frigid air froze the moisture on his face and the snot dripping down his lips. The scenery was unfamiliar, and he wondered when he would arrive. He didn't have to wonder long.

The bus slowed as it turned off the rural blacktop road and into a deserted parking lot at the front of several large metal buildings. Some buildings were expansive—long, tall, and wide—while others looked to be the same size as the hay barn at home. The bus squealed to a stop, and then he heard the door open. Ethan's mind told him to move, but his body wouldn't listen. His knees were frozen in place against his chest, and the handle seemed to be permanently connected to the palm of his hand. Willing himself to step down from the rear bumper of the bus, Ethan could hear his muscles creak and his tendons stretch.

"Jordan!" he called out, but his weak voice only mingled with the swirling wind. Shuffling around the corner of the bus, Ethan scanned the area, searching for Jordan. He wiped the sleeve of his coat against his watering eyes as he turned in place. "Jordan, where are you?"

A small figure walked briskly in between two of the large buildings and then disappeared. Ethan sniffled and then plodded along to chase after his sister. *Just like at Crater Lake*, he thought. *Stupid visions.* After walking between the buildings, Ethan turned left. He found a door but stopped when he heard the sound of rolling metal wheels. He took a step back and stared upward as a large hangar door rolled open. He tried peering inside, but the interior of the hangar made it too dark to see. Stepping to the center of the large door, Ethan walked into the darkness as the deafening roar and harsh wind of dual propellers assaulted him.

Moving out of the reach of the wings and propellers, Ethan's jaw dropped as he saw Jordan sitting in the pilot seat. He blinked once, and then his jaw sagged further. "JORDAN!" The plane began taxiing out of the hangar, and Ethan considered whether he would survive another chase. He shook his head as he assessed the possibility of hanging onto a door handle while crouching on the wing. Exterior travel on a bus is one thing, but on a plane? No chance. Ethan's usual worry and concern for Jordan changed instantly into anger. His muscles tightened, and he screamed with everything he had inside. But the commuter plane taxied forward without hesitation.

The sound of a man cursing over loudspeakers echoed across the small airport, but Ethan kept chasing after Jordan. He figured the man's command to stop was targeted at Jordan, not him. Running up from behind the plane, Ethan searched for a door on what he thought was the passenger's side, but there didn't appear to be any way in. He shifted his run to follow on the driver's side when he noticed a latch near the back of the plane behind the wing. He chased after the plane and grabbed the latch as Jordan taxied onto a strip of pavement that connected the hangars to the runways. As Ethan pulled on the latch, the door fell open, and three steps crashed down, scraping the pavement before bouncing back into their intended position.

Grabbing onto the wire that connected the top and bottom of the door, Ethan hopped onto the step and climbed into the rear cabin. The wind gushed outside, and the steps scraped against the pavement as the plane accelerated. Ethan quickly pulled the door closed and locked it in place before turning his attention to his sister at the front of the plane.

Ethan shook his head. The sound of the propellers increased, and the plane lurched forward as it began speeding down the runway. He braced himself with his hands against the back of a beige leather seat and then worked his way toward Jordan until he stood directly behind her. Reaching forward, he prepared to place a hand on her shoulder to pull her from whatever vision she was experiencing, but before he could make contact, she slammed the throttle down and yanked up on the pitch control. The nose of the plane lifted, and the wheels rose from the ground. Jordan pulled back further on the control, pointing the nose in a steep trajectory. Tumbling, Ethan set his feet and tried bracing himself. But when Jordan maneuvered the aircraft into a sharp turn, Ethan lost his hold on the seat and fell backward, somersaulting through the aisle with his feet over his head until he crashed against the back of the cabin.

The last thing Ethan remembered was the buzz of his cell phone. Then, everything went black.

-7-

A RENO STATE OF MIND

ALLIE CLIMBED OUT OF MARIA'S BLACK HONDA MINIVAN and stepped onto the sidewalk in front of a strip mall. She held her arms and shivered, surprised that Reno could be so much colder than Vegas. She looked at the building behind her, and then turned around and hunched over so she could see Maria through the open passenger door. She smiled at Maria, waved, and then closed the door. She heard the sound of the window lowering, so she hunched over again and rested her arms on the door.

Maria smiled but her eyes expressed worry. "Are you sure you want me to leave you here?" she asked in her thick accent. "When will your brother be here to pick you up?"

"Yes. Thank you, Maria. I'm sure he'll be here soon," Allie lied.

"Would you like to wait at my home?" Maria asked, but Allie just shook her head to decline. Maria's smile turned into a frown. Grabbing her purse from off the floor between the two front seats, she rummaged around and pulled out her wallet. "Let me at least give you some money for dinner. You know, in case Ethan is late."

Allie shrugged away the offer. "You've been kind enough. Thank you."

"No. You take it," Maria said with some sharpness. She

26

shoved her hand toward the window. Allie was hesitant, but she reached in and took the cash. "My prayers will be with you, Allie."

Allie nodded and then watched as the window rolled up and Maria drove away. Turning around, Allie studied the storefronts and then looked at the cash in her hand. She quickly counted the cash and gasped when she realized she had eighty-five dollars. "That will be some awesome dinner," Allie mumbled. She reassessed the storefronts and then chose her first stop, but she wasn't hungry.

Thirty minutes later, Allie emerged from the thrift store wearing shoes, socks, jeans, a heavy sweatshirt, and a puffy silver winter coat. She made her way to a dollar store farther down the line and picked up some snacks. Then she walked to the intersection in front of the strip mall. She looked at the afternoon sun high overhead, and then she darted across the street between the stop-and-go traffic. She stood so that the cars she was facing were heading toward the north ramp to US 395.

Allie ran her hands through her long blonde hair and tied it in a messy bun behind her head. She bit her lip and then extended her thumb. Her chest heaved as her breathing raced with anxiety. Her dad would kill her if he knew she was hitch-hiking; that is, if some psychotic ax murderer didn't pick her up and beat him to it. Her lips quivered as she thought about never seeing her mom and dad again. She closed her eyes and listened to the rumble of traffic passing by. She felt alone and hoped for another sweet woman heading in the direction of Crater Lake to pick her up. But what were the odds? She'd been lucky once, which was more than she deserved.

Opening her eyes, she thought about her dragon breath and pitied any driver with foolish intentions. Allie plastered a smile on her face and stuck out her thumb with renewed confidence. The draw she felt toward Crater Lake was intense and confusing. She didn't know why she felt such an urgent need to return, but it didn't matter. She would get to Crater Lake no matter the obstacles. It was the only home she had left.

8

TURBULENCE

T HE VEINS IN ETHAN'S TEMPLES PULSED AS HE STRUGGLED to open his eyes. When they finally opened and the haze cleared from his mind, he noticed he was lying upside down with his butt against the wall. His neck bent unnaturally into his shoulder as it held the weight of his body. He tried moving his arms, but except for the intense tingles he couldn't even tell if they were still attached. Looking ahead to the front of the plane, Ethan saw the pilot's seat with only Jordan's elbow sticking out from behind it.

"A little help here," Ethan pleaded. As expected, there was no response from Jordan. Kicking his legs against the rear wall of the cabin, Ethan pushed off and freed his body, which promptly changed from a crumpled heap against the wall into a crumpled heap in the middle of the floor. Progress. Ethan turned his neck slowly and rolled onto his stomach. Placing his hands beneath him, he tried lifting himself up by doing a push-up, but his arms collapsed, and his cheek smacked the floor. "Ouch!" he moaned. Then, he attempted to lift himself again and was finally successfully.

Walking between the two rows of dual passenger seats, Ethan approached the back of the pilot's chair. But before he could rest his palm on the headrest, the plane lurched violently to the right, causing him to slam into the side wall and flop into one of the seats. He stood again and approached the pilot's seat for another try, But the plane went into a sudden dive as it made a sharp roll to the left. Ethan fell again, this time smacking his head on an armrest. Rubbing his head, Ethan climbed into the seat and buckled in, preparing for more turbulence.

Jordan's sporadic flying shouldn't be too much of a surprise, considering she's eleven, Ethan thought. He didn't know how much more physical abuse he could take. He leaned back in the seat and tried to forget the throbbing in his head, the kink in his neck, and what was sure to be a lovely bruise across his face. The more he thought about his aches, the less he was able to think of any body part that didn't hurt in some way. Ethan waited for the next jerky movement of the plane, but the aircraft remained stable. It didn't rise or fall or lurch to any side. Maybe Jordan was getting the hang of it. After waiting another few minutes, Ethan unbuckled his belt and tried again, but as he reached slowly for Jordan's seat, the plane lurched to the side and Ethan stumbled to his knees.

What the . . . ? That's not turbulence. Whoever or whatever was controlling Jordan didn't want Ethan waking her from her vision. Ethan sat back in his seat and thought as he massaged his aching body. *Who's controlling her? And why? What's the purpose? Where are we going? How do they know that I want to wake her up?* Ethan swiveled in his seat and searched the interior of the plane for some kind of a camera someone could use to monitor him, but he found nothing.

Scooting into a window seat, Ethan took a moment to stare out the window, hoping to see a landmark of some kind. At twenty thousand feet, most everything looked small except for the mountains and a giant lake. They were landmarks that told him he was nowhere near his Midwest home, but there was nothing specific that he recognized. Leaning forward, Ethan strained to look past the pilot seat into the cockpit of the plane. Even though he was farther away, he had a clearer view of his sister. He saw the kinky lion's mane sticking out and Jordan's hands gripping the handles on the control column.

Before he could think enough to talk himself out of another attempt, Ethan leaped from his seat and lunged toward Jordan. He saw her hands crank the column to the left, and the plane shifted violently, but Ethan's course was already set. Smashing between the cabin wall and Jordan's seat, Ethan reached until it felt like his arm would dislocate. Then he felt the cool flesh of Jordan's arm. A smile crossed his lips but disappeared when he heard Jordan's horrified shriek.

Jordan usually remained calm when she emerged from a vision, but Ethan understood the reaction to this one. He fell to the floor and pried his arm from in between the seat and the cabin wall. As terrified as Jordan sounded, the screams of fear were music to Ethan's ears because it meant his sister was back. The clanking of the metal seat belt being released accented Jordan's screams and cries. "Jordan. I'm here," Ethan said as he stood and waited for his sister to emerge from the controls.

On cue, Jordan squeezed from between the two pilot seats and wrapped her arms around Ethan. He kissed her forehead. "You're okay, Jordan. Everything is going to be just fine."

Jordan whimpered. "Ethan?"

He held his sister tighter. "Yeah, what is it?"

"Who's going to fly the airplane?"

9

SNOW CAVE

THE FOREST CLEARED INTO A SNOWY MEADOW JUST PAST A frosted boulder that looked like an eight-foot-tall thumb sticking up from the ground. *Mmm, frosting.* The boulder was twice as wide as Brady's muscular frame but only half as firm. To the east of the boulder, the snowdrifts tapered off and then deepened into thick dunes of snow as the meadow led toward the cliffs of Crater Lake. Brady removed the stocking cap from his red head and pulled a folding shovel from his pack to dig into the steep drift.

Removing his outer coat, Brady tossed it to the base of the boulder beside his pack and dug an entrance into the snow hill that was nearly obstructed by the eight-foot thumb. Sweat flew from Brady's brow and dripped down his sunglasses as he dug a three-foot-round opening at the base of the snow pack. He squeezed his broad shoulders through the entrance and dug inward four feet. Then he hollowed out a cave on top of a two-foot ledge. Pulling a flashlight from his pocket, Brady set it in the snow beside him to illuminate the cavern. His shovel scraped the snow from the ceiling onto a blue tarp he laid across the floor. When a thick layer of unwanted snow covered the tarp, Brady shimmied his way out of the cave, pulling the tarp with him to dump it outside.

The tedious process required hours of labor and patience.

When the inner cave was carved to Brady's satisfaction, he smoothed it out with his hands and then lay on his back to stare at the rounded ceiling. Sweat dripped from his face onto the ice, and his warm breath and steam from his forehead rose to attack the snow. The snowy walls and ceiling glistened. Though he couldn't tell if the temperature was rising or if he was becoming numb from lying on the ice, the snow cave seemed to get warmer. A drip from the ceiling startled him.

Brady cursed at his mistake. Taking the shovel, he carved a groove at the base of the wall around the entire cave to catch any condensation and snowmelt that might gather. Crawling out of the cave, Brady wandered a short distance from the boulder and approached a tall pine tree. With the serrated blade of his knife, he cut a thin limb from the tree and then sawed off the branches until it was a smooth pole. He then cut a number of evergreen boughs from the tree and dragged them to the mouth of his cave. Climbing on top of the cave, he jumped up and down to test its strength. He hopped cautiously at first, not wanting the cave to collapse after all of his work. But then he stomped hard, figuring it better to find the weakness now instead of while he was sleeping. When the shelter withstood his weight, he took the carved branch and stabbed the snow where he imagined the top of his cave would be. He repeated the process along the side, creating two vents for his snow cave. Not only would the vents allow fresh air in, but they would also release warm breath and the heat from his camp stove without melting the cave. Instead of dripping and flowing onto his sleeping bag, the water would only go where he directed.

Inside the cave, Brady checked his vent holes. Satisfied with the location of his vents, he wiggled the stick to broaden the holes enough to allow a healthy shaft of light inside. He then dragged in the evergreen boughs and laid them on the floor of the cave, a natural pad for his sleeping bag. After pulling all of his gear inside his new home, Brady removed his snow boots and replaced them with his cross-country ski boots.

Outside, he put on the waterproof shell of his jacket, pulled out the skis he'd stabbed into a nearby drift, and clicked his toes into the binding. He lifted his heels, testing the strength of the binding and the flexibility of his movement. Gripping his poles, he glided toward the crater's rim for a fresh view of his worst nightmare.

After a vigorous five-minute sprint, Brady slid to a stop and stood sideways in his skis at the rim of Crater Lake. He leaned cautiously against his pole as he looked over the cliff. Instead of brilliant blue, the surface of the lake appeared to be a hazy baby blue. Ice crept outward from the shoreline to surround Wizard Island, and thin layers of powder covered the ice, nearly hiding the brilliance of the water altogether. He leaned harder against his pole to get a better look, but he was too heavy. The pole sunk deep into the snow, causing Brady to lose his balance and nearly topple over the cliff. Catching himself and standing upright again, he felt his chest bubble with excitement as he considered his proximity to death. He laughed at the thought of death. *Yeah, right.* Then, he heard the sound of crunching snow and heavy panting.

Twisting in place, Brady saw a gray wolf running to him through the snow. He lifted the sunglasses onto his forehead and watched as the wolf raced right at him. It appeared playful, not hungry, so Brady knelt on his skis and held out his hands like he would to the family dog. Brady smiled as the wolf slowed to a careful stride and then nuzzled up to him.

Brady rubbed the wolf's head and scratched his ears. Then he lifted his jowls to get a good look at the sharp canine incisors. Brady's head nodded with approval as he rubbed and hugged the wolf. But then he pushed the animal away when it nipped at his hand. Brady felt the sharp stab of teeth against his skin.

The wolf's bite shredded Brady's Gore-Tex glove. When the wolf tried to approach again, Brady brushed at the animal with annoyance, knocking it back ten feet and causing it to yelp as it crashed into the snow. "Punk! These are my only gloves," Brady muttered.

Removing his right glove, Brady examined the severe tear and then looked at his hand. There wasn't a scratch or even a red mark. Brady placed the glove back on his hand and then watched while the wolf turned to run into the woods.

Brady pounded his chest with a fist and tilted his head to the sky, whooping and hollering, mocking the wolf's howls and yelps. He then screamed, "I AM INVINCIBLE."

Reveling in his newfound durability, Brady smirked, but then his eyes widened with fear as he felt the ground collapse beneath his skis.

The avalanche seemed determined to take Brady with it as it cascaded down the cliff. Falling sideways, Brady quickly turned his skis to point down the nearly vertical cliff slope. The skis hit the slope and Brady picked up speed as he leaned back so far that he sat on the back of the skis. "WOO-HOO!" he screamed as he barreled down the cliff. He then became silent as the rest of the avalanche caught and buried him from behind. It carried him the rest of the way down to the shore of Crater Lake.

The avalanche slammed Brady's body into the snow-covered boulders that lined the shoreline . . . testing his claim of invincibility.

– 10 –

READING MARATHON

T HE SOUND OF THE STORM DROWNED OUT THE NOISE FROM the propellers. Ethan looked out the window to make sure they were both still working. They were. Wind and rain pounded the airplane with the intensity of a convict trying to break down his cell door. It attacked the windows with spraying sheets of rain, and the wind tossed the small commuter plane like a beach ball. The plane lurched up and then down, leaving Ethan's stomach at the top of his throat. He swallowed hard and tried to keep from retching as the plane swung from side to side with the wings tipping and rolling. He held the column firmly, but it rebelled against his attempt for control.

"Ethan?" Jordan's voice sounded reconciled to certain death. "Can you land this thing?"

His chest heaved as he stared at the instruments on the cockpit dash and then out the window into the pure chaos. "I . . . I don't know anything about planes. I've never studied flying before." Ethan growled under his breath and then chuckled nervously. "Flying is cool. Why wouldn't I have read about flying?" He looked at Jordan. "Why? Why didn't I?" Jordan didn't answer, but Ethan didn't expect her to. How could she respond to a question like that? It was his failure, not hers.

"Can you call for help? Maybe someone on the radio can help us. I saw that in a movie once," Jordan said.

Ethan's head wagged. "No. I mean . . . I don't know. I don't see a receiver or anything. There must be some kind of radio here. Look around and see what you can find." Ethan looked over his shoulder as Jordan ran to the back of the plane's cabin and started opening every nook and cabinet she could find. The plane jolted, and Jordan fell to the floor between the seats. "Be careful, Jordan."

Ethan tried to hold the plane steady as Jordan inched her way to the cockpit. He craned his neck and looked back at Jordan as she searched under the cabin seats and in the back pockets of each seat. She held up various magazines and even a Snickers bar, but no radio. "I don't see anything helpful," Jordan yelled to Ethan.

"Keep looking." He yelled every word, just to be heard over the storm. Jordan continued making her way forward as Ethan tried holding the column steady. He snuck an occasional peek back but tried to stay focused on flying the plane. After a few moments of silence, Ethan looked back but didn't see Jordan. "Jordan!" he yelled.

"I'm right here," she said from immediately behind his seat. "I think I found something," she said.

"A radio?"

"No. A book. It's pretty thick."

"Jordan, stay focused," Ethan chided.

"No. I think this will help. It says, *Pilots Operating Manual. 1983 PA-31-350 Piper Chieftain.* This thing's huge. It's the size of a phone book."

Ethan smiled and let out a "WHOOP!" that could barely be heard over the sound of the storm. "Jordan, give it to me."

Jordan stepped in between the two pilot's seats and sat beside Ethan as he grabbed the thick manual. "Is that going to help with . . . with . . . that?" Jordan asked, pointing at the myriad gauges and controls. Ethan didn't respond. He was already busy reading. "Ethan?"

"Hey, Jordan. Hold this for a minute," he said, nodding to the control column.

"I can't. I'm not strong enough."

"Sure you are." Ethan let go of the column, and the plane started to dip. Jordan reached over and pulled the column back until the plane leveled out.

Ethan flipped through the pages quickly. "Ah-ha!" Ethan reached toward the control panel and flipped a small switch. The jerky control column became steady as it pulled back slightly. Ethan smiled at Jordan. "You can let go now. It's on autopilot."

Jordan smiled back, but the worry returned quickly to her eyes. "What does that mean?" she asked, pointing at a blinking red light next to a round instrument with an outline of a plane set at the center.

Ethan flipped through the *Pilot's Operating Manual*. He found a page and studied a diagram. Then he stared again at the blinking light. He sucked in a breath but muffled a gasp as he recognized the low fuel indicator. He tried to calm his heart and breathing that both threatened to race out of control before he answered. "It's nothing to worry about." At that moment he hoped that he wouldn't be struck by lightning for lying so blatantly to his sister. He cast that worry aside, knowing that causing his sister to panic would accomplish nothing.

"Ethan, are we going to die?"

Ethan stared at his book. "I need to read. Try to calm down and remember what you were thinking about before I pulled you out of your vision. Try to re-enter the vision. That's your job right now, Jordan. If you can do it, we'll be fine."

"You think I can save us?"

"You got us here. Or your vision did. It can get us out." Ethan stretched his neck. "Maybe. Concentrate and relax."

Holding the manual in front of his face, Ethan peeked to his side to look at Jordan. She closed her eyes and breathed deeply. He could see her chest move. In and out. In and out. The lines on her face ironed out into the usual young girl peacefulness, free of worry and fear. Ethan looked into the window but didn't look outside. He focused on his own reflection. Deep lines crossed his forehead, his eyes were squinty and tired, and no matter what he tried, his lips were frozen in a perpetual scowl. He looked back at his sister and tried to follow her example by relaxing. No. He couldn't. There wasn't time. He pulled the manual in front of his face and started his speed-reading marathon. He glanced over diagrams, definitions, and equations, flipping the pages quickly while the plane continued on autopilot.

Ethan read fast, and the knowledge became as much a part of him as his anxiety. He tried not to look at the blinking red light, but he couldn't help it. The light taunted him. There was no escaping it. The Piper Chieftain was going down one way or another. He just couldn't be certain of how, or where.

CRASH LANDING

ETHAN MOANED AS HE FLIPPED THROUGH THE PAGES OF THE *Pilot's Operating Manual,* memorizing everything he read. He glanced at Jordan, who kept her eyes closed. It looked like she was trying to calm herself and reenter her vision, despite the turbulent ride. Her breathing was slow and deliberate. Ethan watched her reach to the side of the high-backed chair and pull down one shoulder strap and then the other. She snapped the two shoulder harnesses into the lap belt, all with her eyes still closed. Maybe she was back in her vision, Ethan hoped, but then he saw Jordan open one eye as she peeked back at him. She shut it quickly. Grabbing his harness, Ethan followed Jordan's example and buckled in.

Placing the manual on his lap, Ethan tested his knowledge of the control panel. At the top of the panel in T-formation, he saw the six basic gauges: The attitude indicator, or the artificial horizon, was at the top center. It verified that the plane was flying level. To the left was the airspeed, and to the right was the altimeter, which showed the airplane's altitude above sea level. At the bottom center of the panel, Ethan saw an outline of an airplane inside a round gauge with numbers circling it to indicate the heading of the aircraft. Except for the low fuel warning light, the plane was flying well, and the autopilot seemed to be working as designed. But it wasn't the autopilot he was worried about. He wouldn't even worry about Jordan flying with her own unique kind of autopilot. He was concerned with the Ethan-pilot.

Two other gauges completed the basic control panel: the vertical speed and the turn coordinator. They didn't seem as important, so Ethan's eyes moved lower on the dash. Below the basic panel, Ethan saw a square, black screen. He pressed a small button, and the color display came to life with a global positioning system and Doppler radar that showed severe thunderstorms. Ethan already knew about the turbulent weather. He felt the jarring reminders every second. On the control panel between the pilot and copilot seats, Ethan located the radio and transponder. He pressed the button on the radio but there was no power. He tried turning a knob, and the tuner nearly fell out of the console. Pulling it out carefully, Ethan studied the multitude of colored wires that had been snapped in half. It was no wonder why there was no radio chatter. The transponder was nearly as bad. "Did you do this?" Ethan asked. Jordan just shrugged. He pulled out the transponder to examine the snapped wiring. The wiring looked simple compared to the radio. But without the transponder, no one would ever be able to find them. Ethan looked over at Jordan and shook his head. "Crazy little girl," he muttered.

Picking up the manual, Ethan turned the pages until he located information about the transponder. He read and prepared to reconnect the wires, but his attention was drawn back to the gauges. A second red light flashed beside the first low fuel indicator, and then the plane lurched. Lightning webbed through the sky in front of them, and the rain continued pounding against the windows. The wind tossed the small aircraft according to its whim.

On the control column, Ethan pressed a button with his thumb as he disengaged the autopilot and took control of the plane. He slowly pulled the stick toward him and watched the altimeter. The nose of the plane rose. Sixteen thousand feet. The storm continued raging outside, shaking and rattling the windows and teeth, so he continued pulling back. Seventeen thousand feet. Eighteen. Nineteen. "Twenty thousand feet. We're at the maximum recommended altitude, going three hundred knots," Ethan said aloud, in case Jordan was interested. "Whoa, that's about 345 miles per hour," Ethan said with a smirk, running the quick calculation he'd read in the *Pilot Operating Manual*.

He looked out the window and scratched his head as the plane continued bouncing around. One layer of storm clouds yielded to the next. There was no avoiding the storm. Ethan shook his head, partly with disappointment that he was unable to rise above the storm, but partly impressed with the speed of his aircraft. "Three hundred knots. How is that even possible? Max air speed is only two hundred and fifteen knots. What do you think, Jordan? Massive tailwind?"

Jordan gripped the arm of her chair as the plane jolted to the left. "Ethan, don't take this wrong, but I don't care."

Resetting the autopilot, Ethan turned his attention to the GPS system. He pressed a couple of buttons, changing the screen display until it showed a map of the United States and the dotted course the Piper Chieftain had flown. A red dot marked the area of the small rural airport where they had taken off. Then it showed them passing over Kansas, the Rocky Mountains of Colorado, and the Great Salt Lake.

"Look," Ethan said, pointing to the screen. Jordan leaned as far as she could and squinted to see. "Hold on." Ethan leaned toward the copilot controls and turned on the GPS on Jordan's side of the cockpit. "We just flew into Oregon. If we've been going this speed the whole time, that would explain why we haven't had to refuel."

Jordan's voice fell into a low monotone. "Crater Lake. We're going back, aren't we?"

Ethan nodded and swallowed the spit that had gathered in his mouth. "Looks like it." His breathing and the pace of his speech became frantic. The plane jolted again, and a web of lightning flashed in front of the plane. "Do you have any idea why?" Jordan shook her head, but Ethan eyed her skeptically. "Well, we're going to be there soon." Ethan looked back at the red flashing fuel indicators. "And we're going to have to land . . . somehow." Ethan buried his nose in the manual and resumed his studies, hoping to find tips for a smooth crash landing.

Ethan read as fast as he could while Jordan hummed one of her favorite songs in an attempt to drown out the pounding rain and thunder. Then, engine one sputtered. Ethan looked out his side window and watched as the propeller stopped.

Jordan gasped, and her voice turned into a high whine. "What's happening?"

Ethan bit his lower lip as he tried to calm himself, but his heart lodged in his throat. "It's time to land this thing."

Placing the manual on the floor between the seats, Ethan disengaged the autopilot and checked his gauges again. "Altitude—nineteen thousand feet. We're dropping."

"It's a plane. Won't it glide?"

Ethan chuckled. "We're four thousand pounds of steel. We're going to fall like a brick if that other engine dies. Hold on." Pushing the stick forward, Ethan lowered the nose of the plane and started what he hoped would be a rapid but controlled descent. He watched the altimeter to stay apprised of his altitude. He also watched the artificial horizon as he struggled to keep the wings level. He made minor corrections on the stick and then reached to the panel and pulled out a small lever. He pressed it down. The back wing flaps rose, engaging the air brakes. Ethan pulled back on the throttle. "We need to slow down. Jordan, where are we? Look at the GPS."

Jordan pointed at the GPS screen as the plane continued downward into a bank of even darker clouds. "Um . . ."

"We're at seventeen thousand feet." The Chieftain lunged to the left as the wing dipped into the heavy wind. Ethan pulled the stick as he watched the artificial horizon.

"Ethan, it just gives me some numbers. I don't know what it means. I think we're still in Oregon," Jordan said.

"Sixteen thousand feet. Yeah, we're still in Oregon. We may never leave Oregon," he muttered. The small commuter plane jolted to the right and then dropped like it had stepped off of a tall curb. The wind gusted, but the rain stopped. Instead, white snow bombarded the Chieftain, making it nearly impossible to see outside the window. "Fifteen thousand feet."

Unbuckling her seat harness, Jordan climbed out and ran to the back of the plane. "I'll be right back."

"Jordan. Sit down!"

Within moments, Jordan was back in her seat and buckled. She held up the Snickers bar she had found earlier. "If I'm going to die, I want to die happy." She opened the wrapper and took a bite.

Ethan glared at his sister as he tried holding the stick steady. "Give that to me," he commanded. Jordan handed it over and then smiled as Ethan took a huge bite and gave it back. He chewed slowly.

"Thirteen thousand feet," he called out with his mouth full. He looked at the magnetic compass that was positioned at the center of the windshield. "We're heading west . . . uh . . . southwest . . . ish. Eleven thousand feet." Ten thousand. Nine. Eight. Seven. Ethan reached forward, pulled a knob down, and listened to a gentle hum from below the plane. "Landing gear down."

Six. Five. Four. "Look!" Jordan called out as she stared out her side window.

"I can't see," Ethan yelled. "What?" He rose in his seat trying to look.

Jordan frowned. "It's Crater Lake. We're here!" Jordan said.

"We haven't made it yet." Ethan turned the stick to the right and pulled out the flaps lever on the control panel as the plane continued to slow. "One hundred and fifty knots."

"Whoa! That looks awesome!" Jordan hollered. "Look at all the snow."

"Snow? Crater Lake gets nearly forty feet of snow each year," Ethan recited. He thought for a moment and watched the heading indicator gauge turn as he continued veering to the right. Then he saw the lake. "Crap!" He lined the lake up directly in front of the plane's flight path. "One hundred thirty knots. Um . . . Jordan, we've got a problem."

Jordan scoffed. "You think?" She waited for a moment. "What?" she yelled.

"There's no airport, and no runway, right?"

"Right."

"That means we need to try to land in an open field, maybe in the sandy desert to the east of the lake," Ethan said.

"So?"

Ethan cleared his throat. "I don't think landing gear and twenty feet of snow really work well together."

"O-o-o-o-h." She drew out the word like it was the longest in the English language.

"Three thousand feet." Reaching over, Ethan pulled the landing gear lever up. "We're going to land on the belly," he said, trying to sound confident. "This is going to work out great." He forced a grin, but raised his eyebrows and scrunched them together. He wiped the sleeve of his coat across his forehead to wipe away the gathering perspiration.

"Look, Ethan. It's amazing."

Straight ahead, Ethan watched as Crater Lake grew larger and larger with each passing second of descent. He could see the snow-covered pine forests along the rim of the crater, and he could even see Wizard Island set inside. "Two thousand feet." Ethan pulled up on the stick, leveling the plane. He peeked out the window at the one operating propeller. "There. Just past the trees. Do you see it?" Ethan asked as he pointed out Jordan's side of the windshield. "We'll try to land there."

"I see it." She looked at Ethan. "Are you sure you can do it?"

"Yeah, that looks good. Nice and smooth." He looked at Jordan. "'Are you sure you can do it?' You're kidding, right?"

He didn't want to be mean, especially right before they were going to die, but it felt like Jordan deserved a little honesty. "Jordan, I don't have a clue if this is going to work." He paused. "We'll probably crash into a flaming fireball. I just hope we die quickly."

Jordan wiped her eye. "Okay."

The snow flew into the windshield, making Ethan feel like they were flying at light speed through space. He pulled back more on the throttle. "One hundred knots." He lined up his landing path to a spot on the other side of the lake, and he pushed forward on the stick, lowering the plane again. Crater Lake loomed large in front of him as he prepared to pass over. "One thousand feet. Is your seat belt tight?"

Jordan tugged at the harness. "Yeah."

The Piper Chieftain lowered as it passed over the rim and into the crater. "Five hundred feet."

Jordan screamed. "Ethan, you're too low!"

"No. We're fine." Ethan checked his gauges and pulled back more on the throttle. He lifted the flaps, reengaging the airbrakes. "Eighty knots. We're at landing speed. Three hundred feet."

The plane passed over the other rim of the crater. Ethan's eyes bugged out as it looked like the plane might clip the tall evergreen forest on the other side, but the plane cleared. Ethan checked the artificial horizon and looked at his intended landing spot in the snow. Two hundred feet. One hundred fifty feet. One hundred. He reached to the control panel and flipped a switch, killing the second propeller.

Memories flashed through his mind at the speed of the flying snow outside. Mom. Dad. Jordan. School. Crater Lake. Allie. He wanted to say something sweet and comforting to Jordan in their final moments. But he couldn't think of anything profound, so he sat in silence. He held the wings level and pulled back gently on the stick, raising the nose of the plane as it continued to descend into the snowy pumice desert past Crater Lake.

"Ethan?"

"Yeah." Maybe Jordan thought of something sweet herself. Ethan braced himself for words of kindness.

"Mom and Dad are going to be ticked if you kill us."

The plane seemed to hover over the snowy field. Ethan grinned. She was right. They would definitely be ticked. Time was up. "HOLD ON!"

The rear of the plane settled softly into the powdery snow. Ethan waited for a jolt that would signify they had landed, but he couldn't tell. The rest of the plane lowered. The nose fell last, tearing through the snow and sending piles of white powder over the window and to the sides like a snowplow. When the windshield was covered, Ethan closed his eyes and waited for the plane to stop but it felt like it never would. The airplane plowed forward, occasionally scraping or grinding on something, sending chills through his body. Then the plane jolted to an immediate stop as the nose lowered and struck something hard and immovable. The rear of the plane lifted and so did Ethan's eyelids. He looked in horror as the plane lifted up onto the nose. Ethan stared through the windshield at the ground below.

The Piper Chieftain balanced on the nose for what felt like minutes and then toppled over. Jordan screamed, and Ethan cried in fear as the plane flipped over before coming to rest. Jordan and Ethan hung upside down in their seats, the shoulder harness ripping into Ethan's skin.

He gasped and let out a whimper that didn't sound very manly. He didn't care. He wiped his eyes and turned to Jordan.

She had never smiled so big in her life. "You did it!"

Ethan exhaled unevenly. He smiled and laughed as he hung upside down. "We did it. We survived. I can't believe it. We're here." He thought for a moment, and then the excitement fled from his voice. "We're here. Oh, crap. We're back."

– 12 –

ACHILLES' HEEL

MUFFLED YELLS AND THE SOUND OF FRANTIC DIGGING awakened Brady from his daze. He tried opening his eyes, but coarse ice crystals and snow were packed tight against his eyelids. The warm feel of his breath hit his palms, and he realized that his hands were cupped in front of his nose and mouth, allowing him a little space to breathe. He tried moving his head from side to side, but it seemed to be locked in place. A panicked sensation smothered Brady like the snow that entombed him. The thumping of his heart echoed in his ears. He swallowed and then yelled into his hands. "I'm here!" The sounds of movement above him stopped, and the voices quieted. "I'm here!" he repeated. The sound of wild digging resumed.

Pushing his hands outward, away from his face, Brady tried digging himself out. He pressed the compacted snow away in a motion like he was swimming underwater. He leaned forward and lifted his knees. The muscles in his neck tensed as he pressed his forehead against the snow, giving him more space and more air as he tried to cure the claustrophobic sensation that had settled in. He opened his eyes and looked upward . . . or at least in the direction that felt like up. Above him, there was only blackness, and then a pinprick of light. He yelled again and listened for a response. Brady's heart raced as he considered

47

the possibility that he might suffocate in a tomb of snow. He hadn't felt this kind of fear in months, and the fact that he felt it at all made him even more afraid. The closest thing he could remember was the despair he felt when the ambulance doors closed and the car hauled his father away after the accident just a couple of days ago. Brady clenched his jaw at the bitter memory. He didn't want to think about it, and he didn't want to think about the declaration of invincibility he had just shouted on the cliff above Crater Lake. Suddenly, that feeling of invincibility felt wildly inaccurate.

Muted male voices descended toward Brady. He listened as he continued trying to dig himself out. But even with his increased strength, the limited motion made it difficult to make much progress. Above him, the pinprick of light broadened as the owners of the voices continued digging. "Hurry!" Brady called. His breaths were heavy.

"We're coming," a boy with a gentle accent called back.

Brady focused on the growing white light that penetrated the snow above him. When a bare hand broke through the snow and pulled away large chunks, Brady lifted his hand to cover his eyes from the light. Tears trickled down his cheek, and he convinced himself that the tears were caused by the sharpness of the light, not by any sense of relief or happiness. He rubbed the inner corner of his eyes with his fingers and then reached up to grab the dark-skinned hand reaching toward him.

It felt like an eternity before enough snow was dug away that Brady truly felt free. He looked at the young Native American faces that surrounded the hole with an emotion he didn't recognize. It was odd; happiness, hope, gratitude, and freedom all wrapped into one intense sensation that he couldn't remember ever feeling before. The boys used shovels, buckets, and hands as they pulled the snow away from Brady. He pushed and kicked the snow back, creating space close to his body. Rising from the slightly reclined sitting position he'd been trapped in, Brady stuck his head out of the broadening hole. He then crouched down and pulled his arms into a compact position at his side. "Get back," he warned.

Without further warning, Brady sprung up, his arms reaching as he exploded out of his snowy grave. Falling onto his back, He pinched his eyes shut, hiding them from the piercing sun. Then he waved his arms and legs to create a happy snow angel. He opened his eyes a sliver as a shadow hovered over him. He knew he should express his gratitude for the rescue, but he ignored the shadow as long as he could. Then he relented. "Yes?" Brady shielded his eyes and then reached to accept the hand that was extended. Brady grabbed hold, and the young Native American pulled Brady to his feet and then wrapped his arms around Brady in a tight embrace.

He dropped his chin as he looked at the top of the native's long black hair. His eyes scurried to the group of four boys who hovered around his grave. They peered inside and appeared to be fascinated by something, but Brady couldn't tell what. The boy finally released Brady and looked into his face with a wide grin. "Welcome back, Brady. Crater Lake has missed you."

Brady blinked in slow motion and then pulled away in an attempt to match the voice with the face. The joyful expression of survival transformed into a bitter scowl. His voice became low and surly as he enunciated his words. "Hello . . . Che-tan."

WARRIOR FRIENDS

Ethan wished he had considered the consequences of releasing his seat harness while hanging upside down. His head hit the ceiling of the fuselage with a thud as he dropped from his seat. Lesson learned.

"That had to hurt," Jordan teased as she gripped her shoulder straps while still hanging in her seat.

Ethan rubbed his head and moaned. He glared at his sister. "Really? You think?" She smiled back. "Undo your belt latch, and I'll catch you." He reached up to his sister, but she just shook her head. "Come on, Jordan."

She shook her head again. "Nuh-uh."

"So you're just going to hang upside down for the rest of your life?" Ethan asked. Jordan's thick, kinky curls drooped low. Ethan waited while she thought.

"You'd better not drop me." She wagged her finger. "Mom will be mad if you drop me."

Ethan laughed. "Jordan, I just crashed an airplane. I'm already going to be grounded for life." He paused. "You have to come down. I won't drop you." He thought for a moment as Jordan's head continued to wag in denial. "But you are making it tempting."

Jordan's face was bright red as the blood flowed to her cheeks. "You promise?"

Ethan rubbed the back of his head again. "Yeah, sure. I promise." He held his hands up as he reached for Jordan. "Undo the shoulder straps first and then the belt."

The metal clicked as the first shoulder strap disconnected. Jordan pushed it off of her shoulder and then unlatched the other. "Ready?"

Ethan nodded. "I'm ready."

Jordan took a deep breath and released her belt latch just as a loud bang sounded at the rear of the plane. Ethan turned toward the pounding and then felt Jordan crash onto the ground near his feet. Ethan looked at his younger sister heaped on the floor. Ethan's mouth dropped and then formed into a smirk. Bending over, he ignored the pounding coming from the rear of the plane and helped Jordan sit up. Tears flowed from her eyes and gentle sobs of pain accused Ethan of his negligence and betrayal.

He tried to devise an excuse that would alleviate his guilt, but he couldn't. "I'm sorry," was all he could say. Jordan's eyes told him she was unwilling to forgive, so he turned away. He looked to the rear of the plane where there was continual pounding and muffled yelling. Then he turned back to Jordan and helped her stand. "Should we see who it is?"

Jordan glared and then nodded in agreement.

Walking along the ceiling of the airplane, Ethan approached the rear door. He pulled the lever and pressed outward, but the door wouldn't open. "Who's there?" Ethan yelled.

"I am called Ha-ida." The voice was soft but crisp. "We will get you out."

"Do you promise?" Jordan yelled.

There was only silence on the outside of the plane for a moment, and then came the response. "Yes. I promise."

Jordan glared at Ethan and then mumbled, "You'd better."

– 14 –

SKELL VILLAGE

ETHAN BURIED HIS FACE INTO HA-IDA'S BACK AS THEY RACED away from the plane wreckage on an Arctic Cat snowmobile that looked like it had been dropped over a cliff. The skis were mostly straight, but the lime green fiberglass casing around the engine was held together with a bungee cord and duct tape. The snowmobile felt like it was hovering above the snow.

Ethan wrapped his arms tight around Ha-ida's waist, and not just because he was trying to stay on. She was pretty cute. Her long black hair flowed behind her in the wind and tickled Ethan's face. Ethan glanced back at Jordan and the other two snowmobiles behind him. The only evidence of Jordan he could find was her small hands wrapped around her driver. The thin body of one of the native rescuers concealed Jordan's even skinnier body.

"How much farther?" Ethan yelled. He peeked over Ha-ida's shoulder across an inclined field of snow. In the distance, Ethan could see the hazy outline of trees and black smoke rising in front of the setting sun. "Is that it?" he yelled. The windblown snow attacked his face, so he hid again behind Ha-ida. He heard some kind of muffled response and couldn't understand it. But he really didn't need to. Crater Lake National Park looked to be a barren wasteland in the winter, and the pillar of smoke was the only visible sign of civilization.

The snowmobile slowed as it entered a grove of trees, but it didn't slow as much as Ethan thought it should. He envisioned a fiery crash into one of the pines, but Ha-ida weaved in and out of the trees as a plume of snow shot from behind her snow rocket. The other snowmobiles followed her trail with exactness.

The grove opened into a field the size of a hockey rink. It was littered with individual shacks and shanties pieced together, connecting like a web from a central building. Ethan skeptically raised his eyebrows because he knew calling it a building was a bit of a stretch. Every shack appeared ready to topple with the push of a single finger that would create a domino chain reaction. Tall trees shielded the shantytown from wind and drifting snow, and Ethan briefly entertained the hope that they would simply pass by on the way to their real lodgings. Not so. Ethan's red, frozen cheeks drooped as Ha-ida stopped in front of the central building.

"We are here," she said as she pried Ethan's fingers from her coat. She stood and led the way inside. "Come. Warm up."

Ethan tucked his hands into the pockets of the jacket that somehow passed as a winter coat back home. He waited until the snowmobile carrying Jordan pulled up alongside the main building, and then he ducked through the short door and rushed inside.

Ha-ida waited at the center of a large common room with her stocking cap stuffed into a side pocket. She stretched out her hands as she huddled around a fire pit. Ethan's eyes wandered around the interior of the room as he shuffled along the plywood floor toward his new friend. The pit was lined with thick stone, and a hole in the low ceiling directly above provided an escape for the smoke. Two-by-fours were lashed together overhead, creating thin beams that somehow kept the ceiling from crashing down. Four rough-hewn benches were placed near the fire pit and there were others against the walls. A long countertop stretched almost the entire way across the back wall, stopping only to allow an opening into some other room or shack.

Animal skins lay on the floor as rugs and on some walls like tapestries, but otherwise, there was no decoration. No color. Just dreary wood that looked like it had been cast off from a lumberyard.

Ethan swallowed as he considered the squalor of the shelter. "Do you live here?" Ethan asked as he took his place beside Ha-ida. He felt a shiver of cold rush in as Jordan and the other snowmobilers hurried through the door. The door shut quickly, allowing the fire to resume its mission to heat the building.

"Yes. We live here. It is nice, no? We built it ourselves." Her English was labored and heavily accented, but she was able to communicate her thoughts clearly enough.

Ethan's eyes wandered around the room as other Native American teens began filtering in from adjoining shack rooms. His eyes then narrowed with confusion as they settled on Ha-ida and noticed for the first time the incongruent gray roots on her otherwise black head of hair. "It's lovely," he said, smirking and catching Jordan's eye. Ha-ida smiled back with apparent pride in her accomplishment. He wiped the smirk from his face. "Yeah, I don't think I'd be able to build anything like this," he admitted.

"Or would want to," Jordan mumbled.

Ethan poked her with an elbow. "Thank you for bringing us here to warm up. Do you have a phone so we can call our parents to let them know we're okay?" Ha-ida stared at him with a blank expression. "Telephone," Ethan said slowly. "Do you understand *telephone*?"

One boy chuckled from the back of the room, and then another. Ha-ida's stone eyes burned into Ethan, and then another girl burst out laughing. Ha-ida joined in with a large smile of her own. "Of course I understand *telephone*." She laughed again as she pointed at Ethan. Her friends all joined in the joke, making Ethan feel like an idiot. "I am sorry to laugh. Sometimes it is better to feel happy instead of sad."

Ethan felt like he would shrivel into nothingness, but then

he felt a hard slap on his back from a boy walking up behind him. "We don't get many visitors," the boy said with no accent at all. His warm smile chipped away at Ethan's unease. "We may live simply, but we're aware of the outside world. 'Telephone,' " he said and then laughed again. "That's good."

"Can we make a call?" Jordan asked.

The boy's smile faded. "We know what a phone is. We don't actually have one, though."

"You have snowmobiles but no phone? A little backward, isn't it?" Ethan asked. The words sounded more condescending leaving his mouth than he expected.

The laughter in the room died. Ha-ida and the young boy stood side by side. Ha-ida spoke without emotion. "We take what we find. We survive in winter. It is cold."

"Besides," the boy began, "we need some way to get our supplies and food. I'm Stan, by the way."

Ethan nodded and grinned. The boy wore jeans and a T-shirt. Instead of a long black ponytail, Stan wore his hair in a short crew cut with a brush of bleached blond in the front. "Stan?" He chuckled and looked for a reaction from the others, but they watched him as if "Stan" was a perfectly normal name in a place like this. *Maybe it is.* Ethan shrugged. "Yeah, I didn't mean to . . . you know . . ." His voice trailed off.

"Don't even worry about it. We've already forgotten. Right, guys?" Stan asked.

Ethan looked around the room and saw a number of reluctant shrugs and nods. "Again, I thank you for all you've done to help us, but we really do need to get home. Could someone take us to the ranger station? My Uncle Bart's a park ranger." No one answered. "Or maybe you could point us in the right direction, and we could borrow one of the snowmobiles," Ethan offered as an alternative.

"No."

The softly spoken word jarred Ethan. He reached down and pulled Jordan closer to him. He looked at Ha-ida. "What do you mean, 'no'?"

The exterior door burst open, and Ethan was surprised by the darkness that was already falling outside. Four small Native American teenagers wrapped in an array of mismatched winter clothes and one large man decked out in trendy ski gear entered the room, bringing the cold with them. The tall one ripped away his hat, showing off his bright red hair. He unzipped the top of his jacket that had been pulled up over his mouth. He removed his sunglasses and winked at Ethan. "She means you're here for a reason, so you're staying." Brady walked up to Ethan and motioned like he would punch him in the face. Ethan dodged the phantom blow as his entire body tensed. Then Brady lowered his arm, and he wrapped Ethan in a hug. Then he squeezed.

"Bra-dy. I can't breathe," Ethan forced out.

Brady chuckled. "Sorry, man." He reached down and rubbed Jordan's hair. "How are you, Jordan?"

"Brady!" Jordan yelled before hugging him around his waist.

"Dude, you're huge. What happened to you? And what are you doing here?" Ethan asked.

Brady glanced around the room at the staring teenagers. His eyes stopped on Ha-ida. "I don't know you," he said with a grin. "But I like it here. I like you." His eyebrows rose in two quick motions.

"Dude, seriously?"

Brady cleared his throat. "I'm here for the same reason you're here."

"Really? And what reason is that?" Ethan asked.

The cockiness drained from Brady's eyes as he thought about the question. The room hushed as every eye watched Brady, waiting for a response. "Crater Lake called me back."

Ethan's eyes narrowed. "Called you back to do what?" He looked at Brady and then at Ha-ida. She looked as confused as he felt. The question hovered in the air.

A young teen still standing by the door slowly unwound the scarf from around his head and face. Che-tan stepped forward.

He rested his eyes on Ha-ida for a moment and then settled on Ethan and Jordan. "Welcome back, friends."

Ha-ida's and Stan's eyes bulged. They clenched their jaws, and their muscles tensed as Che-tan stepped forward. The other three boys, with their chests puffed out, stood shoulder to shoulder next to Che-tan. Ethan shifted in place as he scanned the area. The entire room felt like it was ready to explode with hatred and blood, but then a native teen stepped calmly forward. Without warning, he transformed into an oversized cougar with glossy fur and a white streak near its nose. His growl shook the room.

Brady rubbed his red head as he moaned. "Not this again. Come on, guys. Let's keep Crazyville under wraps for a while. What do you say?"

Then another boy morphed into a bear, and a girl transformed into a flock of three hawks. Then another transformed, and another until the room was filled with cougars, bears, hawks, and even an antelope.

Ethan clung to Jordan in front of him. His head shook. "I never get used to that." His eyes darted to Brady, who looked unconcerned.

Brady stepped over to Che-tan, shoved one of the other boys standing beside him, and then wrapped his arm around Che-tan's neck, holding him in a headlock. "It looks like you've been making friends again, Che-tan," Brady said. "You haven't been playing nicely with others, have you?"

Che-tan shrugged off Brady's arm and stepped toward the antelope version of Ha-ida. With his three cohorts behind him, Che-tan held his palms out in front in a peaceful gesture. "I know why they are here. I can explain."

A bear inched toward Che-tan and then charged. Brady stepped in between the angry bear and Che-tan. When the bear approached, Brady lifted his elbow and slammed it into the bear's head. The bear dropped to the floor with a thud. The other animals became agitated and surrounded Brady. He raised his hands high enough that they touched the low ceiling. "Easy. I'm not trying to start a fight . . . yet. Big, Bad Bear Man will be fine." He grinned. "In a while," he said, glancing down at the unconscious form.

Ethan nodded. He glanced across the faces of Ha-ida's animal warriors, confused by the intense hostility. "Ha-ida, calm down. Let's just listen to what Che-tan has got to say. There's nothing to worry about. He and his Guardian warriors helped us fight against Chief Llao on Wizard Island. He's a friend. If he says something jerkish, then we'll kick him out into the cold," Ethan suggested. "What do you say? Deal?" No one moved.

Ha-ida morphed back into her more attractive human form. She brushed a strand of gray hair behind her ear. "Speak."

Che-tan stepped closer to Ha-ida. He focused on Ethan and Jordan before turning his attention to Brady. "You are here to find the Mystic Gray."

"Huh?" Jordan stared at Che-tan with a puzzled expression.

"Yeah, huh?" Ethan repeated.

Brady bobbed his head in perpetual motion. "Mystic Gray? You're talking about the gray wolf, aren't you?"

"Yes," Che-tan affirmed.

"There is no wolf at Crater Lake for seventy-five years," Ha-ida said sharply. "There is no Mystic Gray."

Every creature remained silent. The only sound was the creek beneath Brady's feet as he shifted his weight. "There is a wolf. I've seen it."

"You lie!" Ha-ida shouted. The animal warriors became agitated. They inched toward Che-tan. "We will rip you apart and throw pieces of your body into lake to feed the fish. You have made a mistake coming here. You are traitor. You fight with Chief Llao. You want to destroy my people." Ha-ida stood taller. "We stand with Chief Skell. Skell protect us from Llao for centuries. Only defenders of Skell are welcome here." Ha-ida stood nose to nose with Che-tan. Her voice was low and intense as she breathed out her threats. "Leave now, and I will save your death for another day."

Che-tan lowered his head. He wrapped his scarf around his face and backed toward the door, never removing his eyes from Ha-ida. He opened the door and stepped into the cold, with his partners close behind. The door shut, and the pall of bitterness disappeared. Ha-ida's animal warriors shifted back into human form.

"I've seen the wolf too," Jordan said, tugging at Ethan's coat. "In my vision. I've seen him."

"He's real," Brady agreed. He held up his glove to show the bite mark. I don't know what any of this 'mystic gray' stuff means, but the wolf is real and he's here. Look what that punk wolf did to my glove. I should have knocked him back into yesterday." Brady growled and looked at his glove one last time as he finished his rant.

"Ha-ida, what do you mean by 'defenders of Skell'?" Ethan asked. "We're all on the same team here, even Che-tan. He and his Guardian warriors fought with us on Wizard Island. He may be annoying, but . . . "

"No. Che-tan betray us all. He is not your friend."

Ethan took a deep breath and stepped next to Ha-ida. He lowered his voice as he spoke. "Okay. Fine. But these are my friends," he said, motioning to Brady and Jordan. "I trust them. They say there's a wolf here at Crater Lake. I believe them." Ethan looked into Ha-ida's unyielding eyes. "I've even read about the wolf myself. It's even been documented in conservation journals and newspapers. There is a gray wolf here at Crater Lake, whether you want to admit it or not." Ethan scrunched his nose and lowered his head with a gentle nod. "Please, tell me what it means. What is the Mystic Gray?"

15

NIGHT RIDER

I<small>T FELT LATE, BUT</small> E<small>THAN COULDN'T TELL WHAT TIME IT WAS.</small> Watches felt too constricting, so he didn't like to wear one. His cell phone batteries had died long before "landing" at Crater Lake. And not only were telephones too high tech for the shanty lodge, it appeared that this was also true for clocks. Ethan was left to wander. Lying on his side atop an animal skin rug next to the fire pit, Ethan watched the firelight flicker onto the ceiling and walls. The other lodgers had separated to different areas and had eventually quieted down. Even Jordan's odd mixture of enthusiasm and anxiety had faded over the last couple of hours. Brady had dozed almost instantly after the lights went out. Ethan closed his eyes as he tried to sleep. He felt beaten and exhausted after a day of chasing Jordan across the country and an intense crash landing. He wanted to sleep, but he knew it wouldn't come. It never did.

Shifting onto his other side, Ethan stared into the face of a skinned bear that Jordan lay upon. "That is so creepy," he muttered in an almost imperceptible whisper. A voice from the shadows startled him, and he flinched.

"You do not think very much of our ways. You think you are better than us." Ha-ida stepped from the shadows near the opening to another room. She walked toward the fire pit and sat on a thick stone. "You think we are simple."

Ethan stammered as he tried to defend himself, but his words felt inadequate. He sat up and faced Ha-ida. He concentrated on his thoughts and then spoke slowly. "No, I'm not better than you. And there's nothing wrong with simple. I just thought that . . ."

"What? We are creepy?" Ha-ida pressed. Her words were soft but piercing.

Ethan smiled. "You . . . creepy? No. But that?" he said, pointing at the bear head connected to the rug. "Yeah. That is big-time creepy. You guys transform into all kinds of different animals, some even into bears, but you keep the dead bodies around." Ethan nodded as he studied the orange flame reflecting in the bear's glassy eyes. "It's definitely twisted. You're kind of taking the whole, 'be one with nature' thing a bit too far, don't you think?" He waited for a response, but Ha-ida stood silent and straight. "Seriously, think about it. I could be sleeping on someone you knew." Ethan shuddered at the thought.

Ha-ida's lips parted into a narrow grin. Ethan didn't know what he had said to amuse her, but her smile was definitely more welcome than her scowl. She leaned over and looked into the face of the bearskin rug. She nodded her head and held a hand to her eye. "Yes. This is my grandmother. She is beautiful, no?" Ethan flinched. Ha-ida waited for a moment as her stern eyes looked into Ethan's, but then her smile returned long enough for Ethan to realize the joke. Then, her mood grew somber. "When we die, we take our human form. When you see a dead animal, it is only an animal." She nodded to Ethan as a sign that everything should now be perfectly clear. "Are you uncomfortable? Why do you not sleep?" she asked.

"Me? I never sleep. Not since . . ." Ethan paused. "What about you? Not tired?"

Ha-ida rubbed her eyes. "Exhausted. I have a responsibility. I wait for a girl." A soft knock from the door near the back serving counter drew Ha-ida's attention away, and Ethan followed her gaze. "Yes?"

A young boy stepped forward. The glow of the fire flickered across his face. "She is here."

Ethan rose to his knees, then stood. "What girl? Who's here?" he asked.

"Would you like to come see?" Ha-ida asked.

The boy at the back of the room cleared his throat. "You should hurry."

Stepping over Jordan, Ethan went to the main door where his coat was hanging. He pulled the hoodie over his hair and then zipped the jacket tight up to his chin. Ha-ida joined him at the door, but the other boy disappeared back into the darkness of the adjoining shanty. The bitter nighttime air assaulted Ethan as Ha-ida opened the door. "Aren't you going to get a coat?" Ethan asked as she strolled out the door and into the snow in short sleeves.

She smiled. "Try to keep up," she said. Then she morphed into a pronghorn antelope. Ethan's cheeks filled with air, and he blew out as he shuddered. He never got used to watching the transformation of human to animal. He would never call it "creepy," at least not in front of Ha-ida, but . . . he blinked as he studied the creature in front of him. She was beautiful.

Ha-ida's antelope stood four feet tall and looked to be about five feet long. Short horns rose from her head and curved inward in the shape of a heart. The exterior light from the building shone on her cinnamon-colored fur and gray belly. She turned to Ethan and pressed her nose against his chest. Then she nodded at the snowmobile.

"Hold on a second." Ethan felt a little foolish talking to an antelope. But what the heck. She seemed to understand just fine. He reached inside the door and borrowed a long scarf that he wrapped around his head multiple times. Only his eyes remained uncovered. He shrugged his shoulders and popped his neck. "Let's go."

Climbing onto what looked to be the oldest of the three snowmobiles, Ethan sat, grabbed the handles, and gulped. He'd never driven one before. He'd never driven anything before, except for a plane, and that didn't end very well. He studied the steering column and located the key. He took a deep breath as he turned the key in the ignition. The snowmobile purred. He pressed a switch that turned on the headlights, and then he found the throttle control near his thumb on the right handlebar. He pressed it. "CRAP!" The Arctic Cat shot off like a rocket with Ethan barely holding on. He removed his thumb from the throttle. The snowmobile slowed, but his racing heart didn't. Then from the left, Ha-ida bounded past him with long strides as her hooves kicked up the snow. He blinked as she entered the trees, and then she was gone.

Pressing lightly on the throttle, Ethan weaved between the trees and followed Ha-ida's tracks. When he was out of the grove and facing the slope into the pumice desert, he prepared himself by taking a deep breath. He tightened his grip and then let loose. Ethan leaned forward in his seat, keeping his eyes below the windshield. The snowmobile flew. He checked the speedometer on the dash: thirty miles per hour. It felt like one hundred. His eyes scanned the darkness. He could still see Ha-ida's tracks in front of him, but no Ha-ida. Pressing harder on the throttle, the Arctic Cat glided down a slight decline; forty miles per hour, and there was still no sign of Ha-ida. Fifty. *Where is she?*

At sixty-five miles per hour, Ethan felt like he could barely hang on. He reduced his speed to sixty. The fresh antelope tracks led past the wreckage of his airplane and veered gently to the left through vast open fields. He hoped there wouldn't be any sharp turns, but he decided he'd better locate the brakes just in case. After another few minutes speeding along at sixty miles per hour, Ethan eased off the throttle and practiced on the brakes as he approached a narrow road. Ha-ida's tracks turned and ran along the road heading north. But then they disappeared. He followed the direction of the road and stopped minutes later when his headlights flashed on the antelope. She was standing in the center of the snow-brushed pavement. Ha-ida pushed her nose against a heap in the road, and then she transformed back into a girl.

Ethan pulled up slowly alongside and then turned off the ignition. "Hurry!" Ha-ida yelled.

Ethan jumped off the snowmobile and ran to the center of the road. Ha-ida held a girl in her arms. The girl wore a silver puffy jacket, but, like Ethan's jacket, it appeared inadequate for the conditions. Kneeling next to Ha-ida, Ethan pulled back the hood and looked into Allie's frost-covered face. He gasped, and his lips quivered when he saw his friend's lifeless expression. "Is she . . . ?"

"She is alive," Ha-ida said. Ethan exhaled unevenly as he reached for Allie's hand. It felt colder than his. "We must hurry. Help me put her on your sled." Ethan and Ha-ida lifted Allie from the middle of the thin road and sat her on the back of the snowmobile. "Get on."

Ethan climbed on in front. "How are we going to . . . ?"

"Give me your scarf." Without waiting, Ha-ida pulled the scarf from Ethan's head and wrapped it around the two friends, binding them together while Ethan rubbed the moisture forming in the corner of his eyes. "This time, try to keep up." Morphing back into a pronghorn antelope, Ha-ida strode off the road and began running.

Ethan looked down to turn the key, and by the time he looked up, Ha-ida already had a comfortable lead. "Hang on, Allie. We're going to get you someplace safe . . . and warm." He turned the Arctic Cat slowly and then pressed the throttle with his thumb. He accelerated to forty-five miles per hour. With a passenger tied to his back, it was the fastest he felt he could manage. Ha-ida maintained a comfortable lead, but Ethan never lost sight of her again until she entered the trees. He followed her tracks back to the shelter, where Ha-ida waited in human form for Ethan. Ha-ida yelled inside, and within seconds, Jordan was also at the door. The two girls and Ethan picked Allie off of the snowmobile and carried her inside next to the fire.

"Take off her coat. I will get warm blankets," Ha-ida said. Then, she disappeared through a door into some unknown area of the shantytown.

Ethan laid Allie on the thick bearskin rug close to the fire. "Brady!" Ethan hissed in Brady's direction, but Brady snored without even a break in his breathing. Ha-ida returned quickly, and they smothered Allie under a pile of heavy blankets.

"Ethan, what's Allie doing here?" Jordan asked. He shook his head because he was wondering the same thing. "Will she be all right?"

"She will be fine." Ha-ida looked at Brady sleeping on the ground in front of her. She frowned and then kicked Brady in the gut before stopping at the door. Brady didn't wake up or even flinch. "Get some rest," she said as she exited the room. "I do not know what tomorrow will hold."

"That sounds real cheery," Ethan muttered.

Jordan snuggled up alongside Allie and closed her eyes.

"Thank you, Ha-ida," Ethan said. "Good night."

16

THE WORST SUPERPOWER IMAGINABLE

WITH NOTHING TO READ DURING HIS LONG NIGHTTIME hours, Ethan lay on his side staring at Allie. Her blonde hair cascaded over her pillow, and the blanket rested below her chin. The firelight flickered across her face. She was just as Ethan remembered. Smoke escaped through the round hole in the roof, and the sky outside brightened from pitch black to a dark gray haze. Ethan could hear the wind whipping above the building, and an occasional gust pounded against the shabby shack. It wouldn't have surprised him if the entire building collapsed. But morning finally arrived. Ethan and his friends were still in one piece.

Rising onto his elbows, Ethan looked down at Allie and studied her thick eyelashes, rosy cheeks, and blushing lips. The added color was a good sign. He sighed with a touch of longing but then flinched when he heard a deep voice from behind.

"You little perv," Brady groaned. Ethan swung around to see Brady rubbing his eyes, smiling. "Hey, I can't blame you. She's a hottie."

Ethan's words tumbled from his mouth. "What do you mean? I was just checking on Jordan. That's all."

"Mmm-hmmm. Right. Whatever, man. I don't care." Brady

tossed his blanket to the side as he sat up and then stood. "You think they've got any food in this dump, or will I have to go shoot breakfast myself?"

Ethan frowned and then pointed toward the back counter. "Check over there. You sleep well?" Ethan asked, thinking of how Brady didn't even budge when they brought Allie in during the middle of the night or when Ha-ida kicked him.

"Me? Oh yeah. Awesome." Brady opened a cabinet and peered inside. He opened a box of crackers and started chomping. "I'm as good as dead when I'm asleep." He found a pitcher of water and poured some into a dirty cup he found on the counter. "So when did Allie get here?"

Ethan sat up and looked through the fire at Brady. "Last night. We could have used your help."

Brady laughed. "If you need something and I'm asleep, you'd better get used to waiting. It's safer that way." His smile faded as he took another bite of crackers. "Besides, this doesn't happen by accident," he said, motioning up and down his body like a game show host. "You've heard of beauty rest, right?"

"Yeah."

"Well, I need my stud rest."

Ethan shook his head. "Same old Brady."

Brady smirked. "Well, yeah. I'm the same . . . mostly." He paused for a moment. "But I'm serious, Ethan. The harder I sleep, the stronger I get. I've got some serious bench-pressing skills." Ethan ignored Brady's bragging words. "What? You don't believe me?" Brady asked.

"Like *you* said before, I don't care."

Brady left his crackers and water at the counter and hurried around the fire to stand in front of Ethan. "No, Ethan. Really. I'm so strong that nothing can hurt me."

"Mmm-hmmm," Ethan mimicked.

"Watch this." Without delay, Brady stepped to the fire pit and reached into the coals. He picked up a glowing red ember and held it in both hands. He snapped it in half and stuck a piece in his mouth. Ethan heard the sizzle. After a moment, Brady spit the coal back into the fire. "Can you do that?"

"Wow. That's pretty cool. You should join a circus or something," Ethan said, trying to hide his fascination.

"Oh yeah? What about this?" Brady pulled a compact knife from his pocket and locked it open. He held it out from his stomach, but paused as he looked at Ethan.

Ethan grinned. "What? Nervous?"

"No. But I like this knife." Brady swung his hand out and then jammed it into his stomach. Ethan flinched as he watched Brady stab the knife against his flesh. Then he heard a clank of something hitting the wood floor. Brady bent over and picked up the blade that had snapped in half. He raised his shirt to show Ethan. There wasn't even a nick in Brady's skin. "And if that doesn't convince you, ask Che-tan next time you see him about where he found me."

Ethan stood and shuffled toward Brady, who was still lifting his shirt to expose his ripped abs. He leaned to get a closer look and pointed at the spot where the knife should have entered Brady's body. Nothing. "Where did Che-tan find you?"

Brady's teeth shone from between his lips. "Beneath an avalanche along the shore of the lake. It was kind of fun actually, but my skis are toast. And that's not the coolest part. After they dug me out, I looked back into the hole and saw this huge boulder with a perfect imprint of my body where I slammed into it." Ethan's jaw dropped. Brady chuckled. "The boulder should probably go into a museum or something. It's pretty rockin'."

"Ha, ha," Ethan said, unimpressed by the lame pun.

"Are you done showing off yet?" The weak female voice surprised Ethan. He looked down to see Allie staring at Brady. "You have muscles. Big deal. You can put your shirt down now."

"Big deal? Yeah, I think it's a big deal," Brady said, walking closer to Allie. He ran his fingers through his hair and then pumped his red eyebrows. "Do you have muscles like this?"

he asked, lifting his shirt again and flexing his abdomen like a bodybuilder.

Allie pushed the pile of blankets from her body and stood next to the fire pit. "No, but can you do this?" She kicked a stone at the base of the pit. She grimaced in pain and opened her mouth. Frozen vapor shot from her mouth and suffocated the fire instantly. The logs and coals that had been burning just seconds before were covered in ice. She then kicked her other foot into the stone. She cocked her neck as she tried to control the pain, and then she opened her mouth again, shooting a blaze of fire back into the pit. The fire roared, and white smoke rose up through the opening in the roof.

"That is awesome!" Brady said. He scooted next to Ethan and nudged him in the stomach with his elbow. Ethan folded over from the impact of Brady's blow. He wheezed for breath. Brady stared at Allie. "You get hotter all the time."

"Grow up," Allie said.

Ethan wheezed some more and then reached up and placed one hand on Brady's back for balance.

"Whoa! I've seen that before," Jordan said, joining the group as she rose from off the bearskin rug. "You're the flute." Allie nodded. "Can you do the light and wind too?"

"Wait a minute. She's the flute? What's that supposed to mean?" Brady asked.

Allie ignored Brady and shrugged. "Maybe I can do the other stuff too, Jordan, but I haven't figured it out yet. I didn't even know about the fire until I burned my stupid house down." She tightened her lips and her eyes looked sad.

"So Allie inherited the powers of the flute?" Ethan asked. "And Brady is super tough and strong, like the dagger."

Brady grinned as he stuck his thumbs in his front pockets. He looked like he might start strutting. "That's right. I'm a deadly weapon."

"Is that what happened to your dad?" Allie asked. "I heard that you put him in the hospital."

Brady's scowl darkened the room. "Shut up. I don't want to talk about it."

"And Jordan keeps having these crazy visions, just like when she wore the necklace. We don't know when the visions will come or where they'll take her."

"That's how we got here," Jordan said. "I actually hijacked a plane." She bobbed her head with excitement, and Ethan shook his with displeasure.

"And a school bus," Ethan added. "I just tag along."

Jordan smiled. "Ooh, a bus? I didn't know that."

"Okay, so we've got all of these powers, right?" Brady asked.

"Yeah," the group responded in unison.

"Why?" Brady asked. Ethan hoped Brady wasn't really as slow-witted as he sounded.

"Brady, it's all about the artifacts we retrieved from the Phantom Ship: the dagger, the flute, the healing bowl, and the translator. Together, they were the key to unlocking the Prison of the Lost. The powers are just . . . well, they're exactly what was promised. The legend said we had to stab the conjurer in the eye and watch him perish. Only then would the prison be unlocked and our parents saved."

"The conjurer would lose his powers, and we would inherit them," Allie finished. "I didn't think it was a literal thing, but I guess it was. We have Chief Llao's powers." The words sunk deep as Ethan felt the gravity of their combined inheritance.

"Yeah, okay. I got it. I was just testing you. So what's your power, Ethan?" Brady eyed Ethan as if hoping to see into his soul. "What can you do?"

"He reads," Jordan answered.

"What?" Allie asked as Brady laughed. "No, seriously. What's your power? The bowl told us to stab the conjurer in the eye and we'd inherit his powers, Chief Llao's powers. The rest of us have powers like the artifacts, so what can you do? What does reading have to do with anything?"

Ethan's head hung low. He didn't want to answer.

"Do you also have mad spelling skills?" Brady teased.

"I read fast," Ethan said. "And it doesn't matter if it's written in Chinese, German, Swahili, or mathematical equations. It's like everything is in English to me. Maybe it's because I had the translator on Wizard Island." Ethan paused, realizing his power sounded like he might qualify to be the king of nerddom. "Maybe the translator power I inherited makes me smart. Really smart. I remember things."

"You what?"

Ethan raised his as he looked Brady in the eyes, and then his gaze wandered to Allie. "I remember . . . everything. I read super fast, and I have an eidetic memory. I read almost the entire airplane pilot's manual in fifteen minutes, and I can still tell you about every gauge and controller. I even remember the formulas for calculating actual air speed and distance. I'm smart."

"Fantastic!" Brady joked. "If I'm ever in battle against a horde of zombie teachers, I'll call you. Eidetic memory? What the heck is that?"

Ethan shuffled his feet and tried to avoid Allie's eyes. "Some people call it photographic memory," Ethan mumbled. Brady was right. Speed-reading had to be the worst power ever.

Allie cleared her throat and looked around the room. "That's great, Ethan." Her voice was weak, and her compliment sounded as pathetic as Ethan felt.

"I bet you're great at parties," Brady said. "Maybe *you* should join the circus or something. Or maybe the Academic Bowl Team at school. They'd probably take you."

Ethan felt like he was shrinking into the floor. Brady towered over him with muscles and toughness, while Allie seemed to inch away as if repulsed by his nerdiness.

Jordan puckered her lips as she looked at her brother with pity, and then she ran to Allie and wrapped her arms around the older girl's waist. "I'm so happy to see you again," Jordan said. "I missed you."

"I missed you too, Jordan," Allie said as she squeezed. She

looked at the boys. "But I didn't miss Crater Lake at all."

"Why'd you come back?" Brady asked.

Allie fluttered her eyelashes as she thought. "I'm not sure, but it's the only place I could think of going. In a strange way it feels like home."

Ethan walked to the counter and stuffed a cracker into his mouth. "We're all here now. Let's try to figure out why."

Jordan's tight curls flung around as she wagged her head. "I know why we're here. We came back to find Jacob. Jacob's here at Crater Lake. And he's alive."

17

THE MYSTIC GRAY

ETHAN RUBBED THE BACK OF HIS NECK AS HE STUDIED HIS friend's reactions to Jordan's theory. Brady placed his massive hand on Jordan's shoulder and shook his head. "Jordan, Jacob's dead. I went to his funeral. I see his family at church every Sunday, and he's not there. Trust me. He's gone."

"No. My vision has to mean something. It has to. I don't always understand them, but I saw a gray wolf sitting behind Chief Llao. When I looked back, it was Jacob. And then last night Che-tan called the wolf the Mystic Gray," Jordan said. "It feels like Jacob. It's got to be him."

"Whoa, whoa, whoa! Hold on there," Ethan said. "You think Jacob *is* the Mystic Gray?" Ethan's shoulders slumped, and then his gaze locked on his older friends with a look of concern for his crazy sister. "Jordan, that just doesn't make sense. Jacob's dead. We all saw him. How could he be a wolf? Why would he be a wolf?"

"I'm eleven. How should I know?" Jordan said with a hint of fury in her eyes. "But I know what I saw, and I know that we all have powers we can't explain."

"She's got that right," Allie agreed.

"Why couldn't he be alive?" Jordan asked. "Why? Because that's not 'normal'?" Jordan started to tear up. "Nothing around here is normal. Nothing!"

Brady stepped next to the fire pit, sat on one of the benches, and stared into the flame. "What artifact did Jacob have? It was the bowl, right?"

Ethan nodded as he thought. Then he smiled. "Yeah, he had the healing bowl." Ethan chuckled as he remembered the miraculous healings he witnessed because of the bowl. "The bowl saved Jacob's life a couple of times that day. Is it impossible to think it could save him again?" He looked at Jordan, raised one eyebrow, and lifted his shoulders. "It's crazy, right?" He waited while the others nodded in agreement. "Yeah, definitely crazy. But," he paused, "other than being totally nuts, it could be possible. Maybe Jacob *is* the Mystic Gray."

"Ethan, I shoot flames from my mouth." Allie emphasized every word. "I think *anything* is possible around here."

"So what do we do? How do we find him?" Ethan asked. "I read about this in a magazine. Scientists have been trying to track the gray wolf for months. They've followed his tracks, but he's pretty elusive. They call him OR-7."

"Maybe Jordan could have another vision and lead us to him," Allie suggested.

Jordan shook her head. "I can't control the visions. They just sort of happen."

Brady cleared his throat. "Guys, as always, you're making this too complicated. But don't worry. I'm here to make things simple."

"You *are* the king of simple," Allie agreed.

"Funny," Brady said with a frown. "Ethan said the scientists follow his tracks. It's snowy out there. How hard can it be to follow tracks in the snow?"

Jordan's eyes widened. She bobbed her head quickly in agreement.

Ethan looked at Allie and shrugged. "I suppose it's possible."

"Agreed," Allie said.

Brady clapped his hands together in a loud bang. "Great. So let's go already," he said. Brady walked to the door and pulled his snow clothes from the hooks. Jordan followed and started getting dressed for the frigid weather, borrowing mittens, a hat, and a scarf from the hooks. Then she pulled on her red snow boots.

Ethan hesitated as the others prepared for the cold. The gleam in their eyes was unmistakable. The idea of finding Jacob alive was thrilling, even if it sounded too fantastic to be true. But Ethan worried about Jordan's disappointment when they failed. The wolf, OR-7, had been tracked over months in areas between Yellowstone National Park, Crater Lake, and all the way down to Mt. Shasta in California. He wanted to believe, but . . . the odds of success were terrible. "Hey, guys, maybe we should wait for Ha-ida. I think we could use her help," Ethan said.

"Ha-ida?" Brady asked. "Why would we wait for her? We've got this."

Ethan scratched the fluffy curls atop his head. "Well, she's an antelope, and she's stinking fast. You should see her run. When we find Jacob . . . I mean . . . the wolf . . . I mean . . ."

"Maybe we should just call him the Mystic Gray for now," Allie suggested.

"Fine. When we find the Mystic Gray, she can help us catch him," Ethan said. "Besides, she knows Crater Lake better than we do."

"Do you think she'll help?" Jordan asked. "She got pretty mad the last time we mentioned the Mystic Gray."

Ethan plastered a toothy grin on his face in an attempt to mask his worry. "Yeah, I don't know what all of that is about." He paused for a moment. "Maybe we won't mention the Mystic Gray. We can ask her to take us to the ranger station so we can meet up with Uncle Bart and call Mom and Dad." That sounded really good. He wanted to call. He wanted to hear their voices. He lost himself in a moment of homesickness, but then he returned to the task at hand. He felt guilty about the conspiratorial lie he was planning to tell Ha-ida, but not guilty enough to change his mind.

Brady grinned. "Okay, go get your little friend, Ethan. This could be fun. Don't wolves eat antelope?" Ethan scowled. "Hurry up," Brady prodded. "Go get her. I know exactly where we should start looking. We'll leave the lying to you."

– 18 –

SNOWSHOES

"TELL ME AGAIN WHY WE ARE WALKING WHEN THERE ARE three perfectly good snowmobiles back at the . . . the . . . what do you call that place?" Ethan asked.

Ha-ida moved quickly over the thick layer of snow. She wore a simple leather pack with four small dream catchers dangling from the back of her wool coat. "The machines are for emergencies. Fuel is scarce. We must preserve it."

Allie lifted one foot slowly and took a long stride, staring at the raised snowshoe on her foot. "It looks like I'm wearing a tennis racket," she said.

"Yeah, we're styling," Brady added.

"It is a primo new fashion," Allie said. "Everyone will be wearing them next season."

Ethan sneered and jogged forward with labored steps to catch up with Ha-ida. "These snowshoes are great," he said with a big smile. "Guys, these are authentic. Check out the hardwood frame with rawhide lacings and web on the bottom. This is quality workmanship. Ha-ida, did you make these yourself?" Ethan asked.

She nodded, but her stoic face didn't show any pleasure at the compliment.

"I don't get it," Jordan said, already panting from the exertion of the long walk through the snow. "What's the point of wearing these things?"

Ethan looked at the others with a glow in his eyes, eager to share his knowledge, but he paused when he saw Brady's perpetually annoyed look and instead awaited one of his usual snarky comments. "Go ahead, Encyclopedia Brown," Brady said. "Tell us about the snowshoes before your head explodes."

Ethan smiled. "Since you asked . . . the snowshoe transfers an individual's weight to a larger area to keep them from sinking into deep snow. It's called 'flotation.' The front of the shoe is curved up slightly to help with maneuverability, and the rawhide netting on the bottom keeps the snow from gathering on top and weighting it down." He looked at Allie and then Brady. "It originated with the fur traders and others who depended on walking through fresh snow and—"

"Dude, are you done?" Brady asked.

Ethan glanced over at Ha-ida and saw her smirk. "You've got to admit, it's pretty ingenious," he said in conclusion.

"Yes, it's magical. How much farther to the rim of the crater?" Allie asked.

Ha-ida stared into the sky, so Ethan did the same. He didn't know what he was looking for, though. "We waste too much time going to rim. We should hurry to ranger station. I sense storm moving in."

Ethan cleared his throat. "Brady lost something important before the avalanche. He wants to find it before it's lost forever. Then we'll go straight to the ranger station to find my Uncle Bart. He's a ranger there." Ha-ida pursed her lips as she turned her head to look at Ethan. The weight of her stare felt uncomfortable, so Ethan looked straight ahead. "So do you want to tell us about you and Che-tan? I got the impression you know each other well. Maybe too well."

Ha-ida frowned and growled softly. "My kind does not like his kind. He is selfish. He is deceitful. He is a traitor."

"But you have the same accent," Brady said. "Not like Stan. Don't hold back, Ha-ida. How do you really feel?"

"And what do you mean, 'his kind'? You all look the same,"

Allie said. "I mean, you're different animals and everything, but aren't you all Guardians of the lake?"

"Che-tan's a punk, but the Guardians are killer. You should have seen our battle on Wizard Island last summer," Brady said. "They were amazing."

"I saw everything. I saw Che-tan trick you. I saw you free Chief Llao from his prison below the lake. I saw you leave. I knew you would be back."

"Whoa! Wait a minute. You watched the battle but didn't help us? And you say Che-tan is a traitor? You've got some nerve. At least he was brave enough to fight."

"I serve Chief Skell. No other. He is good. He protect us." Ha-ida looked over the rest of the group. "Che-tan serve Chief Llao. Che-tan serve himself." She pointed through a thicket of trees to an opening. "We are almost to rim. We must hurry before storm come."

"Ha-ida, we want to understand," Ethan said. "But this doesn't really make much sense. You're a person *and* an animal, just like Che-tan and his people. You seem to be the same."

"Have you seen other hawks at Crater Lake?" Ha-ida asked.

"Yes."

"Have you seen other bears at Crater Lake? Cougars, bats?"

"Yes."

"Have you seen other antelope like me?" she asked.

Ethan thought for a moment. He looked at Allie, who was shaking her head. "No. We haven't seen any other antelope. Why is that?"

"This is what I am explaining. Che-tan's power to transform comes from the same place as mine, but . . ."

"But what?" Allie asked. "Why aren't there others like you?"

The group stepped from the trees into a clearing on a snowy meadow above Crater Lake. They lifted their knees high as they stepped across the barren meadow and toward the edge of the cliff leading down to the lake. "Don't get too close. The snow isn't stable near the edge," Brady warned. "Trust me. I know."

He peered over the spot where he had plummeted over the side in his avalanche.

"Ha-ida, why aren't there others like you?" Allie repeated.

After a brief pause, Ha-ida explained. "I am last pronghorn antelope at Crater Lake. That is why. My kind live short life. Che-tan live very long life. He use power of lake to stay young and hunt my kind to extinction."

Ethan scratched his glove against the blue cap on his head. "How old are you?"

"I am almost sixteen years old."

Ethan lowered his head and his lips curled into a frown. "Oh. I'm sorry," he said as he studied Ha-ida's appearance. Her long gray roots didn't match the youthfulness of her face, but they provided evidence of her advancing age.

"Sorry about what?" Brady asked. "That she's too old for you?"

"Brady, the pronghorn lifespan is only fifteen to sixteen years." Ethan said, looking at Ha-ida. "For your kind, you are very old, aren't you?" Ha-ida nodded. "How old is Che-tan?"

Ha-ida stepped closer to the cliff and looked over. "He is nearly sixteen as well, in his own way."

"'In his own way'? What does that mean?" Allie asked.

"Che-tan lives five hundred years for every one year of human life. He was a baby when the Crater was formed."

"That means he's nearly seventy-eight hundred years old. You're kidding, right?" Ethan asked. "Are you telling us that Che-tan is not really a teenager?"

"No. He is. But he ages *very* slowly. It is Chief Llao's gift to him."

"Why would Chief Llao give Che-tan a gift?" Brady asked.

Ethan thought for a moment while Ha-ida flipped up powder with the toe of her snowshoe. Then, recognition flashed in his eyes, and a frown appeared on his face. "Because Che-tan is Chief Llao's son." He looked to Ha-ida for confirmation. She nodded.

"What?" Brady screamed. "That little creep is Chief Llao's son? He was working against us the entire time he pretended to help?" Ha-ida nodded. "I'm going to break that little punk in half."

"Because he lives long, I live short. I will die soon, and there will be no pronghorn left to lead the true Guardians of Crater Lake in defense of Skell. Che-tan and Llao will reign. The Guardians follow Che-tan. They have been deceived. Their eyes are hollow and pale. My people are different. My people know truth. You can see difference in our eyes, and in the gray of our hair."

Brady grunted and pretended he was snapping something in half. Ethan assumed he was planning for his next meeting with Che-tan.

Ethan walked a few paces from the rest of the group and bent over. He stared at the snow and then walked farther. "So what does the Mystic Gray have to do with all of this? Why did you get so mad when we told you the Mystic Gray was back?" Ethan asked.

"Because it is cruel lie." Ha-ida turned away from Ethan. "The pronghorn and the Mystic Gray were partners before gray wolf was destroyed. Only the pronghorn remains. I am the last."

"Ahh. I see," Brady mused. "So if the Mystic Gray returned, you'd be out of a job. He'd be the leader, not you." Brady laughed. "You and Che-tan aren't so different. You both want power."

"No!" Ha-ida stepped close enough to Brady that she almost bumped her nose into his chest. She tilted her head back and stared into Brady's face. "I want Mystic Gray to return. I will be gone soon. We need him, but it is impossible for him to return to lead. The Gray are all dead. My people have told stories of his return for fifty years, but he does not come. He never comes."

Ethan stepped farther from the group and crouched in the snow. "Brady, does this look like the spot?"

"What spot?" Ha-ida asked.

"The spot where I met the Mystic Gray," Brady said, "and then taught him a lesson when he bit me. Yeah, Ethan, that looks about right."

"That really happened?" Ha-ida asked. "Really?"

Brady smiled. "Yeah, of course it *really* happened, and—"

"We've got the tracks to prove it!" Ethan hollered. He stood and held a gloved hand over his eyes. Even with dark clouds in the sky, the snow reflected the light into a nearly blinding aura as he looked to the north. Ethan pointed. "The tracks lead that way."

Ha-ida's expression turned from confusion to joy to worry in a millisecond. She raced toward Ethan and bent over to examine the tracks. She stood and looked to the north. "We cannot go there."

Brady huffed. "You're one nutty old lady. You just got finished telling us how important the return of the Mystic Gray would be. He's here, but you won't follow? What's wrong with you?"

"What's over there?" Jordan asked. "Why can't we follow?"

"Because she's afraid," Brady suggested. "Just like during the battle for Wizard Island. She doesn't have the courage to fight."

Ethan grimaced at the insult and wondered how she would react. "Dude, just because you think you're indestructible doesn't mean you have to be a jerk," Ethan said.

"What are you going to do about it, Ethan? Talk me to death? Or maybe remember something really important? Maybe you can read to me really fast. That would be scary."

Allie stepped beside Brady and glared at him with her patented squint. Brady took a step back. Allie then turned toward Ha-ida and asked, "What's over there?"

Ha-ida's shoulders rose as she took a deep breath. "Llao rock. That is where Chief Llao and his people settled after escaping from the Prison of the Lost." She turned to Brady. "You may think you are strong, but Chief Llao is stronger. You are not invincible. He will find a way to destroy you."

Brady puffed out his chest. "We'll see." He picked up his right foot and took a long stride as he lumbered in the direction of the wolf tracks. "I'm ready for Llao."

19

SEPARATION ANXIETY

BEFORE THE GROUP HAD PROGRESSED THIRTY PACES, THE dark clouds swirled overhead, and a gentle snow began falling. Within the next fifteen paces, the fat flakes fell like a steady rain. By twenty more, the stinging snowflakes beat sideways against Ethan's face. "We're going to lose our tracks," Ethan yelled over the sound of howling wind.

"Or walk off a cliff!" Allie hollered back. "I can't see a thing!" she added.

Ethan wrapped his scarf tighter around his face and grabbed on to Jordan's hand. "Stay close."

"How far to Llao rock?" Allie yelled as she slogged along, lifting her snowshoes high with each step.

"My legs hurt," Jordan said.

"Mine too," Allie whispered to Jordan as she placed a hand on the younger girl's arm.

Ha-ida stopped at the head of the group and turned. "It is too far. You are not prepared for this weather. We must turn back."

"Turn back? This is nothing. We can keep going," Brady argued.

Ethan thought he was trying to act macho again. But as he watched Brady, it seemed that the weather really didn't bother him much. He didn't appear to be cold. He wasn't panting for breath or sweating profusely like the rest of the group, and he certainly didn't complain about sore legs. Ethan didn't complain either, but he wanted to. "I think Ha-ida's right. We need to rest and get out of this snow."

"We go back to Skell Village and wait for storm to clear," Ha-ida said.

"No way. I'm not stopping. If Jacob's here," Brady said, motioning broadly with his hand, "I'm going to find him." Brady's strong words turned into a momentary mumble and then strengthened again with resolve. "Even if he is just some kind of stupid dog that bit me. He was my responsibility. I'm going to find him," Brady said. "Just point me in the right direction. I can do it myself." Brady squinted at the others. "I built a snow cave close to here. You can take shelter. It's near an oval-shaped boulder." The teenagers stood and stared at Brady with pathetic expressions frozen on their faces. "Go," he said as he turned and continued walking.

"I know the boulder," Ha-ida said. "It is close. Follow me." Ha-ida turned, leaving the trail to Llao Rock, and headed back into the snow-laden trees with Ethan at her side and the girls close behind.

Ethan turned back to look at Brady, but he could only see a silhouette disappear into the shroud of snow and wind as Brady jogged toward Llao Rock.

20

SHELTER

Entering a grove of trees, Ethan could now see twenty feet in front of him, and the sting of blowing ice crystals on his eyes felt less like pricking needles as the snow calmed. Ethan lowered his scarf to uncover his mouth for a fresh breath of air. He looked up into the waving evergreens that were weighed down with clinging snow, and then stepped aside as a large clump of wet snow fell to the ground. Focused on the snow-smothered trees, Ethan grabbed Jordan's hand and held her close to avoid other piles of falling snow.

"It is not far," Ha-ida said. Her voice was calm.

Ethan panted as he tried to keep up while still pulling Jordan along. He looked back at Allie and then relayed the message. "We're almost there. You doing okay?" Allie paused and placed her hands on her knees. She then lifted one hand and gave the thumbs-up signal before slumping again to regain her breath.

The dense pine forest opened up as an eight-foot boulder rose out of the snow. "We are here," Ha-ida said. "Make circle and search for opening."

Allie, Ethan, and Jordan spread out around the boulder, and after a short search, Jordan yelled. "I found it. I think."

Ethan rushed to his sister, dodging piles of falling snow. Then he knelt next the narrow entrance of Brady's snow cave.

He peeked into the darkness inside and looked again to the trees as the sound of howling wind rushed across his ears. The trees swayed, and piles of snow fell steadily from them. Taking a quick breath, Ethan unlashed his snowshoes and squeezed into the opening. He shimmied against the narrow opening and sighed with relief as the short tunnel opened into a larger cavern. He climbed atop the short step and sat on the evergreen boughs Brady had arranged as a mat. "Come on, guys!" he yelled, leaning closer to the opening. "It's kind of a tight fit."

Allie, Jordan, and Ha-ida scurried through the opening in half the time it took Ethan. He patted his belly and grinned with embarrassment.

"So, I guess we wait, right?" Allie asked. Ethan didn't answer, but it wasn't really the kind of question that needed a response. The young teens huddled together and waited for the howling wind and snow to subside. They stared at each other in silence as they slouched in the snow cave.

Then Jordan broke the silence. "I miss my mom and dad." Allie and Ethan both nodded. "And I'm worried about Brady," she said.

Ethan exhaled and watched his breath rise to the ceiling. He tried to ignore the sadness he felt when he thought about his parents a couple thousand miles away. Then, he turned his attention to the situation at hand and tried to hide his worry. "Brady? Nah, he'll be fine. He's pretty tough."

A nearly imperceptible scoff escaped Ha-ida's lips.

"What was that for?" Allie asked. "He'll be all right, won't he?"

Ha-ida's head shook gently. "Every person has strength *and* weakness. Where strength is powerful, so is fatal flaw. Chief Llao will find Brady's flaw just like he will find ours. If you believe you are indestructible or smart or powerful, and you think you cannot be beaten, your fall will be hard. Chief Llao will make you pay for your arrogance."

The group became quiet. Ethan considered Ha-ida's words.

"Are you saying we need to stay humble despite our powers?" Ethan asked.

"I do not know about humble. We must stay realistic . . . honest. When we recognize our weakness, we can turn them into strength. If we recognize only our strength, it will be a weakness."

"So if Brady runs into Chief Llao and his people, you think he's going to need our help?" Allie asked.

Ha-ida nodded as she frowned. "He is following the Mystic Gray to Llao Rock. Brady *will* meet up with Chief Llao, and he *will* need our help if he is to survive."

21

LLAO ROCK

BRADY CROUCHED IN THE SNOW BEHIND A MOUNTAIN HEM-lock, sweat dampening his temples as the wind and snow swirled through the trees and across his face. Removing his stocking cap and gloves, he stuffed them into his side pocket and ran his fingers through his red hair, causing it to stand straight up. Staring at the wolf tracks in the snow, he let his fingers rub gently over the track, as if he were reading braille. Then, he unzipped his jacket to allow the air to freshen him up. Steam rose from his head as he peeked around the tree. The wolf tracks led directly into the heart of a wakening village a hundred yards away.

Women and children were bundled in primitive clothing and blankets. Some crouched on mats of thin woven boughs, while others perched on logs, huddled around fires with large steaming bowls. The smell wasn't very appetizing, and Brady wondered if they were actually boiling laundry instead of cooking breakfast. His stomach grumbled anyway as he thought about food, so he pulled a piece of gum from his pocket and tossed it in his mouth, chomping hard and smacking his lips.

Brady surveyed the scene of primitive huts buried up to the eaves with snow. *Is this Llao's village?* It didn't look like much. The dwellings encircled a tower that reached high into the trees. Thirty feet in the air, ropes connected the tower to the trunks of neighboring trees on two sides, providing stability for the tower. Brady looked to the top of the tower that was nearly even with the treetops. Four men stood on top, wrapped in animal skins and puffing on pipes. Each sentry faced outward in a different direction. Brady didn't know what the men were looking for, but they appeared serious and determined.

Sucking on the bubblegum juice, Brady savored the flavor. He stole a quick peek around the trunk at the women in the village and then stood with his back to the tree. He'd seen all he could from this distance. It was time to move closer. He scampered diagonally, his snowshoes kicking up powder before he took cover, and hid behind a new tree. He peeked around the side of the trunk at the Native American women and then up to the tower. One woman stared directly in his direction, so he remained still, secluded behind the trunk. He looked again, and she had resumed her work. The sentries atop the tower seemed to be looking far into the distance and not paying attention to the immediate area, so Brady decided to move closer.

Keeping an eye on the path of the wolf tracks, Brady focused his attention on the surrounding trees. Brady knelt in the snow beneath a dead pine leaning against another. The sounds of chatter and even the crackling fire grew louder the closer he snuck to the camp. He paused as he considered his options and then chose a path through the trees that circled around the village to the back side behind the small dwellings. Following his course, Brady reconnected to the wolf's path as it led back toward the cliffs of Crater Lake. He didn't fear a fight with the villagers, but he wasn't looking to start one, for once. Besides, who was he going to fight? Women? Children?

Brady slunk through the trees as the blowing snow beat across his bare face and head, and then a pile of snow fell on his head as he ducked beneath a branch. The snow ran down his back. But other than a mild chill, he barely noticed the cold. Continuing on his trail and still following the wolf tracks,

Brady wondered about the absence of men. Surely there must be men. And if these were Chief Llao's people, where was Chief Llao? Brady wanted to know, but answers to those questions weren't his primary concern. They'd have to wait. He needed to find the wolf. He needed to find Jacob.

The incline of the path steepened the farther Brady walked. Then, the trees opened, and Brady found himself standing upon a snowy peak, with Crater Lake before him in all its majesty. The massive, water-filled crater filled his view. The golden morning sun peeked above the horizon and reflected off the snow around the crater's rim, casting the entire scene in warmth and beauty. "Whoa." Brady's chin dropped open. He turned slowly as he took in the panoramic view.

Wizard Island was far below and to his right, and the snow-covered islets that crossed from the shore to Wizard Island blended in with the ice-covered lake. Instead of brilliant blue lake water, the frosty surface looked pale, like the color of the Guardian's eyes when they morphed into animals. Brady shivered, but it wasn't from the cold.

He scanned the ground as he reacquired the wolf's path, but then the chant of a war cry turned his blood colder than the icy lake. Brady turned in place. Forty-five yards behind him, thirty men stood in bearskin robes with red paint smeared across their faces in an array of patterns. They hunched over and slapped their knees in rhythm. Brady cleared his throat. He narrowed his eyes and clenched his jaw. His knuckles popped as he tightened his hands into weapons.

The crowd of warriors separated into two even groups. Their chants grew louder as a man walked through them to the front. His long black hair hung to his shoulders. His stone features and rich eyes looked intimidating, but Brady wasn't scared. He gulped, but then straightened his posture. Maybe he was a little worried, but not scared.

"Chief Llao?"

The man nodded and mumbled something Brady couldn't

understand. Then he repeated, "Llao." The man patted his chest and motioned at Brady.

Brady loosened his right fist and smiled as he waved his arm in an exaggerated motion. "Chief Llao, it's so good to meet you. I've heard tons of stories, but don't worry. I usually assume that half of what I hear isn't true. You know what I mean?" Brady's game show voice carried in the wind. "I'm Brady," he announced, as if revealing the greatest knowledge known to man.

The warriors that surrounded Llao continued slapping their legs in rhythm as their chants grew louder. Chief Llao smiled, raised both hands high, and clapped them together loudly. A warrior to Llao's side stood tall and tilted his head back as he screamed into the air. In unison, the warriors stood tall and pulled weapons from beneath their cloaks. Brady's eyes widened as he studied the warriors' weapons. Some were simple daggers crafted from bone and rock, while others appeared to be forged steel; there were spiked balls hanging from chains and spikes sticking out of clubs.

"There's no need for rudeness," Brady yelled.

Then Chief Llao pointed at Brady with a sinister smile. The men flanking Llao on the left continued to chant while the men on his right broke into a dead run, racing toward Brady, screaming with their weapons raised.

Brady widened his stance and clenched his fists as he watched the men barrel toward him. "Punks. Bring it on!"

22

FATAL FLAW

Brady's fist swooshed through the blowing snow, landing like a sledgehammer across the cheek of the first warrior. The man crumpled facedown into the snow and lay motionless. He'd been the fastest warrior trudging through the snow, which also made him Brady's warm-up guinea pig. Brady pounded him easily, leaving enough time to be ready for the onslaught of the other warriors. Brady bit his lower lip, tilted his neck, and then resumed his fighting position as fifteen warriors converged upon him with weapons in their hands and anger in their eyes.

Their painted faces and fierce screams caused Brady's heart to race, even though he knew they couldn't hurt him. One warrior seemed to have claws extending between his fingers. Brady ducked as the bear claws slashed at his face. The warrior spun in place and slashed again with his other hand, this time connecting with Brady's neck. The claws tore through the clothes and scraped against Brady's skin, but they snapped off without leaving a mark. The warrior's eyes showed fear and disbelief, while Brady's shone with renewed confidence. Brady hit the warrior with an open palm to the chest, sending the man flailing backwards and collapsing into the snow.

Spear tips broke against Brady's body, shredding his winter clothes but barely tickling him as they connected. Brady flung his arms wildly at any warrior foolish enough to step within arm's reach. The men fell around him as Brady's blows connected. They crawled through the snow as they tried to escape. and Brady let them. Fourteen men lay sprawled or in varying levels of crawling as one last warrior stood between Brady and Chief Llao. In each hand, the warrior held two flails, foot-long handles connected to a chain and a ball with spikes. The balls twirled as he swung one over his head and the other at his side. The warrior's muscles bulged from underneath his cloaks, and he hollered into the air with anger.

The man twirled the spiked balls expertly on their chains as he stepped closer to Brady. Looking past the man at Chief Llao, Brady offered an exaggerated salute in mockery of Llao's pathetic warriors. Then he stepped closer to the man, allowing the spiked balls to connect with his head and chest. Brady grabbed the front of the man's cloak with both hands, pulled him close, and then smashed his head into the man's face. Blood gushed from the warrior as he crumpled into the snow, holding his nose while blood made the ground look like a strawberry snow cone.

Brady held his palms up as he faced Llao and then motioned for the waiting warriors to come forward. "Is that all you've got?" Brady taunted. The first batch of warriors littered the snow with their writhing bodies and blood. Brady's head shook with disgust when he noticed the warriors next to Llao appearing content to stand and watch while their buddies got whooped. "What? Are you a wittle scared?" he asked in a baby voice.

Chief Llao grinned at Brady and then nodded to his men. The second wave of warriors rushed toward Brady. But instead of sprinting forward at varying speeds with weapons in hand, they all converged upon Brady in one large group as they reached and grabbed, struggling to gain a hold of him. Brady flung his arms wildly, connecting with his enemies and casting them away with power. They fell to the ground when he landed a punch, but unlike the first group, these warriors immediately arose and resumed the fight. The first group of men lying in the snow also leapt to their feet as they surrounded Brady. They crushed in around him while some wrapped around Brady's legs.

Brady heard squawking overhead and looked up to see four hawks circling. Twisting his body, Brady punched and swung his fists. But with men wrapped around his ankles, he couldn't turn in place enough to shift his position and fend off his foes. The warriors swarmed Brady, limiting his ability to swing his arms until he was held by men on his back, men on his feet and arms, and a cord wrapped around his neck from behind. He felt a strong yank as the cord tightened. The cord yanked again, causing Brady to topple backward into the snow. The warriors then piled on him and rolled Brady onto his stomach. They wrapped strong cords made of braided vines and pulled his arms away from his body. They then bound his legs and pulled them apart, separating his legs like he was being forced to make a snow angel. Four men sat across Brady's body while three men pulled tight on each binding. Brady lifted his head and strained to look as Chief Llao stepped in front of him. Llao knelt in front of Brady, placed a hand on Brady's red head, and then shoved his face into the snow and held it there.

Brady relaxed his muscles to signal his submission. But when he felt the warriors loosen their grip on his body, he pulled against the cords and swung his arms and legs wildly, casting off some of his captors, but the warriors regained their grips on the cords and pulled even tighter.

Grabbing a handful of Brady's hair, Chief Llao lifted Brady's face out of the snow. Brady gasped for air as his reddened eyes stared into Chief Llao's. Behind Chief Llao, Brady saw the four large hawks dive toward the ground and reassemble into Che-tan. He groaned when he saw Che-tan but then refocused on Llao. Chief Llao spoke in what sounded like broken English, but Brady couldn't understand. His blank stare signaled that Chief Llao should try again. Instead, Che-tan stepped forward and interpreted while Chief Llao spoke a fast and fluid language Brady didn't recognize.

"Welcome, Brady," Llao said. Brady concentrated on the words as his mind struggled to interpret the unnatural sounds into understandable speech. Che-tan translated Llao's words. "You are strong, but not as much as you think. I am strong too."

Brady tried pulling against the cords, but the men held him tight. "You hide behind your men. Let's see who's tougher. Just you and me," Brady challenged. Llao only laughed.

"Power grows in you."

"I'll show you power," Brady spat.

"You are foolish," Llao said. Even Che-tan's accent made the interpretation almost incomprehensible. Brady focused on each word as Llao spoke. "That is your weakness. You are not god. You can be killed. I teach you so you learn. Make you better warrior for me."

Brady began laughing. As soon as he did, Llao shoved his face back into the snow and held it. Brady screamed into the snow and jerked his neck as he tried freeing himself, desperate for a full breath. Then Llao released his head and allowed him to breathe. "You can't teach me squat! I'll never help you!" Brady screamed. "You can't hurt me."

Llao's lips tightened as his dark eyes narrowed. "You will help. You will be powerful ally in battle against Skell. I *can* hurt you." Llao shoved Brady's face back into the packed snow and waited. Brady pulled at his cords, and his neck muscles bulged as he tried lifting his head to regain the freedom of breathing. He pressed the back of his head against Llao's hands, but Llao kept Brady's face smothered. "I *can* kill you. I choose not to . . . for now. Remember your weakness," Llao said as Brady's body convulsed with panic. Llao released Brady's head, and Brady gasped for air. "Ah. You must breathe. Isn't that interesting?" Llao said with a chuckle. "That is lesson one."

The men on Brady's back rose as Brady's labored breath filled his lungs. The men climbed off his back and loosened the bindings. The warriors of Llao backed away as Brady slowly arose from the snow. His hard eyes glared at Llao and then Che-tan, and he tightened his mouth into an ugly pucker. He watched Che-tan as Llao and his men turned and walked away toward the edge of the crater's rim. "That's right, you'd better leave," Brady mumbled as he brushed the snow from his body and took another deep breath. He pointed at Che-tan. "You and I are going to have a serious talk later."

Che-tan didn't respond.

Llao turned to face Brady and shouted, "You and your friends must leave Crater Lake. It is not yet your time. I will summon you when I am ready for battle. Until then, you are my enemy." Che-tan translated Llao's words. Then Llao paused as he took one step toward Brady. "My next lesson will not be so gentle." He turned and continued toward the edge of the cliff above Crater Lake.

Then, without warning, Che-tan's flesh exploded as four large hawks took flight and shot into the sky. Brady watched Che-tan circle high above, and then he looked back to the cliff where Llao and his warriors had gathered. They were gone. In an instant, Brady was alone in the snow above Crater Lake.

23

DOOLITTLE

ETHAN LEANED HIS BACK AGAINST THE WALL OF THE SNOW cave while Allie laid her head against his shoulder. Jordan's long, kinky hair lay across Allie's lap, and Ha-ida sat as far from the others as she could while still remaining inside the shelter. Ethan looked at Ha-ida and sniffed his armpit. Nope. That wasn't the problem. The group sat in silence as the wind howled outside. Then, as if someone flipped a switch, the wind stopped.

Hopping up from her seat on the evergreen boughs, Ha-ida crawled out the narrow cave entrance and then yelled back inside to the others. "It is clear. We should go."

Allie climbed out first, and then Ethan followed, squeezing his way through. His shoulders and hips scraped against the tight snowy walls. "Having some problems there, big brother?" Jordan asked from behind him.

"I'm almost out." He scooted the rest of the way until his head poked from the hole. He grabbed the snow outside the cave and pulled himself the rest of the way out. Jordan followed. Ethan shielded his eyes from the blinding sunlight reflecting off the snow. His legs wobbled as he stood, and then he shook out his arms and legs as his eyes slowly adjusted to the brightness. The snowy surroundings were pristine. Ethan looked, but between the thin layer of fresh powder and the windblown snow, he couldn't even see his own tracks from just an hour before.

"What now?" Allie asked. "How do we find Brady if we can't follow any tracks?"

"We should get to the ranger station. Uncle Bart can help us find him and maybe even drive us around the overlook road near Llao Rock," Ethan suggested.

Ha-ida pointed toward the south. "Follow the rim. You will find the ranger station that way," she said, turning her eyes back to the north toward Llao Rock. "But . . ."

"But what?" Jordan asked.

"After that wind and snow, the roads will be closed. You will not find transport at the ranger station . . . if you make it."

Ethan stepped into his snowshoes, bent down, and tied the bindings around his boots. He bit the side of his lip as he thought. "Well then, I guess we should go to Llao Rock," Ethan said in a way that sounded like a question.

Ha-ida stared into the distance but didn't respond. Then, removing her backpack, she pulled out the four items that looked like dream catchers and set them in the snow. She stepped out of her snowshoes and then morphed into a pronghorn antelope.

Allie bobbed her head and shuddered. "I don't think I'll ever get used to that."

"Wait here. I will scout ahead. I will be back," Ha-ida said.

"Okay," Ethan replied. "We'll wait here. How long do you think you'll be gone?"

"Fifteen to twenty minutes," Ha-ida said. She placed each of her hooves into the center of a dream catcher, and the miniature snowshoes locked in place. "It is strange, I know. But it helps my speed if I do not sink into the snow."

Ethan held up his hands and chuckled. "No. It's awesome. Way cool! We'll wait, but hurry." The antelope version of Ha-ida turned and began sprinting across the snow through the trees. Ethan smiled as he watched her scurry and dodge around the trees.

When Ha-ida was out of sight, Ethan turned to the others. Jordan's mouth hung open. "What was that?"

Ethan shook his head. "What? It's not like you haven't seen Ha-ida or the other animals morph before." Ethan grinned. "It is pretty awesome, though, isn't it?"

"No, Ethan, I think what Jordan means, is . . . uh . . ."

"Allie, what? Spit it out," Ethan said, his patience waning.

Allie cleared her throat. "Well, you growled and made this kind of huffing sound, like a horse, or an . . . antelope."

Ethan chuckled. "Yeah, whatever."

"No, really," Jordan said. "She made grunting noises, and then you did, and then you kept going back and forth, kind of like you and Ha-ida were talking in antelope."

Ethan furrowed his eyebrows into one long unibrow as he thought. "She told us to wait here. She'll be back in fifteen or twenty minutes. You heard that, didn't you?"

Allie's eyebrows shot to the sky, and she parted her lips as she shook her head. "Nope."

Ethan looked at Jordan, who shook her head softly. Then she smiled as she ran up to her brother and wrapped her arms around him. "Now you have a real power," Jordan said with excitement. "Happy birthday!"

With everything that had happened, Ethan had forgotten his own birthday. He smiled at his sister's reminder and then acted as if it was no big deal. "Yeah, great—I can read, remember things, *and* I can talk to animals. That is *super* helpful. They have asylums for people like me."

Allie covered her mouth as she suppressed a chuckle. "Well, it's something . . . I guess."

Ethan scoffed at his newly discovered ability to translate for animals, but he considered the possibilities of his new gift. A satisfied grin covered his face and he nodded. "Yeah, it *is*."

24

PURSUIT

ETHAN LEANED AGAINST A TREE WHILE ALLIE AND JORDAN doodled in the snow with their gloved fingers. Ha-ida returned to the group quickly and morphed back into her human form. She placed her pack on her back and reattached the mini-snowshoes. "I found Brady," she said, panting for breath. "He is past Llao Rock. He is following tracks."

"He can still see the wolf tracks after that storm?" Ethan asked. "Excellent!"

"No. He does not follow the Mystic Gray. He follows the tracks of many warriors. I do not know where they lead."

"That dude's got a death wish," Ethan said.

"And the attention span of a goldfish," Allie added. "Did you talk to him?"

"I turned into my human form and tried to speak with him. He has anger in his heart. He would not listen to me. Perhaps he will listen to you," Ha-ida told Allie.

"Brady's a fighter. He wants to battle," Ethan said, scratching at the stocking cap on his head. "I can understand that."

Allie glared at Ethan. "That's just stupid. We have a plan to find Jacob. That's what we need to do, not chase after an army of ancient warriors to pick a fight." Allie shook her head. "It's major dumb. Big time."

Jordan giggled. "Maybe that can be Brady's new name . . . Major Dumb."

Ethan lowered his eyes and chose to ignore his sister's lame comment. "Think about it. Llao's our enemy, right? He's the reason we're here. He's the cause of our ridiculous powers."

"Only yours are ridiculous," Allie mumbled.

"Llao is the source of the danger we face. He's ruining our lives. You burned down your house," Ethan said, glaring at Allie. "If I had a chance to take out Chief Llao, and put an end to all of this, I'd do it . . . in a heartbeat."

"That is the mistake," Ha-ida said. "You cannot 'take out' Chief Llao until the appointed time. You may have inherited his powers, but do not think he is weak. He will destroy you if it serves his purpose. He *will* find a way."

"So, what . . . if Llao's standing at the edge of a cliff, I shouldn't push him over to end this whole thing? He's mortal right now, right? Let's destroy him while we can," Ethan said. "Doing nothing would be absurd."

"No, doing what Chief Llao wants you to do is absurd. If Llao taunts you to do something, you should do the opposite. He has a purpose for all he does. You may not understand his design, but he uses you," Ha-ida said.

"Ethan, think. Ha-ida's right. Last summer, Llao played us. We did exactly what he wanted us to do. He's like five steps ahead of us all the time, and we're just trying to catch up." Allie placed a hand on Jordan's shoulder and then looked at Ethan. "We can't allow him to distract us from our purpose. Right now, that purpose is finding the Mystic Gray. That's all. Nothing else. Fighting Llao will have to wait."

"Allie is correct. We must be patient. The Mystic Gray can help us defeat Llao," Ha-ida said.

"Lao isn't stupid. He must know that," Allie said. "Llao is probably leading Brady away from the Mystic Gray as a decoy."

Ethan stared at the two teenage girls: Ha-ida's dark skin and black hair contrasted with Allie's fair complexion and long blonde hair. But both of their expressions were resolute. Ethan shook his head. "No offense, but I don't think you guys have a clue."

Allie scoffed. "How could I possibly take offense at that?" she asked with an annoyed smirk.

Jordan gasped. "Ethan!"

"No. Seriously. You have no way of knowing what you just said, and just because you can make up some explanation about what you think Brady and Llao are doing doesn't mean it's true." Ethan paused for a moment. "Maybe Brady lost the wolf's tracks but picked up the tracks of Llao's warriors, so he's making the best of it. Maybe Llao's warriors are tracking the wolf themselves. If that's true, it would make sense for Brady to follow them."

"Brady's just doing what Brady wants, as usual," Allie said.

"You don't know that," Ethan countered. "That's my point."

"Then why wouldn't he talk to Ha-ida?" Allie asked.

"Because he's a jerk," Ethan said. The girls all nodded. "Look, I'm not trying to defend Brady if he's doing something harebrained. Maybe he is, but we don't know. And guessing about it isn't going to accomplish anything. The facts remain the same. Llao is our enemy, and we need to find the Mystic Gray. Do you agree?"

Allie and Ha-ida both nodded in consent.

"What are we supposed to do?" Jordan asked.

"We need to catch up with Brady and find out what he's up to. If he's found Llao and his people, we should keep an eye on them. But we also need to find the Mystic Gray. That's our first priority."

Allie closed her eyes as she inhaled a deep breath. "So your idea is to do exactly the same thing Ha-ida said we should do. Wow. Genius."

"We need to catch up with Brady and find the Mystic Gray. And we need to keep our heads. Chief Llao *is* smart. We can't let him have the upper hand. We need to be smart too and not make foolish assumptions."

Allie faced Ha-ida. "That's Ethan's way of saying you're right, but in a way that makes him feel like he's in charge." Ethan clenched his jaw as Allie flashed an "I gotcha" smile. Ethan wasn't amused.

Ha-ida's face showed little emotion. She looked to the north and pointed. "I know a faster path. We can catch Brady if we hurry. Follow me."

25

ROUND TWO

BRADY SUCKED ON SOME CLEAN SNOW WHILE STANDING alone at the edge of the Crater's cliff. Then, after a moment of uncertainty about where Llao's warriors had gone and what his next move should be, he followed a set of tracks into the pine forest. He sidestepped from tree to tree, and then a rumble of clomping steps and incoherent chatter drew his attention back to the cliff. Brady crouched behind a narrow trunk at the edge of the forest and peered back across the snowy field. A small contingent of warriors tromped through the snow. The warriors' heavy breathing rose from their mouths in a foggy mist. *Where'd they come from?*

Brady counted the men as he scratched his head. Ten. "I can take ten," he muttered as he spied their movements. He recognized some of the men from the skirmish earlier, but Llao was nowhere to be seen. Squinting at the brightness of the snow, Brady considered his options as he maintained his slow, easy breaths and his position in the shadows along the edge of the pine forest.

When the group made sufficient progress forward, Brady scurried along the treeline to a new cover. *Ten men. I can take out ten punks while picking my nose. Yeah, I can definitely take ten.* He repeated the phrase in his mind, trying to convince himself. The memory of his near suffocation in the snow caused his heart to race and his confidence to waver. Brady kept his distance, content to watch and follow his adversaries from a safe distance. With the tracks of the gray wolf destroyed by snow and wind, he found himself with a new mission: study his enemy.

The group of warriors bustled through the snow along the rim of the crater to the north but then made a sharp turn to the west. They entered the forest and continued their hike for a few minutes before making another sharp turn to the left. Brady knelt in the snow and watched the men change course. He held his position, squinting. The men hiked through the trees, turned left again, and prepared to exit the forest near the crater's rim.

"Weird." Brady hunched his shoulders. He tried to imagine what the warrior hikers could be doing. "Where are you guys going?" he mumbled. They had essentially hiked in a large square. Brady thought some more. It *was* a square . . . around him. He was boxed in at the center. Brady tried focusing on the movements through the trees, but the forest obstructed his view. Still, he didn't dare move. Then he heard a high-pitched moan screeching from behind him. He turned in place and looked in the direction of the sound. A second whine echoed from the side, and then another, and another, until the entire forest was consumed by shrieks and growls. Brady shifted on his knees and looked, but he couldn't see anything. A series of whoops and hollers approached, and he turned back toward the men he had been watching. But the figures were hidden in shadow.

Screams pierced Brady's ears as ten warriors ran toward him. Snow fell from tree branches, but the drifts didn't slow them. The warriors rushed to Brady, their feet sinking deep with each step. Brady set his feet at shoulder's width as he prepared to receive the warriors. But then, from the sides and from the rear, as if completing a net, cougars and bears emerged from the shadows to encircle him. *Were these Ha-ida's friends from Skell Village? Why would they be working with Llao's warriors? Impossible.* Black bears with pale blue eyes swayed their heads and pounded the snow with their paws as they prepared to attack. Brady shook his head and scowled. Che-tan's Guardians had been allies on Wizard Island. Why were they attacking? "Che-tan," Brady said, his lips curling down as he snarled.

Approaching cougars hunched their shoulders low, and their whiskers tickled the snow. They stepped forward in unison, tightening the net around Brady. The growls and howling of the animals rang in his ears. Brady scanned the area, ready to throttle Che-tan. But he was nowhere to be seen, and the annoyance of his usual screeching was absent. Then Brady's eyes darted back to Llao's warriors, who were nearly upon him.

Reaching up, Brady ripped an evergreen branch from its trunk. He swung the limb around him in an attempt to mark the territory that no creature should enter, but the bears, cougars, and warriors continued forward, undaunted by his threat. Brady tensed, his muscles bulging, as he watched the warriors move with an opening salvo. Then, from behind him, a cougar sprung and tried sinking its teeth into Brady's neck. Its claws ripped at Brady and further shredded the clothing on his back. Brady reached over his shoulder with his left hand and grabbed the scruff of the cougar's neck. His grip tightened, and his fingernails dug into the cougar as he lifted the animal over his head and tossed it into the approaching warriors. Three men fell like bowling pins as the cougar crashed into them. Then, from all around Brady, the bears, cougars, and warriors attacked in unison.

Brady swung the tree limb, clubbing men and animals alike as he twirled in place. The cougars slouched lower to the ground as they got closer. They leapt on Brady when his back was to them. His jacket and shirt fell from his shoulders like rotting flesh, leaving his skin exposed to the cold. One bear bit into Brady's right leg and pulled while another black bear grabbed the left. They pulled in opposite directions, throwing him off balance, but he ripped his leg away to keep from falling. He swung again, and the branch snapped as it hit a warrior's head. Brady took what was left of his branch and stabbed the nearest animal. The cougar yelped and then retreated deeper into the woods. Brady's fists landed on the heads of the bears at his feet, causing them to collapse to the snow. Then, he let loose a growl of his own.

Instead of waiting for the attackers to come to him, Brady chose a target and pounced. Crouching low as he leaned forward, Brady exploded into a wall of warriors like a lineman looking for a quarterback. The men fell to the ground and covered themselves while Brady pounded their faces and midsections. Bears and cougars attacked him from all sides, but Brady ignored them until he was finished with his assault. Whenever his bloody victim was unable to continue fighting, Brady moved on to the next.

Rolling on top of a Llao Warrior, Brady planted his foot into the jaw of a bear. He heard a crack, and the bear ran away. Feeling no pain, Brady fought furiously. One bear, two or three, cougars, and several men all fell to the ground bleeding before limping into the woods for safety. But more men and animals still continued their assault.

Brady's chest heaved as he struggled to maintain his balance and position on his opponents. He threw another cougar off him and then stood and backed away. The attackers also regained their feet (and paws) and regrouped while Brady paused for breath. The attackers gathered in front of Brady, forming two battle lines as they prepared for the second round of assault. Brady wiped his arms across his forehead, removing the sweat with a lone sleeve that remained intact. He reached to his back where he felt a cool breeze and then touched his bare skin where the animals had peeled away his clothing. He unzipped the front of his coat and tore the remaining clothes from his upper body. Steam rose from Brady's broad chest, and his pectoral muscles bulged in rhythm. Left, right, left, right. Then he smiled.

Two of the warrior men leaned near each other as they whispered. One man screamed an order, and the other warriors removed braided vines from beneath their cloaks. Brady lifted one finger and wagged it as if shaming them for their desire to bind him like before. His head shook. *No way.*

The cougars stood in front as they sauntered toward Brady. The bears followed closely and spread wide. The men stood in the back as they tied their vines and cords into lassos. The familiar growls of the animals filled the snowy forest, but then stopped as a wall of fire cut a path between them and Brady.

Brady's eyes lit up as the flames sliced through the snow, melting it eight feet to the ground. Brady swiveled his head and his large Adam's apple jumped. "Allie, it's good to see you," he said in the most cavalier tone he could muster through his panting.

She nodded, and then her face grew tense and she opened her mouth. Flames shot out again, melting the snow to create a wide gulf between Brady and his attackers. Brady backed away from the edge as the snow started to cave in toward the gulf.

"Seriously, Brady. It's like twenty-five degrees out here and you can't keep your shirt on," Ethan scolded.

Brady nodded and then looked at Ha-ida. Then he repeated the left, right, left, right flexing of his chest. "Pretty impressive, huh?"

Ha-ida didn't respond, but Brady was sure she was impressed.

"Come on, Brady. Let's get out of here," Allie said.

Two bears tested the edge of the ditch she had melted in the snow. A cougar wandered around the edge to avoid the obstacle. Allie tensed up and then she blew a new wall of flame around the cougar, melting more snow to keep the cougar at bay.

Guardians lined the ditch and pawed the snow. A cougar slipped as the snow collapsed to the freshly exposed mud. The cougar roamed along the wet earth that hadn't been exposed since the first snow of winter in early October. Brady felt Allie grab his forearm and pull him away, but then she stopped. He turned and saw why. Another line of animals formed, but Allie blew more fire to block their attack.

"You know, I had this under control," Brady said.

"Maybe, but we need to get out of here now," Ethan said.

Brady studied the surrounding horde of animals and warriors. Brady, Allie, Ethan, and the others stood on the snow, surrounded by the eight- and sometimes ten-foot drops created by the melted snow.

"What do we do?" Jordan asked, clasping onto Brady's arm.

"Follow me." Ethan grabbed Jordan's hand and walked the only direction he could.

Brady watched as the animals and warriors mirrored Ethan's moves on the other side of the divide.

"Allie, would you mind?" Brady asked, pointing at the attackers. Within seconds, Allie unleashed a fury of fire, causing every creature to back farther away. Leading his friends out of the woods, Brady hurried to the cliffs above Crater Lake while Allie provided a cover of flames to keep the attackers away. The animals followed their prey, mimicking every move until the group arrived at the edge of the cliff.

Brady leaned over the cliff, looking at the steep slope leading down to the ice-covered lake. "What now, brainiac?"

Sweat dripped from Allie's face, and her breathing was labored as she exhaled another wave of fire. "I don't know how long I can keep this up." She shot another blast of flame near an approaching bear, and it backed away. But the circling attackers drew closer. Allie took a deep breath and prepared to blow again but then dropped to her knee and gasped. She removed her stocking cap and dabbed at her face to remove the perspiration.

The attackers moved closer, and Brady readied himself for another round of battle, knowing he could protect himself fine. But the others? "Come on, Ethan. What's the plan?"

The circle tightened around the kids as the bears and cougars inched closer. Then a loud howl arose echoed across the lake below. The animals stopped and lowered onto their front paws, as if bowing. Then out of their midst, the gray wolf strode with its head held high.

Ethan's head cocked to one side, and Brady smiled. "I told

you I'd find him," Brady said. He looked around the group and crinkled his nose as he saw Ha-ida lower onto one knee.

"Yes. Your skills are impressive," Allie said.

The wolf stopped in front of the animals. It perked its ears straight up and growled. The Guardians watched in awe as the gray wolf turned and headed to the kids. Brady stepped to the front of the group as protection. He lowered one hand, inviting the wolf to come closer. The wolf moved slowly toward him. Its eyes gleamed as they reflected the bright snow, and then the wolf passed by Brady and stopped next to Jordan. Ethan held his sister tight against his body, but Jordan shrugged his hands off and reached down to pat the wolf's head. Her eyes brightened as she looked at the other kids, and then she reached around the wolf and hugged it around the neck.

"Jordan, I don't think that's a great idea," Allie said. Ethan nodded as he tugged on her jacket, trying to pull her back. But she resisted. The wolf growled lightly and then pointed its nose at Ethan. It growled again, and Ethan nodded. He let go of Jordan, but then grabbed Allie around the shoulder and pulled her close to whisper in her ear. Allie flinched, and her eyes widened. She turned her head and looked over the cliff at Crater Lake one hundred feet below. Then she gulped. She raised her shoulders rapidly as her shallow breathing raced. Her eyebrows rose and then she nodded nervously at Ethan. "Maybe," she said, again looking over the cliff.

Ethan stepped next to Ha-ida. Her mouth dropped as he whispered. Brady anxiously awaited his turn, and then he felt a rush of adrenaline like he'd just stepped off a roller coaster when Ethan repeated the message in his ear. The wolf growled, and Ethan nodded again. Brady crinkled his nose as he witnessed the strange conversation. He looked back at the bowing animals, and it appeared they noticed too. They didn't seem to like it.

One cougar arose and inched forward as it seemed to study the gray wolf. It growled, and another arose from its position.

The others followed. Whatever awe the Guardians felt for the gray wolf didn't translate into loyalty for his cause. They moved forward, angrier than before, while the warriors at the rear of the Guardians remained still, appearing to be amused by the scene.

"I think it's time, Allie," Ethan said. The animals moved closer, but Allie looked over the edge of the cliff with a sick expression on her face. "Allie, *now!*"

The gray wolf faced the approaching animal army and snarled. Brady clenched his fists as he readied himself for another wave of attack. The Guardian army didn't even pause as it continued forward. The wolf barked and then sprinted toward the woods, leading away a group of cougars and bears while the rest continued to close in on the kids.

"NOW, ALLIE!" Brady yelled. He watched his friend, but she didn't look ready. He could understand why, but he yelled again. "NOW!"

Allie glanced over the cliff at the frozen lake and then swallowed. Her face matched the color of the snow as it tightened. She opened her mouth, blew, and paused, and Brady's heart stopped as she dove over the edge.

26

ALPINE SLIDE

ALLIE KNITTED HER BROW WITH CONCENTRATION AS SHE blasted thick sheets of ice from her mouth. Like a roller coaster track, the sheets gathered on top of the snow before plummeting straight down over the one hundred foot cliff. Allie slid on her stomach with her arms in front of her as she took another deep breath and continued blowing the ice far in front of her. She twisted her body and could feel her foot slipping over the edge of the ice slab. As her body turned, so did the ice spray from her mouth. She widened her eyes with fear, and her heart thumped wildly as she nearly tumbled off the slide to a certain death. She then puckered her lips as if she was blowing out of a straw and changed her breath from ice to flame, which smoothed and rounded the slab into a concave slide. Allie slid back into the center of the slide, blew another light stream of fire to smooth her path, and then returned her attention to finishing the ice slide before she ran out of road.

The incomplete slide stopped halfway down the cliff until Allie connected it with a new blast of ice. With three more deep breaths, Allie connected the slide all the way down to the lake with only minor shifts and turns. She smoothed the slab with a light, steady stream of fire that melted the ice into a comfortable and fast slide. Rolling onto her back, Allie enjoyed the ride as she looked up at her friends still waiting at the top of the cliff near the mouth of the slide. She waved her hands, urging them to follow. A broad smile covered her face as she considered her accomplishment in creating the slide, but then her lips formed into an instant frown, and she gulped down the spit that gathered in her mouth. Overwhelming dread flooded her mind.

Allie flipped back onto her stomach, confused about why she felt such crushing fear. She had already dove from the cliff and created a slide with powers she'd never fully tested. She wouldn't have tried it if she didn't *think* it would work, but what could be scarier than taking flight and sliding down a massive slide that didn't even exist until she blew it into being? Her body slid smoothly toward the lake, gaining speed with each passing moment. At times, the slope of the slide was so steep that it felt like she was free-falling, barely touching the slide at all. Then the realization hit her. The slide took her straight down the mountain, but there was a flaw in her design.

Instead of gradually rounding off at the bottom for a smooth finish, the ice slide entered the frozen lake at a sharp angle. Allie blinked slowly as the finish to her ride became clear. She was about to slam into the ice at a forty-five degree angle. Twisting quickly, Allie looked up at her friends on the crater's edge and saw one of her friends jump on the slide to begin the descent to doom. Allie looked back at the fast approaching ground. Sweat dripped from her temples, but she didn't bother trying to wipe it away. She couldn't control her labored breathing. It felt like a three-hundred-pound weight rested on her chest. She had spent every ounce of energy creating the slide, but there was still more to do—much more.

Taking the deepest breath she could manage, Allie opened her mouth wide and blew an enormous pile of ice at the spot where the slide slammed into the ground. She blew and connected another pile with the first. Her eyes widened as she hurtled face first toward the mountain of ice at the bottom of her slide. She tried to take a deep breath but wheezed and coughed instead. She slid faster and faster as she approached the bottom. All she could see were the piles of ice that looked like icebergs sticking out of Crater Lake. Allie struggled to control her breathing, and just as her head was ready to crash into the ice at the bottom, she inhaled deeply and blew.

Fire exploded from her mouth and cut through the ice like a flamethrower through butter. Allie's eyes widened as she waited to slam into the ice, but a round tunnel similar to the entrance into Brady's snow cave opened up, and she slid through. Her body slid partway up the side wall of the tunnel. Aiming the flames from her mouth, Allie leveled the angle of the slide as she sped through the tube. Then, the brightness of the sun overwhelmed the light of the flame, and she broke through the back side of the iceberg into open air.

Allie's relief was short lived. She burst through the tube. But instead of gliding softly across the ice atop Crater Lake, she flew through the air, four feet off the ground, until she crashed onto the frozen lake cover. Her knees hit the ground first, and her chest and head smacked against the ice as her sliding body came to a stop.

Allie blinked her eyes, trying to focus her vision to the top of the crater. She could still see movement high above, but then she saw another body eject from the tube and shoot through the air. The body crashed to the ground and slammed into her. Allie gasped for air. She tried to rise onto her elbows to watch for the others but white fuzz overwhelmed her vision. She closed her eyes and her head smacked again on the ice with a thud.

27

PARALYZED

BRADY PEERED OVER THE EDGE OF THE CLIFF AND WATCHED as Ha-ida sailed down Allie's slide. He sidestepped the edge and placed himself between Jordan and Ethan and the approaching animal warriors. He glanced back at Jordan and noticed the gray wolf lurking behind Chief Llao's warriors as if corralling them. "Come on, Jordan," he yelled. "Get going." He watched fear fill the girl's eyes, and she shook her head. "Jordan, you can do it," Brady urged. But she didn't budge. Brady planted his feet and clenched his fists as he waited for another wave of attack.

"I'll get her," Ethan yelled, standing closest to the slide. Jordan was inching farther away from the edge.

Brady watched out of the corner of his eye. Ethan rushed toward Jordan, but two cougars leaped in front of him, cutting off his path to Jordan. Their purring sounded hungry. Brady swung around to watch the cougars just as a bear attacked him from behind. It set his teeth into Brady's leg but came away with only a stitch of ripped clothing. Brady slammed his elbow on the bear's head, and it fell to the ground momentarily before stumbling away in a clumsy, diagonal path. "Ethan, get your sister out of here."

"I can't get to her," Ethan yelled as two more cougars separated him from his sister. The gray wolf stepped between Ethan and the cougars. It snarled, and the cougars slowed their approach. "Brady, did you hear me? I can't get her." Ethan's voice cracked. "Help her, Brady."

Brady turned back. Jordan was only fifteen feet away. The cougar and bear warriors didn't seem concerned with her, but they moved closer to Ethan. The gray wolf growled, but the cougars were undaunted. "Go, Ethan. I'll get Jordan."

Ethan backed away as the cougars moved closer. One cougar moved to the side and lunged at Ethan. But the gray wolf attacked, sinking its teeth into the cougar's side and slamming the cougar into the snow. Ethan's mouth hung open, the heat from his breath lifting into the air. He glanced behind him at the edge of the cliff, and then inched to his right until the slide was directly behind him. "Brady?"

"*Go*! There's nothing you can do here, except get killed. GO!" Brady repeated before slamming his fist into another bear. "I'll get Jordan."

Ethan backed closer to the edge as the lead cougar came closer. Ethan glanced at the gray wolf still battling the cougar in the snow, then at Jordan, and then at the lead cougar. The cougar leaped at Ethan, and he raised his hands in front of his face for protection. The cougar scratched his body and toppled him backward.

Brady watched Ethan fall over the cliff. Scurrying closer to the edge, he saw Ethan racing downward, head first on his back, with the cougar lying on top of him. He felt another rip into his pants as a bear grabbed his leg. Brady shook his leg, and the bear detached. He sighed with annoyance and then kicked the bear, sending it over the edge of the cliff. Brady watched until the bear disappeared into a puff of white powder at the bottom of the cliff, and then he looked back at Ethan. Screams of pain echoed across the lake.

Ethan held his arms over his face and cried out as the cougar swiped at him with his claws. Ethan didn't fight back. He couldn't.

There was nothing Brady could do. The gray wolf paced

back and forth between Jordan and the attackers while Brady watched Ethan. The slide approached the shore of Crater Lake, and the large icebergs poked from the frozen lake cover. Brady saw the opening to the narrow tube. He held his hands to his mouth like a megaphone and screamed, "LIFT HIM HIGHER!" He repeated the command.

Instead of simply protecting himself from the attacking cougar, Ethan pushed against the cougar, raising him up. His screams of pain turned to a cry of determination as his hands beat against the cougar.

"MORE!" Brady yelled again.

The cougar was lifted higher; it slammed into the edge of the ice with a splat as Ethan slipped through the opening of the ice tube. A moment later, Ethan flew from the tube and crashed to the ground near Ha-ida and Allie.

Brady turned back to the attacking animals and Llao's warriors. Five bears and three cougars surrounded the gray wolf, boxing it in.

"Jordan, are you okay?" asked Brady. Then he heard her sob. "Come here," Brady said softly, but her feet were paralyzed. She couldn't move. The animals organized into battle lines in front of Brady and pushed him to the cliff's edge. Then a cougar jumped toward the slide. Brady took a quick step and dove at the cougar, tackling it to the ground. He flung it over the edge of the cliff by its tail, but this time, he couldn't watch the result. Another cougar made a dash for the slide, but Brady knocked it off stride. He looked at the slide and at his three friends lying at the bottom. He detected only subtle movements and could tell they weren't prepared to defend themselves if the animal warriors made it to them.

A black bear swayed his head and poked at the snow with his front claws. It charged at Brady. Brady planted his feet in preparation for the contact, but the bear knocked Brady backward into the snow. It straddled him and swiped at his face, but then Brady set his feet against the bear and flipped him backward over the cliff. Brady looked at cadre of animals surrounding the gray wolf, and then he turned his attention to Jordan, who was surrounded by Chief Llao's warriors. Another bear charged Brady, and a cougar dashed for the slide that would take him straight to his prey. Brady swatted the bear and then snatched the leaping cougar from the air. Brady gripped the tuft of the cougar's neck and pulled as another hurried to gain access to the slide.

Brady glanced at Jordan. The warriors had placed a cord around her waist and had tied her wrists together. "Jordan! I'll be back for you!" Brady screamed. Then, looking at the ice slide, he knew what he needed to do. Kicking a nearby cougar because he could, Brady took two quick steps and jumped off the cliff. His fists slammed into the slide as he landed, causing the top five feet of the ice to crumble above him. Brady slammed his fists against the slide again and again as he slid downward. The slide disintegrated with each punch, but this didn't stop two cougars from jumping. They landed farther down the slide in front of Brady. He pounded the ice again, and the slide crumbled more until he was convinced that nothing else could follow.

The gray wolf stood at the edge of the cliff where the slide had been destroyed. It turned in place as if searching for his own tail. But with no immediate threat, it turned back toward Brady on the slide.

Brady's eyes creased as he twisted on the slide, rolling onto his stomach and shifting his body into a forward-facing position. He watched the cougars as they hunched low, preparing to enter the tube at the end. Brady stretched out with his fists clenched in front of him. He ducked his head low and closed his eyes momentarily as he followed the cougars through the tube. Then the darkness of the tube brightened, and Brady salivated at the prospect of continued battle.

28

CIRCUS CLOWN

BRADY SHOT FROM THE TUBE LIKE A CIRCUS CLOWN FROM A cannon. He glided four feet above the icy surface of the lake with his fists clenched and the cougars straight in front of him. The first cougar wobbled as it tried to stand after its landing from the tube. Its head shook, and then its four legs separated as it collapsed onto its stomach. The second cougar regained his feet quickly and walked to the teens huddled in a heap a few feet away.

"AHHHHHHH!" Brady screamed as he flew through the air. The preying cougar paused and turned at the noise. Brady stretched his body as flat and as far as he could, but he couldn't maintain his flight. His belly bounced on the ground, and he slid forward, crashing into the first dazed cougar. He flung the cougar aside and continued sliding to the other. The second cougar turned away from Brady and hurried toward its prey. Brady screamed again. "Guys, get up. Run!"

Ethan stirred as he leaned against Ha-ida. He moved slowly, but then his eyes bolted open. His feet kicked at the approaching cougar in front of him. "Brady! Help! Please!" Ethan shouted.

"Yeah, I got it." Brady brushed the snow and ice from his chest as he climbed to his feet. He took three quick steps forward, setting the toes of his shoes into the ice for better traction. He then dove at the stalking cougar and slid the rest of the way on his belly like a baseball player stealing second base. Brady wrapped his arms around the cougar's back legs and stood. Holding its rear haunches, Brady spun in place, swinging the cougar. Then he let go. The cougar flew through the air and smacked to the ground before sliding to a stop against the giant ice pile, right below the opening of the tube.

Ethan gave a tight smile as his eyes watered. He stared.

"What?" Brady asked.

"Nothing. It's just a shame. That's all," Ethan said.

Spewing out of the ice tube, the gray wolf flew over the cougar and landed on its feet. It slid sideways and then stopped behind the second cougar.

Brady flexed his bare chest and extended a hand to Ethan. He yanked his friend to his feet, but turned in place when he sensed motion from behind. The other cougar was racing toward the group of kids. It leapt through the air. Brady knelt, pounded the ice with the side of his fists, and backed away. The cougar landed in front of Brady, fell through the ice, and sank into the water.

Ethan's eyes widened. "You just killed that—"

"Give it a rest, Ethan. It's not my fault the thing can't swim . . . under the ice." Brady chuckled, then became serious.

"Brady!" Ethan scolded. "That was a person."

"No. That was an enemy. You guys are safe. Maybe you should show a little gratitude." Brady stepped over to Allie and helped her lift her head. He felt sticky blood on the back of her head. But her eyes were open, and she seemed to be aware of her surroundings.

"Is everyone okay?" Allie asked.

Ha-ida rose onto her knees and stretched her back. "I am fine."

Ethan's fingers rubbed over the claw marks in his shredded clothes. He pulled some of the cloth away from his body and studied the claw marks on his chest. "Me too, I guess," Ethan said.

"You're welcome," Brady said with a smirk. "By the way, Allie, that was the coolest ride of my life. *Nice!*"

"Wait, where's Jordan?" Allie asked, wiping her arm across her face and removing the sweat that now caused her to shiver.

Ethan turned in place as he looked for his sister. "Brady, you said you'd get her. Where is Jordan?"

Brady's head hung low as he stared at his shifting feet. His brow furrowed and his nose crinkled. "I . . ."

"Where. Is. Jordan?" Ethan repeated.

"I tried to reach her, but . . ." Brady's head wobbled from side to side, and his voice became subdued. "It was Llao's goons. They took her, but it didn't look like they wanted to hurt her."

Ethan shook his head and clenched his jaw. "Brady . . ."

"I think I know where they took her," Brady said, matching Ethan's gaze. "I've seen their village. I *will* get her back."

Ethan stepped in front of Brady, his nose nearly touching Brady's chin. "You'd better, or I'll . . ."

"What? Quote me some poetry until I die of boredom? I said I'll get her back." Brady clenched his teeth, and then his usual cockiness was replaced by an unusual sincerity. "I promise, Ethan. I promise."

Tears welled in Ethan's eyes. He huffed and turned to help Allie stand. "You said you know where she is, Brady. Let's go."

Brady shook his head as the gray wolf nuzzled Ethan's leg. A soft hum came from its mouth, and Ethan leaned down. He wrapped his arms gently around the wolf's furry neck and then held the wolf version of Jacob by the ears. Ethan stared into his eyes and growled back.

Brady pointed at Ethan as he knelt nose to nose with Jacob, the gray wolf. They growled at each other. Brady wagged his finger and stammered. "Wh-wh-what is this?"

Ha-ida's soft voice pierced the snowy silence. "Shhh. They are talking."

"Talking? You're kidding, right?"

Allied shook her head. "Shhh."

After another moment of shared growling, Ethan released the wolf's ears and stood up. He wiped his eyes, looking down at the gray wolf. Its tongue dangled from its mouth, and its kind eyes looked up at Ethan. "There is something else we need to do first. Jordan is going to have to wait."

"What? Ethan, I told you I'll get Jordan. Let's go. Right now. I'll do it," Brady said. "We can't wait. It didn't look like she was in immediate danger or anything, but there's no telling what those creeps will do to her."

Ethan shook his head as he stared down at the wolf sitting on its haunches. He closed his eyes and paused, and then he nodded. He wiped his eyes again. "There's something we have to do first."

"What do we need to do, Ethan?" Ha-ida asked.

Ethan met Allie's stare and bit his lip while Brady looked on with confusion and bitterness. "It's time we find some real help. Jacob wants us to meet the Mystic Gray."

Ha-ida's jaw dropped. "But *he* is the Mystic Gray," she said, motioning at the gray wolf with her open hand.

"Yeah, Ethan. I thought we were here to find the Mystic Gray. I thought we were drawn here to find Jacob," Allie said.

Ethan shrugged his shoulders and shook his head. "I don't know. Jacob said—"

Brady's upper lip curled as he looked at the wolf. "Jacob, huh?"

"Yeah. We returned to Crater Lake to find Jacob *and* the Mystic Gray." Ethan chuckled uncomfortably as he removed his stocking cap and scratched his head. "I guess." His forehead crinkled as he thought. "Apparently the gray wolf and the Mystic Gray are not the same."

Brady's bare shoulders rose and then fell with exasperation. "You're sure?" Ethan frowned at the wolf and nodded. Brady knelt down next to the gray wolf and grabbed its snout, clasping its mouth shut. "Well, Jacob, if that's really you, you ruined my favorite glove when you *bit* me." He stared into the wolf's eyes.

Finally satisfied, Brady let go of the wolf and stood. He nodded to Ethan and looked back at the wolf. "Okay. Let's go, mutt. Lead the way."

– 29 –

SKELL'S GROTTO

THE GRAY WOLF WALKED IN FRONT OF THE GROUP BY THIRTY paces. Ethan hung his head low as he watched each step, mostly to avoid looking at the landmarks of Crater Lake that caused him to stay awake every night. To his right, the snow-covered Wizard Island rose from the lake. In front and to his right side, the Phantom Ship moored close to the shoreline. Ethan turned his shoulder away from the ship, not wanting to be reminded of the summertime adventure that nearly cost him his life.

The gentle sound of cracking ice greeted every footstep Ethan and the others took, but Ethan was in too much of a daze to worry. Looking at his group of friends, Ethan shook his head as he stared at Brady's bare back. Sure, the attacking cougars had ripped away his clothes, but Brady probably preferred it like that anyway. *What a goober.* Allie pulled the puffy hood of her silver snow coat over her head, hiding the blood matted to the back of her blonde hair. Her steps were still wobbly, and she stayed close to Brady. Ha-ida hiked across the lake with renewed enthusiasm. Her long, graceful strides carried her easily across the lake with a bounce in her step. Far ahead, the gray wolf paused and looked back at the kids. It made a sound, something between a bark and a growl.

Ethan frowned. "Take it easy. We're hurrying." The wolf snarled again, and Ethan actually snickered at the joke the wolf told. He growled back at the wolf and then laughed again.

"Dude, that is so weird. Hey, Doctor Doolittle, do you mind keeping 'crazy time' under wraps? It creeps me out," Brady said.

Ethan smiled again at the gray wolf, and it turned around to continue leading the way.

Ha-ida turned to face Ethan, and he found the grin on her face to be obnoxious. "Ethan, did the wolf say where we're going?"

"Some place called Grotto Cove," Ethan snapped.

"Do you know it?" Brady asked.

Ha-ida's white teeth shined between her lips as her smile broadened even more. "I knew it!" Ha-ida skipped ahead and raised her hands into the air in what appeared to be some kind of celebration dance.

"I'll take that as a yes," Brady said.

"Ha-ida, we really need to work on your moves," Allie said with a grin. She smiled but then winced and grabbed the back of her head.

"We are almost there," Ha-ida said, pointing to the shore-line at the other side of the lake. "Grotto Cove is a special place. It is near a place called Skell Head. It is where we communicate with Skell. It is like a . . . a . . ."

"Church?" Ethan asked.

"No. What is the word? It is big and beautiful. Stone. It is more like a . . . ," Ha-ida said.

"Cathedral?" Allie suggested.

Ha-ida's eyes brightened. "Yes. It is a cathedral."

"What's the difference?" Brady asked.

"It is beautiful. Special."

Ethan quickened his pace, excited to share what he'd read back home. "Grotto Cove is named because of all the caves in the cliffside near the shore." Ethan's enthusiasm died. He paused as he thought about what he was saying . . . he thought about the caves, and he remembered his adventure in the caves below Crater Lake last summer. He moaned. "I hate caves."

The group chattered the rest of the way across the lake, but Ethan walked in silence, slipping back into his previous funk. His lips drooped as he considered the idea of entering another cave. Memories of hiking through the pitch-black lava tubes below Crater Lake flooded his mind and caused his mouth to go dry. Bats. Darkness. Cold. Dread. And really bad smells. There was nothing he missed about hiking underground.

The crunching sound of the ice mingled with the chatter from his friends and the growls of the wolf as they approached the lakeshore. The wolf nuzzled up to Ethan, but he didn't pay attention. He scanned the shore for an opening for a cave, then stepped forward reluctantly as the wolf nudged him from behind. When his feet started moving, they kept moving, following the wolf as he retook the lead position.

Some of the cliffs around Crater Lake entered the water at a gentler slope, but Ethan found himself standing on the icy lake as the nearest cliff entered the water at a near ninety-degree angle. He scanned to the left and right and then looked up. All around him there were small crevices that he imagined opened into larger caves inside the rock. But the wolf didn't approach the openings. It stood with its nose pointed directly at the rock. The wolf stepped closer so that its nose was mere inches from the rock.

"What's that dumb dog doing?" Brady asked.

"Look." Ha-ida pointed to her left. "There is the main grotto my people use. I will show you."

"No. Wait. We followed the wolf, I mean Jacob, this far. Let's see where he's taking us," Allie said.

The wolf growled as it turned back to the kids, and then it faced the rock wall again. It inched forward. Its nose disappeared, then its entire head, and then its entire body except for the tip of its tail. Ethan stared at the tail. It looked like it was connected to the rock wall. But then it disappeared entirely.

Ethan swallowed and cleared his throat. He chuckled nervously. "Ha-ida, do you still want to show us the other cave?"

"Shut up, wuss. This is awesome." Brady stepped in front of the others and stood next to the wall. Ethan surveyed the group. Confusion clouded each face except Brady's. Ethan figured he wasn't bright enough to be confused. Brady lifted his hand and moved it slowly toward the wall. His middle finger looked like it would touch the wall first, but the tip disappeared. Brady pulled his hand back quickly and stared at his finger. Nothing was missing. He pressed his entire hand through the wall and then pulled it back to look. "This is killer."

While Brady continued playing with the wall, Ha-ida closed her eyes for a moment. Then, her face beamed with excitement. She took a brisk step into the wall and disappeared.

Brady continued playing with the wall. "You put your right foot in, you take your right foot out." He sang the entire Hokey Pokey while putting his limbs in and out, examining them each time as if amazed they still existed. Then he got to the part of the song, "You put your whole self in," and he jumped through the wall and disappeared, leaving Allie and Ethan standing on the ice next to the cliff.

Ethan nodded at Allie, as if urging her to go next. "That was disturbing."

Allie grinned. "Yeah, he's not much of a singer. Big shock." She stared at the wall. "Do you wanna?"

Ethan's lips quivered as he tried to smile. "Ladies first."

Allie reached forward to place the palm of her hand on the rock wall. Her hand disappeared into the rock, and she paused. Then her entire body lurched and disappeared into the wall. Then Brady's head stuck out. "Come on, wuss." Then his head disappeared again.

Ethan lifted his shoulders to his ears and dropped them as his breath exhaled with a whoosh. He stepped closer so that his toes nearly touched the wall. He squeezed his eyes closed, and the muscles in his neck tensed as he leaned forward and took a step. He took another step with his eyes closed as he tried to imagine what he would find on the other side. His chin dropped as he peeked. He opened his eyes wide, the cavern view mesmerizing him. His imagination had not prepared him for the vision in front of him.

30

THE REAL MYSTIC GRAY

ETHAN TILTED HIS HEAD BACK AS HE STUDIED THE DOMED rock ceiling twenty feet above. If the other grottos were like this, he could understand why Ha-ida's people thought of them as cathedrals. The floor was frozen lake water, but instead of crusty white, a fluorescent blue light shined from below and lit the entire cavern. He stepped toward the center of the room, oblivious to his friends around him. He stood at the center spot and stared four stories up as another dome piggybacked on the first. It reminded him of standing on the State Seal at the capital and looking into the rotunda. The fluorescent blue light spiraled up the dome and faded into darkness. Ethan couldn't tell if there was anything else up there, so after a moment of staring and guessing, he turned his attention back to the main cavern.

Rocky shores butted against the curve of the smooth stone walls, and at the back of the cavern, the blue light faded to black. He turned quickly in place and looked back at the entrance. From the outside looking in, he saw only rock wall. But from the inside looking out, Ethan gazed out onto the frozen lake. Low clouds hovered above the crater's rim, and a steady stream of smoke rose into the sky from a location near Llao Rock. Ethan remembered Jordan, and his awe of the grotto cathedral vanished.

Ethan looked into the faces of Allie, Brady, and Ha-ida as

they examined the beautiful cavern. "Hey, guys, where's the wolf?" Ethan asked. But no one answered. Placing his pinkies at the side of his lips, Ethan whistled. A tremendous shriek sounded through the cavern and threatened to burst his eardrums. He stretched his jaw and rubbed his ears. "Sorry, guys." Every one stared at him. "Good, I have your attention. Where's the wolf?" Ethan repeated.

"I'm here!" Jacob called out from the darkness. He walked into the shimmering blue light in human form. He wore his usual, Australian-styled cowboy hat with the spaghetti straps hanging from his chin, but he no longer wore his thick, black-rimmed glasses. The hem of his pants hugged tight against his calves and his shirt looked ready to burst at the buttons.

Allie's mouth fell open, and she ran to Jacob, almost slipping on the ice. She proceeded more carefully, wrapped her arms around Jacob's neck, and kissed his cheeks. "You're really alive. I can't believe it!" She kissed him again and hugged him tighter as tears gathered in her eyes and ran down her cheeks. "You've haunted my dreams for months. I'm so happy you're alive." Allie shrieked with delight and then kissed him again.

Jacob grinned, apparently pleased by Allie's attention. Ethan hurried to his small friend, who wasn't nearly as small as he remembered. He placed a hand on his shoulder, smiling broadly as he, Allie, and Jacob all united in a group hug. "It is *really* good to see you," Ethan said, his voice cracking.

Jacob chuckled. "It's good to be seen."

"You bit my hand," Brady called. "You mangy little mutt."

"Oh yeah, that," Jacob said in a deep voice. He chuckled. "Purely an accident, I assure you. I would never bite you on purpose, as I'm sure you'd never deserve it." He winked at Ethan and Allie, and they shared a laugh.

Brady walked close and prepared to slug Jacob in the shoulder, but stopped his fist inches away. He shoved Allie and Ethan away. Then he grabbed Jacob and hugged him tight. Tears cascaded down Brady's cheeks, and for a moment, Brady didn't seem to care. Then, after his hug was finished, he pushed Jacob away and rubbed his red eyes. "Your dad will be happy to see you. I talk to him every week. Your whole family misses you, but especially your dad. He hasn't been the same since you . . ."

"Died? Disappeared? Turned into a canine?" Jacob joked. But his eyes were red too.

"Why did you not transform before?" Ha-ida asked, stepping toward the united friends. Her eyes ran up and down Jacob's body.

"I couldn't."

"Why did you bring us here?" Ha-ida asked.

"And this is Ha-ida," Brady said, motioning to the Native American girl as he rolled his eyes. "Don't you worry, she's always this friendly."

The cavern fell silent as no one laughed at Brady's joke. Then the group assaulted Jacob with rapid-fire questions.

"Have you been at Crater Lake the whole time?" Allie asked. "How did you turn into a wolf?"

"Why aren't you dead?" Ethan asked.

"Are you the Mystic Gray?" Ha-ida asked.

"Why did you really bite me?" Brady asked.

Jacob took a deep breath and answered each question in turn. "Yes. I don't know. I don't know. No." Jacob said, pointing at each inquisitor. He pointed at Brady. "And last but not least, I bit you because I wanted to. What are you going to do about it?"

Brady laughed. "I could probably snap you in half or something."

"I'm a little tougher than I used to be." Jacob's smile faded into a stern expression. "Now that that's out of the way, there's someone you really need to meet."

"The Mystic Gray?" Ha-ida asked as her entire body shook.

Jacob nodded. "Yes."

"Well, where is he?" Brady asked.

Ethan stared into the darkness at the back of the cavern. A narrow pinprick of light emerged and rested on a rock sticking out of the ice. The light grew brighter and brighter until the entire cavern was consumed in white. Ethan closed his eyes and covered them with his hand until the brilliance faded enough that his eyes could distinguish the outline of a figure standing on the rock.

"Friends, I want you to meet Chief Skell."

31

RESCUE PLAN

WHEN THE BURN IN ETHAN'S EYES FADED ENOUGH TO LOOK directly at the man standing atop the rock, Ethan cocked head to one side and stuck out his lower lip. "Interesting." Chief Skell's feet straddled the sharp apex of the rock. He stood tall and still, a warm smile lighting his face with a continued glow. From the corner of his eye, Ethan saw Ha-ida lower onto one knee with her hands outstretched, her palms facing up, and her head bowed like a servant approaching her king. Ethan thought for a moment. That's exactly what she was doing. She was a servant approaching her chief. Embarrassed by his ignorance, an almost inaudible scoff blew from Ethan's lips. He then turned to Jacob and raised his eyebrows as if asking "now what?"

The light around Chief Skell faded further, and Jacob stepped to a position in front of the rock. "Chief Skell has returned. In the past, he's assigned valiant warriors to serve as the Mystic Gray for a period of time, but now he is here at Crater Lake to lead himself. He is the Mystic Gray."

Ethan studied Chief Skell as he jumped down from the rock. Skell's bare feet planted firmly on the ice beside Jacob. His white hair almost glowed, contrasting the beautiful darkness of his native skin. Unlike Chief Llao, whose black hair hung evenly at shoulders length, Skell's white hair brushed straight back and was trimmed neatly around his ears, except for one long braid wrapped in leather hanging behind his right ear. He wore a full-length bearskin cloak that hung from his shoulders like a cape and was closed in front. Ethan squinted, trying to see what the chief was wearing beneath the cloak, but he couldn't tell.

Chief Skell stepped closer to the group, approaching Ha-ida first. He tapped her on the shoulder with his finger, and she arose. Pride and happiness beamed from her eyes as she stared into the chief's face. He nodded to her and then turned toward Ethan.

The closer Chief Skell moved, the more confused Ethan became. Skell's youthful appearance didn't match his white, old man hair, and he looked like the eighteen-year-old twin of Chief Llao. Despite the similarity in appearance to Llao, Ethan felt an unusual sense of peace and safety in Skell's presence. Like no one could say or do anything to hurt him. *Maybe this is how Brady feels all the time*, he thought. The sensation was liberating. Still, despite his newfound confidence, Ethan gulped when Skell stood in front of him. Ethan stared into the kind eyes of the chief, who looked to be only a few years older than Ha-ida, yet whose mere presence seemed to promise success and security.

Chief Skell reached forward and placed one hand on Ethan's shoulder. "Ethan, it is a pleasure to meet you. I apologize for being so abrupt, but we must begin our preparations immediately. I need you."

Ethan stumbled backward, surprised by Chief Skell's perfect English, but even more so by the fact that Skell knew his name and needed him. "Me?" Ethan looked at Brady. His bare muscles bulged. Brady was invincible, strong . . . a warrior. Allie could shoot fire and ice from her mouth, for goodness' sake. Ha-ida could turn into an antelope and run sixty miles per hour. *Sixty.* They all had real power while Ethan could merely perform simple party tricks, like talking to the cat or sharing a story about the history of lettuce or something else completely useless. Chief Skell must be making a mistake. Ethan's heart pounded and then he cleared his throat. "My friends are powerful. I will help them in any way I can."

Chief Skell smiled at Ethan and placed his left hand on Ethan's other shoulder. He leaned close and whispered into Ethan's ear. "Ethan, I don't want you to help. I want you to lead your friends into battle. You must help them prepare." Skell continued whispering so only Ethan could hear while the rest looked on. When he finished, he urged Ethan. "Remember these things. This knowledge provides you power. Be courageous."

"Ah-hem, excuse me!" Brady called as he walked to Ethan and Skell. He did his usual pectoral muscle dance as he leaned close to Skell. But instead of whispering, he spoke in full voice. "Listen, Skell. Don't you want someone who can actually fight?" He stepped back and smirked. "I'm your man."

Skell grinned. "You will be a powerful tool for Ethan to use, Brady. Thank you for your willingness to accept your role."

"Wait, I . . . um . . ."

Allie smiled while Brady stammered for a retort. "Chief Skell, what can I do?"

"Follow Ethan. He will direct you. You must trust him, even if you don't always understand why." Skell faced each of the kids in turn and then lingered on Brady. "All of you. Trust him. You will find safety as you follow Ethan. If you choose not to follow, I cannot protect you."

Ethan's mouth hung open, and his eyes glazed. He shook his head fast enough that his cheeks jiggled. His stomach fluttered as he considered what Skell had said. Then a wave of dread swirled in his head as he thought about his inadequacy.

"You must prepare yourselves for the battle coming at the Summer Solstice. You are here to learn and train. You will have six months to prepare to defeat Llao. Be patient and wise. He will attempt to hurt you. He will deceive and lie to you. Do not believe him. He believes he can turn you to be his servants. He will try many things to trick you, but if you stay close and strengthen each other, and follow Ethan's instructions, you will be protected."

"If Llao is so dangerous, shouldn't we leave and come back when it's time to fight? Can't we train somewhere else?" Allie asked.

"Or take him out now while he's weak," Brady suggested.

"No," Ethan said. "With Llao's escape from the Prison of the Lost, he is granted one year to prepare himself. Skell is bound by the treaty. He cannot destroy Llao until the proper time."

The corners of Skell's lips curled. "Yes."

"We need to stay at Crater Lake if we hope to be strong enough to defeat Llao forever. Our powers are growing because we're here. We must grow into ourselves. We must fully develop as a team," Ethan said.

Chief Skell nodded. "That is correct. And I have two assignments to start your preparations."

"What must we do?" Ha-ida asked.

"Jordan?" Ethan asked hopefully.

Skell nodded. "Yes. That is one mission. Rescue your sister. She is essential to stopping Llao. Time is short. Llao hopes to harness her power of vision. It is only a matter of time before he is able to extract it."

"Extract it?" Allie asked. She raised her eyebrows and crinkled her nose in disgust.

"Saving Jordan will be our first priority," Ethan said. He looked to Skell for approval.

Skell nodded his head gently. "If you must. Just remember, your team is not yet complete. And Llao is dangerous," Skell said.

"What do you mean?" Ethan asked.

"Utilize Ha-ida's people. They can be a strength."

"Of course. What else?" Ethan asked.

"You still have a friend who is not quite himself." Skell looked at Jacob. "He is powerful already, but he has much more to offer. This brings me to your next assignment. You must retrieve the healing bowl. It will complete Jacob's powers and provide him control over his body. You will need every advantage you can get, and you will most certainly want Jacob at full strength. The bowl is the key to making your team whole. Use it only to accomplish the greater good. I will be watching your progress while I make preparations of my own."

Chief Skell walked back to the rock that poked out of the ice floor. He bent his knees, then leapt the four feet back to the top of the rock. His feet straddled the crest, and then he began to glimmer.

"The bowl will be your redemption!" Skell shouted, his glow becoming more intense. "Hurry, but be patient. The bowl, Ethan. Don't be distracted from the bowl."

Ethan watched as long as he could, but then shielded his eyes when Skell's brilliance threatened to blind him. The light lifted from the rock and then shot into the darkness of the cavern.

Ha-ida beamed. "Let us get Jordan and the bowl. Where is it?"

Allie moaned. "It's at the bottom of Crater Lake," she said, defeat sounding in her voice.

"Crater Lake is nearly twelve hundred feet deep. Any diver would be crushed at that depth," Ethan said.

"There must be a way," Ha-ida said. "There is always a solution where there is a willing heart."

Brady nodded. "Does anyone have a fishing pole with twelve hundred feet of line?"

"No," Ethan said. "But we have something better."

"What?"

Ethan winked at Brady. "We have an invincible man, *and* I have an idea."

32

AWKWARD QUESTION

E THAN AND ALLIE HIKED ACROSS THE FROZEN LAKE FROM Grotto Cove toward Llao Rock. His head hung low as he wondered about Jordan and felt the weight of responsibility that rested upon him. He had to rescue her. He missed her. He missed his mom and dad. He missed his normal life.

Ethan watched his feet and then peeked at Allie. Her eyes lacked the usual energy and happiness he was used to. She looked worse than he felt. He wondered if he should ask his question or keep his mouth shut. Ha-ida and Brady walked at the front of the group, both refusing to let the other take the lead. Jacob walked behind them, relegated again to his wolf form. Ethan glanced again at Allie.

Allie's head bobbed, and then her feet stopped as she turned to face Ethan square. "What? Why do you keep looking at me?" Ethan kept walking as he ignored her questions. He wanted to answer but didn't dare. "Ethan?" Allie repeated as she grabbed his elbow. "You're acting goofy. What's up?"

Ethan looked at his friends at the front of the group. He waited while the distance between them grew. When their distance guaranteed privacy, he looked Allie in the eye. "I've been wondering something, but . . ." His voice wavered as he lost courage.

"But what?" Allie prodded.

"It's pretty personal." Ethan waited, hoping Allie would lose interest or get nervous and change the subject. But her sad gaze held him steady, so he continued. "Okay, the night Ha-ida and I found you."

She nodded. "Yeah?"

"You were nearly frozen. If we hadn't gotten there when we did, you'd be dead on the road."

Allie's smile looked like she had pried the corner of her lips up with a crowbar. "Thank you, Ethan. I owe you everything. I should have thanked you before. It's just that I was . . ."

Allie's words were kind but felt empty. Ethan waved away her gratitude. "No, Allie. I'm not fishing for a thank you. I have a question."

Allie gulped, and her body tensed as if she expected to be slammed in the stomach by a wrecking ball. Her voice resisted, but her vulnerable eyes pled for Ethan to continue. After a long pause, she nodded. "What is it, Ethan?"

Ethan stalled with a nervous chuckle. "Well, you can shoot fire from your mouth, and all you needed was warmth. I mean, you were freezing to death, but you didn't start a fire. I was just wondering . . . why? Did you want to die?"

Allie's eyes widened with alarm. Then she her furrowed her brow as a frown overran her face. "You don't know what you're talking about." Allie turned and began a brisk walk to catch up with the others.

Grabbing her arm, Ethan swung her around. He stared into her eyes. "Allie, no one else is here. It's just us. You can trust me." He waited for a response, but none came. His head lowered with shame as his breathing raced. Then his eyes rose again to meet hers. "I know what it feels like. Hopeless. Scared. Alone." He reached down and grabbed Allie's left hand. "That's how I've felt for a really long time, and I'm pretty sure Jordan feels the same. Brady—who knows? But we have all of these terrible memories from last summer, battling zombie thingies and nearly dying I don't even remember how many times. And it was all out of our control. Now we have these insane powers, and our lives are still trapped in chaos. We're here at Crater Lake. I crashed a plane, and my sister's been kidnapped by an evil spirit chief. Brady put his father in the hospital, Jacob's a wolf, and you burned your house down." Ethan let Allie's hand drop. "I just want you to know that, I know how it feels. We're in this together. You're not alone."

Allie leaned forward, kissed Ethan on the cheek, and resumed her hike. "That's sweet." Ethan stood behind her and watched her head bobble. She seemed unwilling to accept the madness that controlled them.

From the front, Brady yelled back with an impish grin. "Hurry up, birthday boy. Are you hitting on her or talking her to death?"

Ethan stood still, glaring daggers at Brady. But then Allie turned back around. This time her smile seemed genuine. "Come on, Ethan. We're falling behind. We need to save Jordan."

- 33 -

THE CENTRAL PLATFORM

ETHAN STOOD AT THE BASE OF THE SNOWY CLIFF WITH HIS head cocked back. He stared at the white clouds and wondered where the cliff ended and the sky began. Shielding his eyes from the splendor of the snow cover, Ethan gulped and tried to sigh, but he was too tired. He considered the height they had to climb to the rim of the crater.

Tears of exhaustion gathered in Allie's eyes as she followed Ethan's gaze. She plopped onto the ice and lay down as she covered her eyes.

"Allie, what's wrong? What are you doing?" Ethan asked.

Allie sat up. She looked at Brady, then Ha-ida, Jacob, and finally Ethan. "Are you serious? Look." She motioned up the crater's cliff with her hand. "How do we get up there? How?" The group remained silent for a moment, but then Allie continued. "I just thought I'd take a little rest. Is that a problem?"

Ethan turned in place as he studied the massive cliffs of the crater surrounding them. It felt like he was trapped at the bottom of a bowl with no means of escape. There were no roads out. He couldn't even see a visible trail anywhere. The hike down to the lake had been exhausting enough in the summer when there was a path to follow, but now there were only sheer cliffs, snow, ice, and rocks jutting from the side of the cliff.

142

Brady frowned, looking at Ethan. "So what's your plan, boss? Your exceptional leadership brought us here. Now what?"

Ethan sat down on the ice next to Allie and closed his eyes. "We rest."

"Brilliant," Brady grumbled.

The gray wolf stepped beside Ethan and sat before placing its head on Ethan's knee. It growled as Brady wandered closer. Ethan rubbed the wolf's head and squeezed his eyes tight, resting them from the glare of the snow.

Brady towered over Ethan, wearing only his semi-shredded pants, boots, and sunglasses. His sweaty, red hair spiked up when he ran his hands through it. Steam rose from Brady's bare chest and head. He took a deep breath in, and then exhaled. "Okay, I'm rested. Now what?"

"How about you get dressed?" Ethan murmured. "Seriously, dude, aren't you freezing?"

Brady puckered his lips as he shook his head. "Nope. I feel great, and sadly, I forgot to pack a change of clothes."

The wolf growled again, and Ethan growled back. They traded barks, howls, growls, and snarls for a few minutes while the others watched and listened. Then Ethan rose to his feet and stepped beside Ha-ida. He whispered into her ear, and she nodded.

"Are you going to share?" Allie asked. "What's going on?"

"This is just a minor setback. Our main plan is the same, but we're going to need to adjust it a bit. I don't know how much energy we'll have to rescue Jordan after we get up the cliff. *If* we can find a way up the cliff."

"So what are you saying?" Allie asked.

"He's saying he's too much of a wuss to climb the mountain," Brady said.

"No. Well, maybe. But I'm suggesting that we split up."

"Split up? Why?" Allie asked.

"We have two missions. We need to rescue Jordan, and we need to recover the bowl artifact at the bottom of the lake.

We're down here, and Jordan's up there somewhere," Ethan said, glancing up the cliff.

Allie's head shook. "Yeah. I'm still not following you."

"Come on, professor. English, please."

Ethan's lips tightened. "Jacob knows where Llao Village is, and he thinks he can climb the mountain easier than the rest of us. Ha-ida will change into her antelope form, and they'll climb together. Jacob will watch the village, and—"

"They're going to 'watch' the village?" Brady said, cutting him off. "Wow, that sounds like a great plan. Jordan's probably feeling safer already."

"Jacob will locate Jordan and keep an eye on her until the rest of us can join. You've seen Llao Village, right, Brady?" Brady nodded. "So you could lead us there?" Brady nodded again. "Good."

"So, what will we do down here? Nap?" Allie asked.

"Unfortunately, no. We've got a lot to do. We're going after the bowl."

"Wait a minute. The bowl's at the bottom of Crater Lake, genius. How will we possibly get to it?" Brady asked.

"That's where you come in, Brady. Are you up for an adventure? Or are you scared?"

Brady scoffed. "Me, scared? Whatever."

"So you're in?"

"Yeah, I'm in," Brady said.

"And I need you too, Allie."

"Just tell me what to do." Her voice sounded sure, but her face looked worried.

"Good. Let's get going." Ethan nodded to Jacob and Ha-ida.

Ha-ida instantly morphed into a pronghorn antelope. She huffed and nuzzled against Ethan. Ethan nodded, and then Ha-ida raced across the frozen lake with Jacob trailing behind. She slowed as she began the arduous ascent up the mountain with Jacob bounding past her.

"This is going to be tricky." Ethan said. "Allie, I'm going to need a couple of things from you. Are you up for a challenge?" Her face contorted into a scowl, and she shrugged. "Come on, Allie. Are you up for this?" Ethan asked with newfound enthusiasm. Allie nodded subtly. "Good enough. Thank you."

"What do you want me to do?" Brady asked.

"We need a rock." Ethan stared at Brady as if challenging his manhood. "The biggest, heaviest rock you can hold."

Brady scoffed. "You want a big rock? I'll get you a big rock. What are you going to do?"

Ethan stared ahead. He looked at Wizard Island and then at the Phantom ship in the distance. His eyes wandered up to the Devil's Backbone and then in the direction of Danger Bay. Then he looked at Cleetwood Cove. "I'm going to calculate the location where the Old Man sank. The bowl will be nearby. It should be at the edge of the central platform."

"The central platform?"

Ethan chuckled. "I've studied a *ton* about Crater Lake over the past six months; rock formations and topography, both above and below the lake. The central platform is essentially a shelf below the water so it's not as deep as the basins, which can dip to almost two thousand feet." Allie and Brady's expressions remained blank. "Hey, you asked."

"Way to go, professor. We're proud of you."

Ethan raised his left eyebrow as he looked at Brady. "The good news is the water is not nearly as deep above the central platform, so it will be easier to access."

"What's the bad news?" Allie asked.

Ethan coughed and cleared his throat as he stalled in answering. "Well, the water's still eleven to twelve hundred feet deep. At that depth, there would be so much pressure against a diver's chest that he wouldn't be able to breathe. His lungs wouldn't be strong enough to inflate. An average diver wouldn't be able to breathe, even with oxygen."

Brady puckered as if eating a lemon. "Why do I get the feeling I'm *really* going to hate this plan?"

Ethan grinned. "We'll find the bowl at the edge of the central platform. Trust me. My plan will work." He winked at Allie. "Probably."

SURVEILLANCE OF LLAO VILLAGE

JACOB SAT ON HIS HAUNCHES AS THE COOL BREEZE RUFFLED his gray fur. His ears stood straight as he listened to every sound the forest made, and his canine nose noted every smell. Bright beams of sunlight shone through the evergreens, but Jacob hid in the shadows, far away from the chatter of the village. He turned his head with each new sound or interesting smell, but there was still no evidence pointing to Jordan's whereabouts.

At the center of the village, the tall tower rose to the treetops with sentinels standing on top, searching, watching. A low rumble escaped from Jacob's mouth as he licked the short fur around his mouth. Then he lowered his head onto his front paws. He still watched and listened, but the exhaustion he felt after hiking up the crater's cliffs was more than he expected.

A series of small fires burned near the edges of the camp, and Jacob watched the people shuffle through the snow in their thick, animal skin coverings. Some children played, but most stayed close to the adults huddled near the fires. The frigid air remained calm, and the beautiful day dragged on toward mid-afternoon. There was no sign of Llao or his warriors. Even stranger, there wasn't even a dwelling that looked impressive enough to be Llao's. *Where are you?* Jacob lifted his head off his paws and swiveled as he heard a branch rustle. He looked, but nothing was there.

Desiring a different vantage point, Jacob stood and pawed his way across the snow-crusted ground, flirting with the edge of the shadows. He circled the village until he found a comfortable, new place to hide himself. Then he sat, extended his front paws, and lay his head down again as he watched, listened, and sniffed his surroundings. Though he enjoyed the heightened senses his wolf form provided, Jacob longed to return to his human form permanently. Or at least to have the control of his own body to assume his human form outside of Skell's grotto. Jacob thought about Skell, and then about the pleasure of seeing his friends with his own natural eyes, speaking with his natural voice, and touching and hugging his friends with his natural arms. It provided warmth and comfort he hadn't felt in over six months. He wanted to be himself again. He wanted to be normal, human.

Jacob closed his eyes, but his ears remained perky. Then another brush of evergreen foliage alerted him to movement to his right. Standing, he backed behind a tree as his nose went into overdrive. He recognized the musky odor of a warrior's sweat mixed with the coppery fragrance of blood. He keenly watched as four men entered the village. They walked in single file. Behind them, two girls who looked to be about Jordan's age followed, brushing away their tracks with fluid waves of evergreen branches against the snow. Two men hurried up a ladder on the exterior of the tower, while two other men waited at the top to be relieved of their duty. The two sets of warriors exchanged places. At the bottom, they strode into a small dwelling, and the track brushers lay down their boughs and joined a group at one of the fires.

Satisfaction rumbled from Jacob's mouth as he watched the men. Then his gaze diverted to the path they had walked. Arising, he bounded along the shadows toward the path that had been almost entirely hidden by the brushed snow. His nose hovered above the ground as he inhaled the scent of the men. His wolf mouth separated, and his tongue hung out as he panted with excitement, recognizing the faint smell of Jordan. His nose locked onto the smell, and he ran, his paws flipping up snow with each stride. His tongue flapped to the side, eager to find Jordan so he could bathe her with safety and comfort.

- 35 -

ICE FISHING

BRADY STOOD AT THE EDGE OF THE HOLE AS HE STARED INTO the water. Two inches of white ice crusted the lake top, while the brilliant blue water shone from beneath. The four-foot round hole opened into the crystal abyss of Crater Lake. Brady clenched his jaw and then loosened it. In a steady rhythm, he bit repeatedly into his tongue as if it were chewing gum. He leaned further over the hole, considering Ethan's request, and turned to Allie. "This is crazy, right?"

Allie's eyebrows rose to meet her hairline, and she bobbed her head slowly. "Big time."

Brady shook his head. "Ethan, I have limits."

"Do you?"

"I saw a movie once where a submarine imploded because it went too deep," Brady said as he looked at the palms of his hands. He clasped them together slowly, interlocking the fingers into one super-fist. He squeezed. Brady's voice raised an octave as he imagined what the water pressure at twelve hundred feet would do to his body. "A submarine, Ethan. *Imploded*. Crushed like an empty soda can." He paused for dramatic effect. "Are you listening to me?" Brady kicked at the large rock he'd collected from the cliff and carried it to the middle of the lake. "I'm not even sure I can fit into that hole carrying this thing. It's just not going to work out."

"Allie, would you please?" Ethan asked, motioning at the hole. Allie's body tensed, and she opened her mouth as flames shot toward the hole, broadening it to an eight-foot-wide diameter. When the flames disappeared, she nodded to Ethan. "Thanks, Allie. See? Problem solved. You'll fit great."

"Do you have any idea of how cold that water will be?" Brady asked. "Remember swimming to the Phantom Ship in the summertime? We nearly died of hypothermia. Do you remember?"

Ethan nodded. "Oh yeah. I remember well." Ethan looked up and down Brady's body. "You must be freezing right now," he said, pointing to Brady's bare chest. "I know I am." Brady didn't say anything. "Well, are you cold?"

Brady shook his head. "Not exactly." He paused as he thought.

"You mean not at all, right?"

The words raced from Brady's mouth. "But that doesn't mean I won't be freezing when I'm submerged twelve hundred feet below the surface."

"True. But you do have an incredible tolerance for heat and cold. Remember what you showed me when you put the coal in your mouth? Heat didn't bother you at all. And it doesn't look like cold will either."

"But, Ethan, even *if* you calculated correctly, and I'm right over the bowl, how will I see? It's going to be pitch black at that depth."

"Excellent point." Ethan nodded again toward Allie.

She knelt on the ice with her face near the water inside the hole. "I've been practicing." She squeezed her eyes together with concentration, then filled her cheeks with air. She leaned closer to the water and opened her mouth. Just like the flute, brilliant white light exploded from her mouth and shot into the watery depths.

Brady partially covered his eyes to protect them from the intensity of the light as he stared into the round entrance to the lake. The light from Allie's mouth radiated deep, and Brady could see fish swimming far below. "Hmmm. Cool."

"What else, Brady? What are you most afraid of?"

"Afraid? I'm not afraid."

"Of course not. What I meant to say is, what are you most concerned about?"

Brady sidestepped closer to Ethan and leaned close. "I have to breathe."

"Yeah, definitely," Ethan said.

"No, Ethan. I get a little . . . woo-hoo," Brady said in a sing-song tone as he motioned with his dancing fingers. "You know, a little nuts . . . panicky." Brady pulled Ethan close. "I like breathing."

With one sharp nod of his head, Ethan stepped back and forced a smile. "No one can blame you for wanting to breathe. We have a solution for that as well."

Brady's eyes bulged. "Really? What?"

"This is another job for my trusty assistant." Ethan parted his lips but continued to clench his teeth. His horsy smile signaled for Allie to begin.

After a moment of concentration, Allie opened her mouth and spewed out a small mountain of ice next to the hole in the ice.

"What's that supposed to be?" Brady asked.

"Just watch."

Allie stepped to the front of the mountain she had formed. Her forehead creased with concentration, and then she blew a steady stream of flame into the ice, melting away the center. She stepped inside as she focused large flames and small flames alike, rounding out the interior of the ice mountain. Nodding her head with satisfaction, she exited the cave she had built and then smoothed the exterior into an oval-shaped capsule that stood ten feet tall. "Take a look."

Brady moved closer to the capsule and stepped up as he ducked inside. The thick ice was so pure and clear that he could see through the capsule like it was glass. He saw Allie waving to him, so he waved back. "And what's this stupid thing supposed to do?"

Ethan grinned from ear to ear. "That's your ride." All expression from Brady's face disappeared. Ethan examined the interior of the capsule and nodded. "This is going to work great. Nice job, Allie."

Allie curtsied. "Once you hit the central platform, you can just break through the bottom of the ice so you can move around down there. The rock will keep you anchored. I'll be blasting light down to you so you can see. You'll need to find the bowl and then float back up to the top. Voila. We've got the healing bowl. Simple."

Brady laughed and then wiped the cheer from his face. "Simple?" He stepped to the hole in the ice and stared again into the water. "For you, maybe."

"I estimate you'll have approximately thirteen minutes worth of air. How heavy do you think your rock is?"

"Three hundred and fifty pounds. Give or take."

Ethan closed his eyes and moved his lips quickly but silently. "Okay. It'll be close, but I think it will do. You'll reach a maximum descending speed of about 260 feet per minute. At that rate, it will take you just over four and a half minutes to reach the bottom. That will leave you ninety seconds to find the bowl and seven minutes to get topside."

A wispy moan escaped Brady's mouth. He stared back into the depths of the water. "Four and a half minutes down, ninety seconds to find the bowl, and seven minutes back up."

Ethan nodded. "That sums it up. Are you ready?"

Brady laughed. "No." His chin hit his chest, and his entire body tingled with nerves. He started to talk, but the high pitch of his voice caused him to clear his voice to sound more manly. "Just one more question."

"Shoot."

"If my maximum descent speed is 260 feet per minute when

I'm holding a 350-pound weight, how will I rise to the surface in seven minutes?" Brady wished he'd taken math class more seriously as he tried calculating the necessary speed of his rise. *Twelve hundred feet divided by seven equals 171 feet per minute.* "Ethan?" he yelled. "How is that even possible?"

"Buoyancy."

"English! Speak English!"

"Ice is less dense than water and is naturally buoyant. It floats."

Brady nodded. "And . . . ?"

"The entire top portion of the capsule will have air trapped beneath it, which will allow you to breath. Air is also lighter than water. So if you drop the weight and hold tight to the top of the capsule, you won't have any choice but to shoot up to the surface."

Brady looked to Allie. "Is that true?"

She nodded quickly. "Oh, yeah. Definitely. I even carved out some handholds inside to help you hang on to the capsule. But, um, it probably wouldn't hurt for you to kick as you're rising. The faster you get back up, the better."

"Okay, Brady. You can do this. We may not understand it completely, but Skell said we need the bowl if we want to defeat Llao and get our lives back. Think about it. Once we have the bowl, we can even help your dad in the hospital. Are you ready?"

Brady leaned over the hole in the ice as he stared into the deep, blue water. He shook his head and took rapid, deep breaths, worried he'd never get another.

Allie placed her hand on Brady's shoulder. "You're very brave. I know you'll be okay." She stood up on her tiptoes and kissed Brady's cheek. "It's time. You know what you need to do. You *are* ready."

Brady shuffled his feet. "No, I'm really not."

36

ALARM!

Tufts of snow kicked up behind Ha-ida as she raced through the trees and stopped at the front door to Skell Village. Morphing back into her human form, Ha-ida ran inside, past the fire pit to the back counter where the food was stored. Panting, she searched the cabinets; then, from underneath the counter, she pulled a large brass bell and a mallet. She held a thick leather strap from which the bell hung, and she pounded the bell with the mallet in rhythm.

Yells and the anxious bustle of teenagers rose to accompany the clanging rhythm of the bell. The main room flooded with Ha-ida's friends as they gathered around her. Her labored breathing caused her shoulders to rise and fall, but she concentrated on banging the bell as she studied the faces of the friends rallying to the alarm. Once satisfied with the assembled crowd, Ha-ida set the mallet and the bell on the counter. The room fell into utter silence.

"What is it?" Stan hollered from the back of the room.

"It is Llao. He has taken the little girl, Jordan," Ha-ida said. Disappointment spread across her face as she noted the indifference of her friends. Some sighed and looked away, avoiding eye contact, while others looked uncaring. "All of the visitors have special powers. Llao is trying to claim the girl's power. He is trying to steal her visions. We must save her before it's too late." Ha-ida voiced her anxious plea to little effect. A girl at the back of the room turned to walk out, but Stan grabbed her arm. They shared some words, and then Stan let go as she walked away. Two boys exited through a side door. Ha-ida's eyes locked on Stan, pleading with him to stop the walkout.

Stan shrugged his shoulders and yelled to Ha-ida, "They don't get it!" But his words barely rose above the clamor in the room. Climbing atop the counter, Ha-ida yelled to the assembled crowd. But the harshness of the rumble drowned her voice. Then, from the back of the room, an ear-splitting whistle penetrated every ear. Stan stood on a bench with his pinkies in his mouth and whistled until every eye was on him. He lowered his fingers from his mouth, and then ran his fingers slowly through his crew-cut. He licked his finger and spiked the bleached yellow streak at the front of his hair. He lowered his hands and waited as he scoured the room with his eyes. Then he unleashed his verbal attack. "What's wrong with you people? This is the moment we've been training for. This is why we're here. We must defeat Llao. Come on, guys, this is it." He studied the crowd. "Now shut up and listen." He motioned back to Ha-ida.

She nodded and mouthed the words. "Thank you."

"We're not here to fight for some little girl," a female voice called from the middle of the group.

Ha-ida searched the crowd until she identified the speaker. Her eyes locked on the girl. "Yes, we are. It may begin with just one girl, but Llao will destroy us all if we don't stand up together."

"That is foolishness," the girl yelled back. "We must reserve ourselves for the final battle. We cannot afford to lose strength by fighting meaningless battles."

Ha-ida shook her head. "The war has begun. We either choose to fight or we choose to lie down and accept our own deaths. If we will not fight for the girl, who will fight for us?"

The girl in the middle of the group grumbled and pushed

her way to the door. "I will wait until the battle matters."

"It matters now!" Ha-ida yelled. Her voice shook with emotion. "I met Skell." The rumble of the crowd went silent. "He is here." The opposing girl stopped pushing her way to the door and turned back to Ha-ida. "The war is now. We must be with him."

"What do you need?" Stan yelled from the back. "I'm with Skell, and I'm with you."

Ha-ida took a moment to calm her breathing, forcing a smile. "We need everyone. Skell told me to rally my people. I need you to follow. I need you to be obedient and vicious as we take the fight to Llao. Summon your courage. Prepare for battle, and follow me. Llao underestimates us. He *will* be sorry."

37

LLAO'S LAIR

LIGHT SNOW STARTED FALLING, AND THE WIND GUSTED AS Jacob sniffed along the ground. Jordan's faint scent disappeared for a moment, so he refocused his nose on the more powerful odor of the warriors. Leaving the cover of the woods, Jacob padded along the trail his nose could detect. The visual trail had disappeared completely in the falling snow and wind. Cool air tickled his nose, and he paused when the squawk of birds sounded overhead. He pointed his nose skyward at the birds, and then he resumed his chase, increasing his pace as he followed Jordan's scent and the stench of her captors.

The four hawks circled above, gradually falling below the crater's rim directly in front of Jacob's path. His mind raced as he wondered about the bird's connection with Llao and his warriors. Ha-ida was convinced of Che-tan's treachery, but Jacob wasn't as sure.

The trail headed toward the edge of the cliff and disappeared over the edge. Jacob stood at the edge and watched the birds spread into single file and fly into the cliff. Jacob's tail wagged, and he growled. It looked like the birds had crashed into the side of the cliff. He stared over the edge, and then a face appeared from a recess in the rock twenty feet down. Jacob's head lurched back when Che-tan smiled at him.

Knowing his instruction was merely to find Jordan and keep an eye on her until the others arrived, Jacob's mind raced. *What should I do? Che-tan saw me, but does he know it's really me? Is he working with Llao like Ha-ida thinks? If so, he'll alert the warriors to my presence and Jordan may be in greater danger.* Even as a wolf, Jacob's mind was clear as he considered his options. Deciding that Che-tan's presence couldn't be helpful, he decided he couldn't wait. Jordan could be in greater danger. The image of Che-tan's smiling face burned in Jacob's eyes, and he snarled as he considered the treachery of his former colleague.

Far below on the crusted lake cover, Jacob saw his friends preparing for their mission to retrieve the bowl. Jacob longed to have the bowl back. Alone, the energy it provided was valuable and worth any effort to recover it. But its healing properties were truly magical. He needed it if he was ever to return to his human form full-time. Jacob lifted his nose to the sky as he sat back on his haunches. A mellow howl flowed from his mouth and echoed across the lake. Then, eager to find Jordan and protect her from Che-tan, Llao, and the other warriors, Jacob ran along the crater's rim until he found a split in the rocks that led further down the cliff. He bounded along the path and over the cliff as he found the warrior's scent and saw the remnants of footprints the wind and brush strokes hadn't fully wiped away.

Following his nose along a rocky, snow-covered path, Jacob slowed when he observed the dark shadow of an opening. The mountain cliff separated into a narrow passageway, barely the width of two men standing shoulder to shoulder. Jacob stood beside the fissure. His ears perked up as he heard chatter coming from inside. His instinctive growl rumbled as he heard the shrill echo of laughter. He bared his teeth and stood at point as he listened and sniffed, trying to determine the distance to his enemy. With the echo of so many voices bouncing off the rock walls, it was impossible to accurately guess. Jacob surrendered caution because he didn't care about what he might face. Jordan

deserved action. Striding into the opening, he snarled and prepared his sharp canines for action.

Jacob stepped into the darkness. His eyes searched to iden-
tify every sound—a shuffle of feet on the stone floor, a drip of
water, the sound of breathing. A yellow glow from deeper inside
seeped toward him. He looked left, then right, up, and down as
he studied the passageway, surprised not to find a sentry keeping
watch. Going deeper into the tunnel, he stopped and flinched.
He stepped back as a figure emerged from a recess along the
wall. Jacob growled at the man standing between him and the
brighter light just beyond as the tunnel lowered and seemed to
open into a vast cavern.

Che-tan held a finger to his lips, crouched low to the floor,
and motioned downward with his other hand. "It is I."

Jacob wasn't impressed. He flashed his teeth with a snarl to
let Che-tan know.

Che-tan whispered in earnest. "Shh. You should not be
here. They will hear you." Jacob showed more of his teeth,
so Che-tan tilted his head at the wall in front of the broad
opening. His black ponytail brushed against his ear. "Come.
Look."

Jacob followed Che-tan to the wall and stuck his nose
around the corner to look. The passageway opened into a broad
cavern sunk into the mountain. Crude steps lowered from the
passageway to the stone floor below. Jacob looked at Che-tan
and then refocused on the mass of warriors gathered below.

Smoke from two small fires hovered at the top of the
cavern, which went at least three stories high. The dome
shape of the cavern reminded Jacob of Skell's Grotto, but
it lacked the smooth finish and beauty. The flickering fires
pasted orange and yellow light against the andesite walls and
mingled with the shadowy movements of the men. Jacob
sniffed quietly, but with so many warriors gathered together,
the stench of their poor hygiene mixed with smoke completely hid Jordan's scent.

Che-tan leaned close and whispered in Jacob's ear. "She is there." He pointed to the far corner of the cavern. "Behind the altar."

Jacob watched. He studied the thin stone slab that rested on a rectangular rock. The entire altar appeared to be a little smaller than a child-sized casket. Then, from behind the slab, he saw a thick mane of hair poke up. A low hum warmed Jacob's throat, and he felt the sudden urge to attack, to rip his teeth into the flesh of the warriors. But then he felt Che-tan's hand brushing against his back.

"You must leave. If they find you here, they will escalate the plan for Jordan." Che-tan's warm breath tickled Jacob's ear. "We do not want that."

Jacob backed away from the entrance to the larger cavern. His nose crinkled as he faced Che-tan. He backed up slowly. Che-tan nodded, took a deep breath, and walked through the entrance to the lower cavern. Jacob heard Che-tan being greeted by the others, but the language was foreign. He heard Che-tan say something and laugh as he joined the men. Jacob watched Che-tan mingle with Llao's warriors and was concerned by the familiarity and apparent camaraderie.

Creeping back to the cavern opening, Jacob stuck his nose around the corner and watched as Che-tan walked to the left side of the cavern where a throne was carved in rock. Chief Llao sat on his throne and stood to embrace Che-tan. Mumbled words gathered with the smoke at the top of the cavern. Jacob shook his head and backed away from the cavern, unsure of what it all meant.

Jacob's breathing raced with anxiety, causing his mouth to drop open as he started to pant. The sound of his panting echoed on the stone walls, so he quickly exited from the passageway. Standing on the rock and snow outside the narrow tunnel, Jacob gazed out over Crater Lake as he fantasized about what he should have done to Che-tan. *I could have sunk my teeth into Che-tan's neck and torn out his throat. Or I could have . . .*

No. Maybe Che-tan is still a friend. Jacob couldn't be sure, and the confusion made him angry.

He'd seen Jordan, and she didn't appear to be in immediate danger. Che-tan was either conflicted about working with Llao or was maybe working as a double agent. Jacob thought about it. Maybe he was a triple agent. The thought made his brain hurt.

As he made his way along a ledge that led away from the fissure into the mountain, Jacob found an alcove where he could hide and still watch the entrance to the cavern. He lay his belly on the rock and laid his head on his paws, forcing himself to wait. He watched the entrance with one eye and his friends on the lake with the other. He hoped Ethan and Allie were having more success than he was. He hoped Ha-ida would be able to follow his tracks from Llao Village to Llao's inner mountain lair. He closed his eyes, hoping for the quick arrival of reinforcements.

38

ANCHORS AWAY

BRADY WATCHED SKEPTICALLY AS ETHAN POSITIONED HIM-self inside the ice capsule. Ethan looked up, down, and to the sides. Then he placed his hands in the ice grips Allie had created at shoulder level. "This is fantastic, Allie. Great job!" He waved to Brady and Allie through the crystal-clear ice. "Come on, Brady. Check it out." Ethan stepped out of the capsule and motioned for Brady to take his place, but Brady shook his head vigorously.

"You have no idea what you're asking me to do. Do you?" Ethan nodded his head in rebuttal. "I'm not invincible. I'm just not." Brady swallowed hard, leaning over the hole in the ice to peer into the water. He had always liked swimming, but this? "This is *nuts*."

Allie placed her hand on Brady's shoulder. "He's right, Ethan. He can't do it. You're asking too much. He could die. It's not worth the risk."

Ethan's chest heaved. He closed his eyes and rubbed them with his thumb and middle finger. "We've got everything we need," he said. He pointed at the rock Brady had chosen to weigh himself down, then at Brady, then at the capsule, and finally at the hole in the ice. "It's risky. I know it is," Ethan said, shaking his head. "But it is worth it."

"It's easy to accept risk when you're not the one taking

it," Brady said. He paused for a moment while he studied the expressions on his friends' faces.

"I just don't know what else we can do," Ethan said. He chuckled nervously as he looked at the rock. "But you're right. To think you could hold that boulder all the way down to the bottom of the lake. It's insanity. I'm sorry, Brady."

"Yeah, it's impossible," Allie agreed.

Brady's eyes narrowed. *Ethan has no idea what I'm capable of.* Holding the rock would be simple. He felt like he could bench press a Volvo. A stupid rock would be nothing. Still, he was skeptical of Ethan's motives. "The rock isn't the problem. I can hold it all the way down," he corrected.

Ethan made a face and shrugged his shoulders. "Whatever. If you say so. The rock would help with the descent, but getting you back up quickly is what really worries me. I'm not sure you could kick hard enough to propel yourself up fast enough."

Allie nodded her head. "Seriously. I'd freak out. I'm not exactly a fan of the dark . . . or cold. And if I thought there was a chance I could run out of air . . ." She shook her head. "Don't worry, Brady. I'd be way too scared to try it too," she said, patting Brady's back.

Brady huffed, annoyed at his friends' lack of confidence. "No. I'm a good swimmer, and it's not that I'm scared. I'm not scared of anything."

"Well, Brady, that's obviously not true," Ethan said. "You won't even step inside the capsule. That's fear, but there's no shame in it. You don't have to get defensive about it. We understand."

"Shut it, you little punk." Brady picked up his rock and scooted his way inside the capsule. "See. No fear. That's not the problem."

Ethan opened his mouth to speak but stopped. He looked at Allie and opened his mouth again. The words were slow tumbling out. "Then I don't get it." Brady and Ethan locked eyes as they stared at each other. Then Ethan continued. "I've got an idea. Allie, blow some ice and seal up the capsule. Maybe Brady's nervous because of the confined space. Maybe a little claustrophobic," Ethan suggested. "Maybe he needs to get used to it for a little bit."

Brady started yelling at Ethan for insinuating—again—that he was afraid. But Allie concentrated and blew ice at the capsule, sealing the opening. She gave it a quick spray of heat to melt the seams together and smooth out the capsule. "Maybe if you just wait in there for a moment you won't be so scared," Allie suggested.

"I'M NOT SCARED!" Brady yelled through the ice.

Ethan frowned. "Good. Just remember to hold on to the grips so you keep the air trapped inside as you rise. Oh, and kick as hard as you can when you come back up."

"What?" Brady yelled.

Ethan nodded at Allie, and then Brady read Ethan's lips as he said. "Do it."

Allie closed her eyes for a moment and furrowed her brow with concentration. Then her mouth opened and a spray of flame shot forth, melting the lake crust directly below the capsule. A large, round hole opened up, and the capsule slid into the water with a splash.

Brady held his rock and looked up through the top of the capsule. He saw Allie's head appear above the hole, and she mouthed, "I'm sorry."

Brady peered upward through the clear ice and water at Ethan and Allie standing beside each other. Their expressions were grim, but not nearly as gloomy as they'd be when he got back to the surface. He leaned his head back and screamed, but the sound echoed against the ice walls and died before it could escape the capsule. Brady's shoulders rose and fell quickly with each shallow breath. He'd heard of people being accidentally buried alive before, but this was a burial at sea. It was like dropping an anchor in an ice casket . . . and he was still conscious. For a moment, Brady wished he wasn't aware of his situation.

Every muscle in his body flexed with anger. But as much as he wanted to pound Ethan into oblivion, he focused his mind on his two immediate missions—survival and the retrieval of the healing bowl.

39

A SINKING
FEELING

BRADY CONTINUED TO LOOK THROUGH THE TOP OF THE capsule at his two friends. "Friends?" he muttered. He growled as he tightened his grip on the rock. All he could see were Ethan's and Allie's silhouettes against the bright sun as his capsule blasted down through the water. His stomach settled in his throat and he tried to control his breathing to keep himself from up-chucking. He was breathing shallowly and was light-headed.

The deeper the capsule sank, the darker the water became—and the faster Brady sucked down his oxygen supply. For a moment, he thought he saw a giant Kokanee salmon swimming by. But then the darkness became total except for the pinprick of light where the sun shined through the ice hole. He stared out of the clear ice capsule, but there was nothing to see except the water's blackness that wanted him dead. Brady had his own homicidal thoughts as he considered Ethan's trickery in getting him into the capsule. His stomach fluttered and gurgled, and he thought he would vomit. But then he gained control again.

He didn't know how long the capsule had been in the water, but it felt like it had been twenty minutes already, and he hadn't hit bottom. The thought made his heart race, but he calmed a little when he reminded himself that he hadn't run out of air either. Brady focused his mind, willing himself to breathe slower, deeper. He imagined his father's soothing voice talking to him. He closed his eyes and tried swallowing, just as the speed of his capsule seemed to max out.

Brady thought about the bowl and what it would mean to turn Jacob back into a boy again. He thought about Jacob's family, their smiles and relief, and the excitement and uncontrolled joy they would feel when they saw him again. Brady hoped his family would feel the same way when they were reunited, but he doubted it.

For a moment, Brady forgot he was sinking one thousand feet below the surface of Crater Lake, but then a noise jolted him back to reality. His eyes burst open when he heard the sound of the first crack, but the complete darkness made it impossible to see any problem. Then he heard another crack. He and Ethan had discussed his body's ability to withstand the water pressure deep in the lake, but he'd never considered the possibility that the capsule would fail. But then, Ethan hadn't really given him a chance to think about it. Brady remembered the submarine movie where the water pressure squeezed the sub into oblivion. He moaned, and his pulse quickened as he heard another crack in the ice.

Then, high from above, through hundreds of feet of water, a bright light shined into the depths of Crater Lake. Brady squeezed his eyes shut and slowly opened them, allowing them to adjust to the light. "It's about time, Allie," he muttered. The water appeared even more brilliant than the blue sky. Looking out of the capsule and into the lake, Brady saw a blurry shadow swim past. Then, the capsule crashed to a stop as Brady landed on the central platform. The boulder fell from his hand, and the lower half of the capsule shattered and drifted away. The top half of the capsule shot upward, and Brady reached for it with his right hand. Grabbing one of the ice handles, he pulled the top of the capsule lower so that his head touched the top. The toes of his shoes searched for a hold. He gripped the boulder he had been holding, keeping him anchored to the bottom of the platform floor.

Despite a large crack in front of his face, Brady held to the top of the capsule, pulling it down with him as he struggled to scoop up the boulder in one hand. The light from above shined on the floor of the central platform, and Brady scooted his feet across the coarse rock. He scanned the expanse below the lake. He turned in place, looking, hoping to find the healing bowl, but it was nowhere to be seen. The coldness of the water pressed against him, and although he could tell it was chilly, the temperature didn't bother him. But the pressure did. The water crushed against his chest. Every breath felt like he was bench-pressing a three-hundred-pound barbell. It felt like his lungs would collapse—or worse, like he would suffocate even though he had air inside the capsule to breathe. His lungs refused to inflate fully. He flexed his chest as he held the boulder against his stomach with one hand and held the top of his capsule with the other.

He shuffled over the hard ground and scanned the area for the artifact. Every breath sounded like a combination of a balloon letting its air out and a smoker's cough. His eyes widened with panic when he realized these incomplete breaths were the best he could hope for. He shuffled faster, and his eyes darted from side to side as he walked across the bottom of the lake.

In the distance, a shimmer caught his eye. So he made a slight adjustment to his right and hurried toward it, his chest burning from the stress of breathing. Brady blinked as blackness formed around the corners of his vision. Looking up, he could see the light still beaming down on him, yet his vision faded. He picked up his feet and moved more quickly, stopping when he stood directly over the source of the shimmer. Crouching down, he placed the rock between his legs and picked up his dagger. His eyes brightened with happiness. He had found his dagger. He'd never even considered the possibility, but there it was. Raising the dagger in front of his eyes, he studied the black obsidian blade with the appreciation of a father finding his lost child. Then he set the dagger in his pocket, the bone hilt down, and resumed his search for the bowl.

He didn't have to look far. To his left, the flute sat on top of a rock, and the bowl lay beside it. Brady considered gathering up the flute, but decided Allie's big mouth was sufficient for blowing fire, ice, and light. Besides, his hands were full. He wheezed for breath as the water crushed against him. Ignoring the flute, Brady reached for the bowl. His fingers knocked it away at first, but eventually he was able to pick it up and pull it into the capsule. He stared at it, but his raspy breathing made it impossible to smile. Holding onto his capsule handle with one hand, Brady looked for a way to secure the bowl in his pants, but it was too big. He balanced the bowl on top of his head, and grabbed the other handle on the capsule, and pulled it tight against the bowl. Releasing the boulder from between his legs, Brady pushed off from the bottom of the lake and started kicking.

Brady focused on the light above him, blinked, and then closed his eyes momentarily until he forced them back open. The light burned into his eyes, but it was better than the cold darkness that would consume him if he allowed it. The trapped oxygen contained beneath the top of the capsule pulled Brady toward the surface like a beach ball trying to escape from below the water. His legs kicked. At moments, he couldn't breathe, and additional cracks continued to splinter the capsule, but Brady kept kicking faster, ignoring the pain and exhaustion threatening to destroy him.

The higher he floated up, the less the water pressure constricted his breathing. His lungs inflated with air, and it became easier to breathe with each passing moment. The light grew brighter . . . and larger. But once again, the darkness began filling in around the corners of Brady's vision. He took deep breaths that felt increasingly empty. Brady knew his air was almost depleted, so he kicked harder and faster. With each passing moment, the temptation to close his eyes and give in to his exhaustion threatened to overpower him.

The clear water seemed to last for miles, and the panic of suffocation caused Brady's ears to tingle as he gasped for each partial breath. He kicked and kicked, and the light grew brighter and brighter until he burst from the surface into the sunshine. He kicked so hard that his body flew from the water and landed on the ice crust of Crater Lake. His lungs burned, and the ice capsule shattered around him as he slammed onto the ground near Allie and Ethan. Brady's fingers dug into the icy crust, and he pressed his face against the hard surface of the lake as a tear fell, mixing with the splashed water all around him. His eyes squeezed closed as he kissed the ice. "Thank you, thank you, thank you, thank you."

***

Ethan stepped back with wide eyes as Brady flew through the air like a penguin returning from a swim. He watched Brady crash to the ground, the ice capsule shatter, and the bowl skitter away. Ethan's eyes focused on the bowl as it slid across the ice toward one of the other holes Allie had blasted in the ice. His heart stopped. The bowl slid to the edge of the ice, teetered, and then toppled through the hole. Springing forward, Ethan dove for the bowl, but his fingertips couldn't grab it before it fell through and started sinking back into the depths. Ripping off his jacket, Ethan yelled, "Light," and dove into the water. He reached and pulled at the water as he swam deeper, chasing the sinking bowl until his fingertips grabbed the rim. He kicked his feet, righted himself, and pulled himself with one hand back toward the opening.

The terror of drowning enveloped him. So he kicked and pulled harder until he slammed into the ice covering the lake. The ice was trapping him! His eyes widened, and he prayed for help. His hands and feet pressed against the ice, looking for an opening. Then a burst of red-and-orange light engulfed his view. The heat was unbearable, so he allowed himself to sink farther away until a powerful hand reached in and grabbed him by the scruff of the shirt.

Ethan stared into Brady's eyes as his friend yanked him out

of the water. Spitting up lake water, Ethan set the bowl carefully on the ice and continued to gag, spit, and choke. When his coughing fit was complete and he could feel the comfort of regular breathing, Ethan climbed to his knees. He looked at Allie and attempted a grin. Then he stepped up to Brady and gave him the tightest, heartiest hug he could manage. "You d-d-d-id it, B-b-brady!" The weakness of Ethan's voice couldn't convey his true excitement. His body shivered, and the shock of cold hit him. "I kn-kn-knew you'd d-d-do it."

Brady wrapped his warm body around Ethan to convey some of his body heat to his friend. "Yeah. I did, didn't I?" he said, smirking. "I rock!"

Allie cleared her throat. "Ehhemmm. I think we *all* did it," she corrected.

"Yeah, whatever."

– 40 –

DRAFTED

HA-IDA, IN ANTELOPE FORM, LED WARRIORS FROM THE SHAN-tytown of Skell Village toward Llao's new home base. Stan walked beside her, his head swaying. He scratched his claws at the snowy path. Ha-ida paused and turned in place. The other trekkers also stopped and huddled together. She watched the stragglers who were falling further behind. She lifted her nose and huffed, turning fully to face her comrades. Then she waited.

Stan turned, grunted to Ha-ida, and stood on his hind legs, rising to his full and intimidating stature. Ha-ida morphed into her human form and issued her command again. Then Stan bared and attacked the stragglers with a roar that punctuated Ha-ida's command. He waved his arms and paws over his head as if shredding an enemy.

"Quicken your pace. Do not be afraid. Do not waiver in your commitment to serve Skell," Ha-ida yelled to the gathering troops. Once most of the animals had assembled, Ha-ida morphed back to her antelope form.

She nudged Stan with her heart-shaped horns, and he lowered onto all fours. She lifted her nose again and huffed with acceptance as the stragglers in the line caught up to the rest of the group. They gathered around, and Ha-ida approached a cougar who still had a bad attitude. She lowered her head and pressed her nose against the cougar's. She stared, never blinking once. Finally, the cougar lowered on its front paws and bowed its head. Ha-ida nodded as the rest of the stragglers lowered their heads in submission. She huffed and continued the march toward Llao Village.

41

PROCESSION

T HE CLAMOR INSIDE LLAO'S LAIR INTENSIFIED, AND
screeches and hollers echoed in the entire cavern. Jacob
raised his ears as he listened and worried about his captured
friend inside. What had Jordan done to deserve abduction and
assault from Llao's band of warriors? Jacob pondered the question but was unable to come up with a reasonable answer. Still,
he knew enough about Chief Llao to know that everything he
did served a purpose. He wanted Jordan for a reason. What did
he plan to do with her? Jacob wondered but was pulled from
his thoughts as the echoed screams of hate blasted from the
entrance to the lair.

Jacob backed away along the cliff's ridge above Crater Lake.
He crouched behind a boulder, ready and alert, prepared to
attack the warriors as they exited the lair. The uproar inside the
cavern finally blew out. Llao exited first, staring straight ahead.
He held a rope wrapped around his waist that connected him
to the next exiting warrior. Jacob cocked his head as he watched
Llao. Instead of the usual, simple garb of tanned animal skins,
Llao wore flamboyant apparel dripping with brilliant colors of
indigo, mustard, and pine, all capped with plumes of feathers
that rose three feet above his head.

Jacob was ready. His nose and eyes peeked out from behind
his boulder when he saw the next warrior step from the shadows

of the cave onto the ridge of rock and snow. Jacob watched while warriors filed out of the cavern in their traditional dress, each connected by the same long rope wrapped around their mid-sections. Llao marched with dignity and pomp at the front of the group, never turning to speak to the men behind him. The warriors moved slowly as they shuffled their feet along the icy ridge. Jacob began to lose patience. He imagined attacking the warriors. The ridge was so narrow that they would have to fight one at a time or risk falling over the edge of the cliff. If one fell, maybe he would pull the rest down with him. The fur on the back of Jacob's neck rose as he considered his options and his chance for success.

But then he paused. Jacob turned his head to the side as two men exited the cavern mouth standing side-by-side. The men were dressed like the others. Heavy furs hung from their shoulders like capes, and animal skins covered their nakedness. Thick poles rested atop the furs on their shoulders. Two more men exited directly behind the first with poles lying across their shoulders. A three-foot-high, four-foot-long rectangular stone balanced on top of the poles. Behind them, two other sets of warriors pulled up the rear with the weight of the rock slab distributed on the poles across their shoulders. They inched onto the ridge, moving slowly as they made the turn out of the cavern and onto the narrow pathway.

Jacob raised his head, his tongue lying across his sharp teeth and out the side of his mouth. He focused on top of the stone slab. Jordan lay atop the altar, tied down with a multitude of cords. Her hair dangled over the back of the slab, and her head moved from side to side. Jacob noticed her shoulders bounce as she sobbed quietly.

The procession continued moving forward in silence until the last man exited the cavern. Che-tan looked around and grinned as he shook his head gently at Jacob. Jacob slunk deeper behind the rock, but then stepped forward when it appeared Che-tan had no intent to alarm the others. The line of warriors marched slowly along the ridge and up the path to the rim of the crater, all while Jacob watched helplessly. His sharp eyes watched Che-tan, and he gained confidence when Che-tan remained silent, never speaking to the men in front of him.

Creeping from behind his hiding place, Jacob followed way behind Llao's warriors as the procession moved toward Llao Village. Atop the crater's rim, Llao tried pushing his men to go at a faster pace but eventually settled for the slow and steady movements of the men weighed down by the rock slab.

Jacob looked over the cliff at his friends far below. They gathered at the base of the cliff but didn't climb. He wondered why. Then he continued following Llao and his men.

42

CRYSTAL STAIRCASE

ETHAN CRINGED AS ALLIE FACED HIM AND TOOK AIM. SHE opened her mouth, and Ethan ducked, covering his head with his shivering hands. "S-s-stop!" he pleaded. But Allie didn't listen.

Allie fluttered nervously, but the mixture of breath was just what Ethan needed. Ethan sighed in relief when Allie's breath didn't yield fire or ice, but instead shot out a hot desert wind. The warm gust blew against Ethan, causing his cheeks to flap and his clothes to tighten against his body. He took a step back to brace himself and then leaned into the hot breeze. After a moment, Ethan's clothes dried and the chill abandoned his bones. He no longer shivered but rather felt like removing his shirt to catch some sun.

"Have I told you lately . . . you *rock*!" Ethan said, smiling at his beautiful friend. Allie tucked a strand of blonde hair behind her ear and pulled her hood back over her head as she blushed at Ethan's compliment. "Seriously, Allie, how'd you do that?"

Allie knit her eyebrows together, making her look like she was concentrating hard. "I just have to think about what I want," she said. "I wanted to mix a little bit of fire—for the heat—and wind. I'm glad it worked. I was afraid I'd barbecue you."

Ethan laughed. "Very cool. You're amazing."

Brady's triceps bulged as he sat on the ice and leaned back.

"Yeah, who would have thunk that a girl would be full of hot air?" Brady laughed, but he was the only one.

Allie squinted at Brady and then blew a stream of ice that covered the muscular boy's entire body up to the nape of his red neck. "You're a funny guy," Allie teased as she watched Brady struggle in the confining ice. He wiggled, shrugged, and twisted. Finally Brady poked his hand through the ice, shattered the rest of it, and rose to his feet.

Ethan zipped up his jacket and placed his stocking cap on top of his curly head. "Come on, guys. We're on the same team here. And we've got work to do. We've got to help Jacob and Ha-ida. We've got to find Jordan. Time's running out." Ethan cocked his head as he stared up the side of the sheer cliff.

"And how do you plan on getting up where the action is, professor?" Brady taunted.

Ethan scratched his head. "Allie, any ideas?"

Allie smiled. Her white teeth matched the snow. "Oh yeah. Leave it to me." Allie studied the cliff side. She tilted her head and stared again. Without further delay, Allie opened her mouth and spewed out sheets of thick ice at the base of the cliff to create a wide platform. She created another platform ten feet higher, studied it, nodded her head with satisfaction, and then approached the lowest platform. Her mouth opened as she sprayed fire from one side to the other, creating a step. She repeated the process nine more times until she had a full line of ice steps leading to the raised platform.

"Nice!" Ethan cheered.

"Not bad for a girl," Brady offered. He stepped up first and reached back to grab Allie's hand to help her up, but Allie ignored the offer as she bounded past him.

The upper platform of ice hugged the side of the cliff. Standing on top, Allie took aim and began spraying diagonally a steady line of ice, fifteen feet up the side of the cliff. She rotated heat and ice, creating a crystalline staircase. Taking her first step up the narrow stairs, Allie slipped and fell forward.

Her chin slammed on the step, splitting it open. Blood gushed from the wound.

Ethan helped her up and wiped his hand across her chin, removing the blood and wiping it off on the snow beside him. But Allie's split chin continued to bleed. Tears formed at the corner of her eyes, but she wiped them away. "I'll be fine," she said, standing on her own and shaking off the daze. Allie took another deep breath and connected a thin beam of ice four feet above the stairs.

Ethan poked her with his elbow. "Handrail?"

"Yep." Allie rubbed her chin and wiped a handful of blood across the sleeve of her jacket.

"Hold on a minute." Ethan bent over, unzipped his coat, and removed the healing bowl from his side. Holding the bowl next to a snowy patch on the cliff, he brushed the snow and ice into the bowl and held it out for Allie. "Just a touch of heat please," he requested. Allie blew onto the ice, turning it to water. "Let's see if this thing still works." He extended the bowl in his hand toward Allie. "Here. Drink."

Allie looked at the bowl and then accepted it. She held it to her lips, her eyes peering over the rim of the bowl at Ethan and Brady. She tipped the bowl and slowly sipped. The pained expression on her face changed to an exuberant smile. The cut on her chin closed in on itself, and the blood vanished from her face as if she had never been injured at all. Allie ran her hands across her face and rubbed her chin, testing the effectiveness of the bowl. Her smile grew.

"Not bad, huh?" Ethan said.

Allie nodded fast. "Don't take this wrong, but I always just assumed you exaggerated about what the bowl could do. But this is incredible. I feel better than . . . than . . . ever."

Ethan scowled. "Seriously, you didn't believe me about the bowl?"

"Don't worry, professor. She believes you now."

Allie chuckled and grabbed the handrail as she started

walking up the slick staircase, carefully placing each foot. "It's not that I didn't believe you. Not really. I mean . . . you told me about it . . . but this feels even better than you described."

Ethan scraped more snow into his bowl and hurried up the steps closer to Allie as she prepared to blow the next set of steps. "Hey, Allie, would you?" he asked, holding out his bowl. She blew in a way that sounded like a sneeze, and the snow turned to water. Ethan drank.

"Dude, that's seriously gross," Brady said, stepping up from behind. "She blows her nose, and you drink it? Nasty."

Ethan ignored Brady and followed Allie closely.

Allie continued her ascent along the staircase, creating the ice base. She used flame to etch the individual stairs and then finished the creation with the safety handrail. After walking to the top of the stairs, she turned the other direction and zigged a new line of stairs the other direction. She continued her process up the cliffside, Ethan bounding behind her with newfound energy from the bowl.

As the group neared the summit, Allie created two additional platforms that dangled out into the expanse of air. The staircase led to the first platform, and then a few additional stairs led to the final platform, which was positioned level with the rim. Allie motioned toward the rim of snow and rock with a flourish of her hand. "We're here."

Ethan bit the side of his lip as he glanced at Allie. He tried not to stare, even though he wanted to. At the edge of the top platform, he leaned over and looked down at the staircase glistening in the sun. Then he looked back at Allie, who seemed to be sparkling with pride for her creation. Stepping beside her, Ethan nudged her shoulder lightly as they stared past Wizard Island. He glanced sideways and then turned and pecked Allie on the cheek. He turned back to gaze over the lake. "Sorry," he said, nearly out of breath as his eyes shifted to the side, trying to see Allie's reaction. He swallowed, fighting to find the courage to speak. "I just think you're awesome. That's all." He chuckled nervously.

Allie's cheeks turned red, and her eyelashes fluttered as she turned away.

Ethan clapped his hands together and stepped from the ice platform back onto the crater's rim. "Okay, Brady. You're up. Take us to Llao Village . . . fast."

-43-

THE LEGEND OF LOHA

HA-IDA'S ANTELOPE FORM REARED BACK ON HER HINDQUAR-ters as she morphed back into a human. "Form a perimeter. I want to know everything that comes in or out of the village," Ha-ida said to the group of animal warriors gathered around her.

The thick streak of blond fur on Stan's face swayed in the breeze. He growled and grunted. The other animals separated, some heading to the left and others to the right. Stan led the group to the left while Ha-ida wrapped her scarf around her neck and face. Stan grunted again and wiggled his black nose.

"No. Do not worry. I am going to get a closer look inside the camp," Ha-ida said. She walked from the safe and secluded cover of the woods directly into the center of Llao Village. She turned her head from side to side as she studied the village, but aside from a young boy building a fort in the snow and the female elders sitting around the campfires threading thick needles through animal skins, the village appeared to be deserted.

As Ha-ida approached, the women around the fires stood and backed their way into the nearby dwellings. One hollered at the young boy, who quickly abandoned his play and joined her inside. Only the eldest looking of the women remained seated next to her fire, so Ha-ida approached her with slow, deliberate steps. She loosened the wrapping from around her face and felt the cold wind blow across her nose, causing it to run. Ha-ida motioned toward an open seat. "May I sit?"

The old woman nodded, so Ha-ida sat. The seat still felt warm from its previous occupant. Ha-ida held her hands closer to the fire for warmth, lifting her head and studying the village. She twisted in her seat to look at the dwellings behind her and saw the young boy peeking from inside a leaning shelter that appeared ready to topple over. She then focused on the tower at the center of the village to her left. The trees had been cleared around it, providing a small but open field surrounding the tower. She looked at the strong cords that lashed the poles together and at the ropes higher up that connected to mature trees for additional sturdiness. The tower reached to the treetops.

Ha-ida turned back to the old woman, who continued sewing her animal skin clothing. Ha-ida spoke in her native tongue. "I am Ha-ida."

The woman ignored the introduction for a moment and then mumbled in response, "I know."

"What do they call you?" Ha-ida asked.

The woman's busy fingers paused as she turned toward Ha-ida. Her lips formed a wispy smile. Her long, gray hair was tucked behind her ear and pulled into a loose braid. "I am called Loha."

Ha-ida's eyes raced from side to side, looking for any sign of Llao or his warriors. But the village remained calm. The wind whistled through the evergreen branches overhead, and the crackle of the fire added to the peacefulness of the village. "I do not intend to hurt you," Ha-ida said quietly as her eyes returned to the old woman.

"Then why do your warriors surround my village?" Loha asked, returning her fingers to sewing.

Ha-ida listened. She didn't hear a single grunt or even the sound of paws sinking in the snow. She looked over the perimeter of the village, but she didn't see any sign of her people. How could the woman possibly know? Ha-ida thought about denying the accusation but decided not to lie. "We are looking for a girl. Her name is Jordan. She has thick hair. She was taken by Llao and his men. She is innocent."

The woman smacked her lips together as she concentrated on her sewing. She appeared uncaring or, at the very least, bored with the conversation.

"Have you seen this girl?" Ha-ida asked.

Loha grinned at Ha-ida. She shook her head. "No."

"You have not seen her?" Ha-ida confirmed.

"No. She is not innocent. She has power. Power was taken." Loha's eyes refocused on her agile fingers. "Llao will take it back."

"How? Where? When?"

Loha's smile broadened. She set the animal skin and needle on her lap and folded her arms across the top. She made a *tsk-tsk-tsk* sound with her tongue.

Ha-ida frowned and crinkled her nose as she studied the old woman. "You are not like those other women," Ha-ida commented with dry accusation. "You are not afraid."

"No. I am not afraid."

"Why not?" Ha-ida squinted as she watched the old woman fidget on her log seat. "You do not look like them. Your hair. Your clothes. They are different." Loha nodded. "And your name 'Loha' means *princess*."

Loha fidgeted more. "You do not know."

Ha-ida's eyes softened, and she tilted her head to one side. "I know of only one legend about a princess named Loha. It is *the* legend."

Loha nodded. "Tell me."

"Loha was daughter of the first Klamath chieftain. Llao fell in love with her and desired her for wife, but Loha refused. She rejected him." Ha-ida looked into the woman's eyes, hoping to find a glimmer of recognition.

"Go on."

"She was in love with another man: Skell." Ha-ida spoke

slowly, emphasizing every word. "He loved her too. Loha's father rejected Llao's offer for union and accepted Skell. Llao became angry. Under cover of night, he abducted Loha and hid her away on Mazama. This is the root of the conflict between Llao and Skell. They fought for Loha. They fight still."

"Is that all?" Loha asked.

Ha-ida shook her head. "No. When Loha and Llao's son was born, Llao gave Loha a gift."

Loha's craggy voice brightened. "Yes. What was the gift?"

"A necklace. Three round, interlocking stones."

"A necklace? No. That is not the gift," Loha said. "He gave her the gift of vision."

"Do you mean sight? Was she blind?"

The old woman wagged her finger and her head at Ha-ida. "The necklace means nothing without the gift." Loha leaned forward and untied a strap that held the fur-skin shawl around her shoulders. She reached underneath her robe near her bosom and pulled out a necklace of three interlocking stones. They hung around her neck and rested against her chest. She repeated herself. "It is beautiful, but the necklace means nothing without the gift."

Ha-ida blinked rapidly as she thought about the legend of Loha. *Could it be true? Is it possible* she *is Loha? Could this old woman be the cause of the feud between Llao and Skell? Could the great battle, the destruction of Mazama, and the centuries of imprisonment and warfare between Skell and Llao all be her fault? Does Crater Lake exist because of her? Impossible.*

As if she sensed the inner conflict of Ha-ida's thoughts, Loha shook her finger at Ha-ida and poked her in the chest. "I am not responsible for Llao's choices."

Ha-ida scoffed. "Yet you sit in Llao Village. You help him?"

"The necklace means nothing without the gift. My gift. The gift the girl took."

Ha-ida's attention returned to her original purpose. "Jordan. Where is she?" Ha-ida stood over Loha. "Tell me."

"She is not far. The gift will soon be returned to me."

Ha-ida chuckled nervously as she sized up the old woman. Her eyes became narrow slits. "Why are you telling me these things? What will happen to the girl?"

Loha's cheeks sagged. "I tell you because I want you to stop Llao. He will be stronger when the gift is returned."

Ha-ida squinted at Loha. "What else?"

"I tell you because I do not want that cursed gift back."

PERIMETER BREACH

A T THE EDGE OF THE PINE FOREST, JACOB WATCHED THE procession of Chief Llao and his minions wind its way into the woods toward Llao Village. He remained hidden in the shadows and observed both this group and a separate group of animal warriors move into position. Jacob lowered his belly onto the snow and watched while Ha-ida's warriors, all easily identified by their streaks of gray, or blond in one bear's case, positioned themselves around the perimeter of the village. Ha-ida was nowhere to be seen, so Jacob focused his attention on a black bear who seemed to be in charge.

The black bear with the blond streak across his face quietly grunted to a nearby cougar, and then he motioned with his head. The cougar backed away into the woods where it hid behind a downed tree with piled snow on it.

Llao's warriors marched slowly to the forest while the chief continually yanked at the rope wrapped around his waist. Despite all of his pulling, his men did not speed up. The black bear backed further into the trees and lowered himself onto the snow.

Jacob watched from his hiding spot as Llao's warriors hiked deeper into the forest in silence. The men balancing the heavy stone with Jordan struggled in the deep snow. Jacob listened to Jordan's panting sobs from the top of the slab.

His gaze shifted from Jordan, and his ears stood straight as a deep growl rumbled from the black bear. He hoped the bear and all of Ha-ida's warriors would remain calm and wait for the right moment. But still, not knowing how his presence would be received by Ha-ida's warriors, Jacob decided to remain hidden in darkness and silence.

After Llao's men passed, the black bear nodded to the cougar on his flank and grunted. Without hesitation, the cougar sprinted back along the perimeter.

When the final man in the procession was far enough ahead, the black bear followed at a distance. His head shifted, and a quiet growl sounded like wind rustling through the trees. Then the dark head of another black bear poked from behind a tree and followed from the other side of the trail.

The black bear's head swayed, and his tongue rubbed against his sharp teeth. He stretched his jaws wide enough to fit around the head of one of Llao's warriors. Jacob watched closely, and then shifted his gaze from Ha-ida's warriors back to Llao's men and Jordan. Sadness replaced curiosity as he heard Jordan sob for help. He stared at Jordan, his head shaking in disbelief at the barbarity displayed by Llao and his men.

Jacob turned to Che-tan at the rear of the procession. He gnashed his teeth in silence, wondering about Che-tan's true allegiance. How could he be sure of Che-tan's intentions? Ha-ida and her warriors had made up their mind about Che-tan, but Jacob felt conflicted. He knew he would need to make a decision soon, because Ha-ida's warriors considered Che-tan a traitor and were likely considering gruesome ways to end his life. Rising from the snow, he took another look at the procession entering the village and at Ha-ida's warriors positioned strategically around the perimeter. He stared at Jordan as her screams faded in the distance. Then, leaving his hiding spot, Jacob raced through the woods, weaving between trees and keeping his distance from Ha-ida's warriors as he searched for the right opportunity to make his move.

– 45 –

COLLISION

THE NOISE SOUNDED LIKE BIRDS SQUAWKING TO HA-IDA AT first, but it turned out to be Jordan screaming for help. When she recognized Jordan's shrieks, it was nearly too late. Ha-ida turned on her seat and looked between the dwellings and the tower at the center of the village. On the other side, she saw the procession marching into camp with Llao in the lead. Standing, she glanced back at Loha.

"Go!" Loha whispered. The force of her breath and the intensity of her order nearly knocked Ha-ida from her feet.

Ha-ida looked in the direction she had entered the camp and saw a cougar entering the village. Jordan's shrill screams grew louder. Then, with one last glance at Loha, Ha-ida dove over the fire pit. Her hands sank into the snow first as she morphed back into a pronghorn antelope. Within moments, her sprint slowed as she entered the snow-covered trees. She turned around and stared at Loha, who was still sitting at the center of camp, sewing calmly as the warriors marched in and circled the tower. They stopped and turned so their backs were to the tower. Llao then untied the rope from his waist. He adjusted the plumage in his headdress and smoothed the flowing, indigo cape covering his shoulders. He walked to the next warrior in line and unwrapped the rope. Then he moved to the next and to the next, but he stopped as he approached the men holding the stone slab with Jordan on top. From the other direction, Che-tan untied the warriors until all the men were able to move freely and the ropes remained connected only to the slab of stone.

The men carrying the poles grabbed them in unison as one man counted down. Then they all lifted and stepped to the side, and the altar sank one foot into the snow. Ha-ida got a good look at Jordan and the layers of rope binding her to the rock. Then, her eyes wandered to the back of the village where the procession had entered. Stan waited just beyond the shadows.

Self-doubt flooded Ha-ida's mind as she realized she didn't know what to do next. She was told to locate Jordan and offer support to Jacob, but what then? *Where is Jacob?* Bounding in a wide circle, Ha-ida sprinted around the perimeter of the village, her sinking hoofs kicking up dustings of snow. Her fighters were spread at varying distances around the border. With each one she passed, she ordered them to follow, and they did—until she came across a cluster of six gathered together. They had not spread out as commanded earlier, and they ignored her new command to follow. Refusing to waste her time, Ha-ida ran past her disobedient allies to the far edge of the village.

***

Jacob approached the edge of the village with caution. He could still smell Ha-ida's animal army, but he didn't detect her nearby. He also wasn't prepared to make his presence known yet. The warriors didn't know him, and he didn't know them. Introductions in this kind of volatile situation were too unpredictable. He padded through the thick evergreen forest, watching, listening, and sniffing his way. One hundred yards away, at the edge of the village, the black bear, two cougars, and a flight of hawks gathered. The black bear with the blond streak gathered additional fighters close to him as they arrived to join the group.

Jacob watched from the anonymity of distance, downwind from his supposed allies. With his tongue dangling from his mouth, he lay on his belly with his head up and his ears on point. Then a familiar face comforted him. Ha-ida rounded a bend between the trees at a full sprint and stopped beside the black bear. Moments later, additional animals joined.

Jacob kept his head low and crept quietly toward the group. He paused as they all morphed into their human forms. The muffled sounds of nervous chatter helped him approach undetected as Ha-ida and the boy who had been the black bear engaged in earnest discussion. Jacob waited behind a tree, and then, at an appropriate lull in the conversation, he strode into the center of the group. Ha-ida smiled, which made Jacob feel good. But the ghastly expressions on the other kids' faces made him wonder if he had a squirrel tail dangling from his teeth. He swept his broad tongue across his mouth. All clear.

Jacob nuzzled Ha-ida and then sat, facing her.

"Jacob, this is Stan," she said, introducing her right hand man. "Stan, this is . . ."

"The Mystic Gray," he said, completing her sentence in a reverential tone. Stan gaped. "I didn't . . . I mean, we . . . uh . . . we didn't know you were real."

Jacob shook his head and let out a low grumble. "The gray wolf is *not* the Mystic Gray," Ha-ida explained. "But he is the Mystic Gray's envoy." Ha-ida paused as she surveyed the group. "We all serve Skell. He is the true Mystic Gray. He is the one who will save us from Llao." Heads nodded, and Jacob growled in approval.

"So what do we do?" Stan asked. A few of the other kids mumbled, repeating the question that dominated everyone's thoughts.

Jacob growled, but no one understood. He motioned with his head toward the village, where two men were climbing the side of the tower with ropes slung over their shoulders. The ropes all connected to the sacrificial altar upon which Jordan lay.

Ha-ida took a deep breath. "We must stop them, but we need more help. Some of our friends do not believe the importance of saving Jordan. They drag their feet. They are not committed."

The words burned in Jacob's brain, and before he could control himself, he rose onto all fours and growled loudly as he faced each of the gathered youth. How could they not believe? Why wouldn't they help?

Reaching down, Ha-ida placed a hand on Jacob's head and scratched his ears. She lowered onto one knee and held the sides of Jacob's furry face. "These are strong," she said, motioning to the kids around her. "There are others. Before we can take on an outside enemy, we must first be united together. Come with me." Diving onto the ground, Ha-ida morphed and began running. Jacob followed closely, leaving the rest of the group behind.

Arriving at the group of malcontents still waiting at the spot outside the perimeter, Jacob and Ha-ida approached. They were far enough from the village that Jacob didn't feel the need to be as docile and polite as he had previously been. Ha-ida morphed into her woman form and approached the ringleader of the group. She pointed, and Jacob attacked. He leapt from the snow onto the back of the cougar and sunk his teeth deep into the shoulder. The cougar yelped and bucked, but Jacob held firm, digging his claws into the cougar. The cougar was alone. None of its friends gave aid or comfort. Finally, the cougar gave up the fight, lowered to its belly, and covered its face with its paws. Then Jacob climbed off.

Blood dripping from his teeth, Jacob growled at the other warriors.

Ha-ida spoke. "The Mystic Gray has commanded us to this mission. Are you with us, or are you against us?"

The bears, cougars, and even the hawks stood a little taller, rigid and at attention. Jacob approached the cougar he had attacked and nudged it with his nose. Then he licked its face with his long tongue.

Ha-ida lowered to her knee and lifted the cougar's head. "You too. Are you with us?"

The cougar rose onto all fours and nodded its head.

Pleased with the change in attitude of his fellow animal warriors, Jacob turned to Ha-ida. He hoped their commitment was genuine and lasting. If not . . . well, he dreaded the thought.

"Good," Ha-ida said. "Let us join the others." Without any further discussion, she morphed and led the way back to the group to gather her army in full strength.

– 46 –

ATTACK!

L LAO'S WARRIORS STOOD IN A TIGHT CIRCLE WITH THEIR backs to the tower. Their eyes roamed. Che-tan and Llao stood at the front of the tower next to the eastern pole of the foundation. They worked with the lashings that bound Jordan to the altar. Jacob gazed upon the four climbing men with the ropes hanging from their shoulders but then looked again to Jordan bound to the slab. He shook his head and prepared for battle.

Stan morphed into his human form, and so did Ha-ida. Jacob wished he could transform from a wolf, but he remained caged in the canine body next to the other animal warriors. Jacob padded to the front of the group and faced Ha-ida, Stan, and the others. A gentle growl seeped from his jowls as he tried to communicate, but the others couldn't understand. Nipping at the back of Ha-ida's pant leg, Jacob tried to refocus Ha-ida. But her attention remained locked on the tower.

"What are they up to?" Stan asked.

"I do not know," Ha-ida said, shaking her head. "But I do not like it."

Duh! Jacob thought, but it came out as another growl. He yipped at Stan and motioned with his head toward the tower. *What's to like? She's tied to an altar where Llao will sacrifice her to obtain her power.* Then Jacob took three quick strides toward the tower as if to say, "Let's go. Follow me." But the others didn't pay attention.

Atop the tower, two men ran their ropes over a broad beam extending from above the platform like a hangman's gallows. The climbers threaded the thick ropes through a pulley system, and then let it drop partway down the tower. The first climber tied a loop at the bottom of the rope and set his foot inside. The second climber wrapped one arm around the other and placed his foot in the same loop. Chief Llao yelled something from below as the men sat on one of the tower crossbeams, staring downward. Llao yelled again, and then the climbers slid from the tower, each gripping the rope tightly as they faced each other.

The men lurched to a stop five feet lower. The slack in their rope tightened. Then, slowly, they lowered as Jordan and her slab of stone began rising from the ground.

"I know what they're doing," Stan said.

"Duh," Jacob said again, but it came out as a low yip. Jacob growled louder, bit into the hem of Ha-ida's coat, and started pulling her out of the woods toward the tower. He snarled as he pulled and yanked at her coat. Finally, her eyes met his, and he released her coat. Running to the edge of the forest cover, Jacob turned around to face Ha-ida's small army. Ha-ida snapped her head toward Stan, and he morphed back into a black bear. They stared at each other, then Jacob turned from them and ran full speed toward Llao and his men.

47

INTO THE FRAY

A ttack!" Ha-ida yelled as she waved her arm forward. Stan stood tall, waving his paws over his head. Then he lowered onto all fours and chased after Jacob. Wind brushed past as Ha-ida's animal army joined the race, running past her on either side to join Jacob and Stan in battle.

Cougars and bears rushed forward on a collision course with Llao's band of Native American warriors. Draped in cloaks of furs and skins, the warriors braced for impact. Two of Llao's men separated, allowing Chief Llao to step between them to stand in safety beneath the tower. Stan raced toward his nemesis, but Che-tan burst into a flock of four hawks and circled the tower as he rose into the sky and out of sight over the treetops. A girl from Ha-ida's army morphed into three hawks and burst through the snow-covered canopy of trees as she gave chase.

On the ground, the warriors removed weapons from beneath their cloaks. They pulled daggers and scimitars from sheaves on their backs, while others gripped the carved handles of their flails with heavy spiked balls dangling from woven chains. The largest of Llao's warriors held a massive wooden club that curved at the end like a hockey stick. The crook of the club would bludgeon any opponent silly. But even more deadly was the sharp piece of stone that looked like a railroad spike sticking out of a fish mouth carved into the end. This warrior waited patiently to inflict death. One warrior swung his flail, but most warriors held their weapons still, calmly waiting to absorb the force of the animal attack.

Ha-ida's gaze shifted to Loha, who remained next to her fire as she sewed. All the other women and children stayed inside the shelters, peeking to watch the action. It appeared that Loha ignored both the approaching force and Llao's warriors, but then she raised her shoulders as she turned away from the fire and faced the action.

Ha-ida's chest rose as she took in the scene. Jacob, Stan, and the other animal fighters raced toward Llao's warriors while Llao hid inside the protection of his men. Two men dangled from the tower on a rope as they slowly lowered to the ground. Jordan and her slab met them halfway up the tower and continued to rise higher. The field of battle seemed to linger in eerie silence. The cries and roars of the attacking animals were muffled like a child yelling underwater. Everything moved in slow motion, and Ha-ida could see every tuft of snow flung up from their paws as the animals lowered their heads and sprinted into battle.

Then, to the left behind Loha, a door opened and a boy emerged. His black hair hung straight across his forehead and around the collar of his leather cloak. His mother reached for him, but he raced to the tower to join Llao's men. His leather moccasins sunk deep into the snow, and when he lifted his feet to continue running, he was barefoot. Ha-ida blinked once and then saw Loha yell at the boy as she tried to stand. Ha-ida blinked again. She swiveled back to Jacob, who was nearly upon the enemy with his teeth gnashing. Stan was close behind. She looked back at the boy, who had slowed down because of the deep snow and a lack of warm clothing. Loha reached for him, and a woman from inside the shelter held her face in her hands as she screamed. Ha-ida saw the anguish, but she couldn't hear the woman cry.

Ha-ida stood still, her feet unable to move. Then Loha looked in her direction, and Ha-ida stared into the old woman's eyes. Without further delay, Ha-ida leaped forward, her hands hitting the snow as they morphed into hoofs. Within four steps, she hit full stride and picked up speed. Running toward the boy, she noticed a crude weapon in his left hand. Growls and screams echoed in Ha-ida's ears as Jacob jumped onto a Llao warrior and dug his teeth into a shoulder. The boy drew closer to the erupting battle as Stan hurried forward, bulldozing over three of Llao warriors to breach the interior of the lower tower where Llao hid.

Ha-ida raced forward, her eyes on the boy. She ignored the battle to her right and the crying mother and Loha, screaming for help, to the left. Cutting off the boy's path to the tower, Ha-ida stood in front of him and nodded with her heart-shaped horns for him to return to the safety of his shelter. He stood and watched her, his bare feet sinking deeper into the snow. She urged him back as the battle waged on the other side of her, but the boy stepped forward. Then, with a tight grip on his weapon, he slashed at Ha-ida. She reared back on her hind legs and then fell toward the boy until her nose connected with his chest, knocking him into the soft snow. He gripped his weapon and took another stab. He climbed to his knees, but Ha-ida lurched toward him, forcing him to the ground again. The short knife fell from his hand as he scampered backward with his hands behind him. Ha-ida moved closer, forcing him to quicken his escape until the boy's mother ran from the shelter, grabbed the neck of his cloak, and dragged him back inside.

Ha-ida looked at Loha, who barely acknowledged her presence. Instead, Loha looked past Ha-ida to the battle. Turning in place, Ha-ida gasped as she witnessed the destruction taking place near the tower. A girl she knew well lay facedown, her crimson blood seeping into the snow. Another of her warriors was in cougar form, blood matting its silky fur as it attempted to crawl away from the onslaught of battle.

Anger boiled inside Ha-ida. She didn't know what kind of damage she could cause to the enemy as an antelope, but that concern felt unimportant. Her friends were fighting. Some were hurt and dying. She would hate herself if she didn't try.

She took an angry step toward the battle, but her left front leg buckled, and she toppled face-first into the snow. She tried to stand, but her leg wobbled and collapsed again. She twisted her neck as she tried to see the wound that prevented her from standing. Then the pain of her wounds washed over her as the sight of blood-soaked snow came into view. Her eyes widened as she tried to examine her body. Through her peripheral vision, she could see a gash across her lower leg where the boy must have connected with his second stab. She hadn't noticed at the time but now she also felt a deep throbbing in her breast. She could see the blood oozing from the wound, running down her leg and into the snow.

Ha-ida attempted to stand again but was unable to rise. Fatigue and pain urged her to morph back into her human form. *Perhaps it will help me see and treat my wounds*, she thought. But then she looked at the girl lying facedown in the snow. Despite the desire to change, Ha-ida held tight, maintaining her antelope form. The pathetic corpse of her friend lying just yards away reminded her that every death was preceded by a return to the weaker human form. It urged her to stay strong and hold on as an animal warrior. She wouldn't give in. But coldness seeped into her body as the warmth of her blood seeped out.

Ha-ida lifted her head and tried to watch the battle, but she didn't have the energy. Her vision faded at the corner of her eyes. Her eyes glazed, and the individual warriors in her line of sight melted into blurs. She blinked again, and her eyes refocused momentarily when she felt a warm tongue licking across her black nose. The gray wolf stood above her, blood drenching his fur coat. Despite his wolf form, his eyes appeared human . . . and sad. Then Ha-ida lost sight of Jacob. The darkness swept across her as she shivered in the snow. Then all sensation disappeared.

48

JACOB RETURNS

T HE FURY OF JACOB'S GROWL PULSED ACROSS THE SNOW. Ha-ida's body quivered on the ground in front of him. He licked her antelope face again and then looked at the tower as two of Llao's warriors scurried to the top, replacing the two men who had ridden down on the rope as Jordan's counterweight. Llao also climbed the ladder on the tower's frame, making his way to the top. Jacob couldn't tell if Llao had plans once he reached the top or if he was merely escaping the danger of battle. The two climbers pulled themselves onto the platform beside Jordan and her dangling slab. Pulling at the ropes, they forced the slab over the platform and lowered it. One man pushed against the altar while the other pulled on the rope until it was set at the center of the platform. Jordan's sobs and cries for help lofted downward, but they were muffled by the time they reached Jacob's keen ears.

Leaving Ha-ida twitching in the snow, Jacob reentered the fray and leapt onto the back of a Llao warrior, biting his wrist. The warrior stopped swinging his flail when Jacob clawed at his back and bit into his shoulder near the neck. The bear that had been the warrior's target lunged forward and scraped away the man's cloak, leaving only deep scratches against his chest. Double-teamed by Jacob and the bear, the warrior fell to the ground. Jacob jumped off while the bear finished the gruesome task.

The warrior perimeter around the tower extended outward as Ha-ida's army clashed with Llao's. Human bodies littered the ground. Some were the remains of Llao's fierce warriors, while others were the small, teenage bodies of Ha-ida's army. Their human form testified to Jacob that they had sacrificed all they had to give.

Both sides continued to battle with brutal blows and gnashing teeth, inflicting pain and death. Blood matted Jacob's fur. He looked at the top of the tower and then refocused on a bulging warrior stomping toward him. The warrior swung a flail in one hand and held a dagger in the other as he approached. Jacob lowered his head and calculated his move. He timed the rotation of the spiked ball at the end of the flail chain. He bobbed his head as he followed the motion of the ball. Then, when the man was close enough, Jacob lunged forward. He kept low to the ground as he squeezed between the man's legs and bit into his calf, removing a hunk of flesh. Jacob spat it out and dug into the other leg. The warrior moaned and writhed in pain as he and his weapons crashed to the snow. In turn, Jacob bit both of the man's wrists, forcing him to loosen his grip and release his weapons. Jacob snarled, bared his teeth, and moved in slowly for the kill, but he stopped when he heard the familiar voice of a friend.

Turning in place, Jacob looked to the tree line where Ethan, Brady, and Allie stood.

"Fall back!" Ethan yelled again. Without hesitation, Jacob abandoned his foe to escort his animal comrades back to the trees.

Allie held the healing bowl in her hands. She leaned down, setting the egg shaped tip into the snow for balance. "Drink," she said quickly as Jacob approached, limping on his right-front leg. Leaning forward, he prepared to sip from the bowl, remembering the way it had saved his life during the summer. He wanted it badly, but he stepped back as a cougar inched closer and collapsed. Allie set the bowl closer to the cougar. It drank. Within seconds, the blood-crusted fur shined as if it had just come from the groomer. The cougar rose and stood at attention, glancing back at Llao's warriors. His paws inched toward the edge of the forest as if unable to wait for a chance to get back into the fight.

Each cougar and bear sipped from the bowl until it was empty. "Back away," Allie said. Her lips pursed with concentration and then she opened her mouth. Instead of fire, ice, light, or even wind, she mixed the elements of heat and ice as water shot forth with incredible force and accuracy. The water settled at the bottom of the bowl, and then the animals continued to drink. The other bears and cougars made way as Stan limped to the front of the group, lowered his mouth to the bowl, and sipped. The instant healing from the bowl gave him strength to lift the bowl with his paws and guzzle the rest. His body quivered with energy and excitement. Standing tall on his hind legs, he faced Llao's warriors and growled ferociously.

Jacob watched the warriors' reactions and smiled with pleasure as they headed back to the tower.

"This is for you, Jacob," Ethan said. He nodded to Allie, and she spewed out more water to fill the bowl. "This is what Chief Skell commanded. Retrieve the bowl to make you human again."

Jacob stared at the bowl but hesitated.

"Quick. Drink," Ethan urged.

"Yeah, you won't be a freak anymore," Brady muttered.

Jacob inched closer and looked at Ethan, but Ethan's attention was squarely on the tower platform. Jacob saw him wipe at his eyes. "Let's save Jordan before I turn back," Jacob suggested with a growl he knew only Ethan would understand. "I'm a lot tougher this way."

Ethan shook his head, but then his lips quivered. He tried to speak. "No. Drink first. Skell said you will be stronger once you are turned back. We . . ." His voice cracked. "We have to trust that. Drink. Hurry," he said, motioning toward the bowl.

Leaning down, Jacob lapped at the cool water inside the

bowl. The instant the first drop entered his body, Jacob could feel an effervescence bubbling inside. He lapped up more of the water as his right paw turned into a hand. He kept drinking, and the other front paw turned into a hand. He drank faster and faster as the fur fell from his body to reveal his scout uniform and pale skin. His long, lapping tongue became short, and when he could no longer drink like a wolf, he picked up the bowl, tipped it, and slurped every drop of water.

Jacob knelt in the snow, dropped the bowl in front of him, and stared at his own hands. He brushed his fingers through his hair, touched his face, and then ran his hands down his chest, stopping at his bare midsection. His scout shirt no longer covered him.

"Hey, shrimp, it looks like you grew a bit," Brady said. "But if you don't mind putting your self-reunion on hold, we've got a girl to save."

Jacob dropped his hands to his side as he remembered the reason for their fight. The cold mountain air whisked against him, causing him to shiver. His shorts were too short, and his shirt left him exposed. He looked at Brady standing barechested, but then he looked at Allie, and he longed for the warmth of a coat like hers. He already missed the comfort of his fur, but energy and hope made every inch of his skin tingle.

"So, what's the plan, boss?" Brady said, pulling Ethan by the shoulder. "This is the big game. This is what we're playing for. It's Jordan time."

Ethan's eyes met Brady's as he spoke with authority. "Let's get her."

The group rumbled with excited chatter, but Allie grimaced as she took a deep breath. "Is there more to the plan than that?"

Brady smiled, but Ethan remained silent as he stared at Chief Llao standing over Jordan on top of the tower. Then Ethan snapped his head back to meet the gaze of his friend. "We're not only going to take Jordan back, but we're also going to get rid of Llao forever. This ends now."

Ethan's newfound confidence made Jacob smile. But then he remembered Ha-ida lying in the snow, bleeding to death. "We need to help Ha-ida too. She's hurt."

Ethan clasped his hands together and pulled them apart while keeping the fingers interlocked. His knuckles popped, and his eyes narrowed. "You guys ready?" He looked into Brady's and Allie's eyes, but Jacob looked away. "Chief Llao is going to be sorry he ever met me."

"Us," Allie corrected. "He'll be sorry he met *us*."

"Ethan, I'm sorry, but can I . . . ?" Jacob started, but Ethan waved away the question. He stared at the top of the tower and at the two warriors climbing down. Only Llao, with his colorful, ritualistic garb, stood atop the tower with Jordan tied to the slab of stone.

"Do it. Save Ha-ida and the others. We'll get Jordan."

Jacob cupped the healing bowl in his hands. "Allie, fill me up."

Allie breathed water into the bowl, and Jacob ran across the snow toward Ha-ida, careful not to slosh the water onto his already cold skin. He focused on Ha-ida, but his ears lingered on Ethan and the rescue plan he was describing to the others. "Tower . . . crash . . . Llao . . . dead." Jacob couldn't make out everything, but what he could hear with his keen, wolf-like ears was enough to get his heart pumping even faster. The tower was going to come down, and Jacob smirked at the thought of Llao crashing down with it.

49

OPERATION TIMBER

"So what do you think, Brady? Can you do it?" Ethan asked, his speech clipped and fast.

Brady flexed his muscles and pulled the dagger from his pocket, careful not to stab himself. "Dude, just let me at them."

"I'll take that as a yes. Allie, any questions?" Allie shook her head. "Good." Ethan turned in place as he glanced over the remaining animal warriors. "You, you're with me," he said, pointing to Stan. "You two, you flank Brady. And you, cougar boy, you're with Allie. Don't let any of those thugs near her. The rest of you—circle around, and when I give the sign, create total chaos."

"What about Jacob?" Allie asked. "What should he do, and who's going to protect him?"

"He's on his own, but he's doing exactly what he should be." Ethan noticed the twist of Allie's lips and the skepticism plastered on her face. "Trust me. Jacob's got some surprises left in him. He'll be fine." Ethan nodded to the group, swallowing a lump in his throat. His heart fluttered, but then his eyes narrowed as he focused on Jordan's screaming. Brady cocked his arms back in ready position and turned his head to watch Ethan. "*Go!*"

Brady exploded from the woods, gripping his dagger tightly in his right hand. The black obsidian blade gleamed as it caught a ray of sunlight. A cougar and a bear ran next to Brady. Then Allie stepped from the shadow of the tree cover into the snowy field. Ethan watched the entire scene and glanced once at the old woman near the fire, who seemed to be enjoying the show. Allie ran to the shelter houses, passing by Jacob on the ground next to Ha-ida.

Ethan halted when he saw Jacob. Ha-ida's long, black hair lay across the white and crimson ground. Her chest heaved with labored breaths. Ethan watched from the shadows as Jacob attempted to pour the contents of the bowl into Ha-ida's mouth, but the water drizzled out the sides as she coughed and sputtered. Jacob tried again and then set the bowl down. He grabbed the back of his head with both hands and pulled at his hair. Ethan cupped his hands to his mouth and shouted. When Jacob turned around, Ethan continued yelling. "You have the power!" Ethan waited and then continued. "The bowl is the conduit! But YOU have the power!"

Ethan swallowed hard and wiped his wrist against his brow as Jacob stared back at him with a befuddled expression. But then Jacob's eyes brightened. Setting the tip of the bowl into the snowy ground, Jacob closed his eyes and dipped his fingers into the water. After a moment, he opened his eyes, removed his fingers from the water, and placed them on Ha-ida's face. He squinted, and his body tensed, but his fingers pressed into Ha-ida's face. She slowly rose into a sitting position, looked at Jacob, and wrapped her arms around his neck. She kissed him on the cheek over and over and then stood.

Ethan smiled as Jacob helped Ha-ida stand. He had an expression of shock and realization, happiness and confusion. Ethan understood the expression because it felt like he was wearing the same one. The bowl provided instant healing and vigor, but Ha-ida moved slowly as if the healing was incomplete. Ha-ida grabbed on to Jacob's arm, but he hurried over to a girl in the snow. Ethan brushed aside his worried thoughts about Ha-ida and turned his attention back to the tower and Jordan.

One—two—three warriors. It didn't matter how many there were. Brady sliced his way through them with his dagger. They slumped to the ground, and then Brady's animal friends finished the task. Those warriors wouldn't be causing any more trouble. Ethan shook his head, amazed as one warrior connected his spiked ball with Brady's head. The steel ball shattered, and Brady just smiled. He picked up the man by the neck and tossed him to the ground, where the cougar and bear dug in.

Ethan could see Allie's face sticking out from behind one of the shelters. She took a deep breath and spewed fire out of her mouth. The blaze connected with its target as one leg of the tower caught fire. The flames licked up the side of the tower for a moment, and Allie let it burn. But then she quenched it with a blast of ice. She scorched it again with fire. Then ice. Then fire and ice again. Only one warrior dared approach her, but after she turned him into a Popsicle, no others dared. Ethan nodded with approval and then scanned the sky as four large hawks squawked from high above. The hawks flew to the top of the tower and hovered above as they circled. Then the hawks aimed down like a missile—a missile aimed directly at him.

The first hawk pulled up before crashing into Ethan, and the other three slammed into the first, returning Che-tan to his human form. Stan reared back on his hind legs, prepared to take a swipe at Che-tan, but Ethan stepped between the two adversaries. Additional squawks floated down as another flock of three hawks approached Ethan, Che-tan, and Stan. The hawks morphed into a slender girl, who pulled her hair back behind her ears, wiped the perspiration from her forehead, and hunched over with her hands on her knees as she gasped for air.

"What do you want, Che-tan?" Ethan asked.

Che-tan started to speak, but Stan growled a murderous threat. Ethan growled back, "No, it will be fine. Let's hear what he has to say."

"Your sister is in danger, and time is running out." Che-tan fidgeted with his hands as he spoke. His eyes wandered to the tower.

"No kidding. We're working on it." Ethan looked into the eyes of the young native girl. "Can you distract Chief Llao?" She nodded, and without saying a word, she turned into her flock of three birds and flew to the tower.

Stan morphed out of his bear form and stepped nose to nose with Che-tan. "We can't trust him. His heart is black."

Ethan nodded. "Maybe." He circled Che-tan and studied him. "Tell me. What's Llao doing with my sister?"

Che-tan cleared his throated and lowered his gaze to the ground. "He plans to destroy her."

Ethan shook his head. "No. I don't have time for riddles. Explain. What's he up to? Why does Jordan matter to him, and why should we believe you?"

"Jordan possesses a gift."

"The visions? More like a curse."

"Yes," Che-tan agreed. "It is a gift, or a curse, that Llao gave to another. It is a gift that provides him control and power. He wants it back. If he is able to complete his ritual extraction, he will return the gift to its proper holder. Jordan will be destroyed permanently, and my mother . . ." Che-tan cleared his throat. "And the proper holder will be cursed once again."

Ethan's eyes narrowed. "We're stopping Llao, no matter what." He glanced to the tower where the left leg was bursting in a cycle of flame and ice. "The tower will fall. And we have a secret weapon to protect Jordan." Fifty yards away, Jacob continued his rescuing work with Ha-ida at his side. Death and injury presented no challenge to his healing powers. Ethan grimaced as he thought about the desperation of his plan. It seemed crazy. But if all else failed, Jordan's death would merely be a temporary obstacle.

Che-tan shook his head as if he knew Ethan's thoughts. "No. Jacob will not be able to save Jordan if Llao extracts the gift and kills her. She will be gone. Not even Jacob can save her." Ethan's eyes widened as he stepped closer to Che-tan. He grabbed Che-tan by the scruff of his cloak and pulled him close. Che-tan continued, speaking faster. "She lies on Llao's sacrificial altar. If she dies at his hand, only he will have the power to raise her. Llao will soon finish his work."

"So you're saying we should hurry," Stan said, annoyance smothering every word. "I think you're just trying to slow us down with ridiculous stories and threats." Ethan watched for Che-tan's response.

"No, I do not want the gift returned to the rightful holder. I want her to be free of the curse."

"So you want Jordan to hold the curse instead. That's big of you," Ethan said.

"This is what I'm trying to explain." Che-tan's dark brown eyes bored into Ethan. "You have a choice. She will be cursed, or she will be dead. That is your choice."

"Death is not an option," Ethan spat.

"Then hurry. Once Llao's incantation is complete, and his blade penetrates Jordan's heart, there will be no hope. You must free her . . ." Che-tan paused. "Or . . . kill her before Llao does."

Stan's eyes bulged, and Ethan's mouth fell open. Ethan's gaze rose to the tower and the altar. He was too far away, and his angle was too bad to see what was happening, but Ethan smiled as three hawks dive-bombed and swirled around Llao, distracting him from his plan.

The hardest part of Ethan's plan was the patience it required. And with Che-tan's warning, he no longer felt he could wait. Jacob and Ha-ida continued their healing work, rushing to each animal warrior who had either been wounded or killed. In turn, they each arose and rejoined the fight, pushing Llao's warriors deeper into the woods. The second leg of the tower burst into flames, and then ice and flames again as Allie aimed her breath of destruction around the base of the tower. "It's time," Ethan said calmly, his fists clenched at his side.

Raising his fingers to his mouth, Stan whistled. The shriek

filled the battlefield, but when he stopped, the cacophony of chaotic sound grew even louder as animal warriors rushed the field from their positions surrounding the tower. With the new wave of chaos providing cover, Ethan rushed from the edge of the forest to the tower. "Brady!" he yelled.

Brady turned around as a spear broke against his back. "Now?"

"Now!" Ethan confirmed. Finding a handhold where two poles were lashed together, Ethan struggled to scale the exterior of the tower until he located a ladder to ease his climb. He reached frantically for the next rung, and his foot slipped as he hurried up the ladder. Despite the slip, he didn't slow his ascent. He climbed recklessly, but fast. Foot—hand—foot—hand. He panted from the exertion, but his will and adrenaline pushed him upward. Looking down, he saw Brady braced against one leg of the tower. Ethan hoped that Allie's fire and ice treatment had sufficiently weakened the leg for Brady to take it the rest of the way down. Brady pushed, and Ethan could hear the grunts of his effort, but the thick pole appeared solid. Then, backing away from the pole, Brady set himself in a three-point stance as if waiting for a football to be hiked before obliterating the offensive line on his way to the quarterback. Ethan's hands and feet raced up the slender ladder, but his eyes watched Brady.

Brady blasted from his stance and lowered his shoulder into the pole. Ethan felt the entire tower shake from the impact. Brady repeated his effort, lowering his hand to the ground and ramming the base of the tower pole with his shoulder. Then Ethan heard a crack. Brady set himself one more time and then blew through the vertical pole, snapping it in two. The tower listed to Ethan's left, but the support cords that connected the tower to mature trees held it upright. Ethan's feet and one hand slid from the ladder, but he held on tight with the other. He quickly regained his hold and continued climbing.

Jordan's screams grew longer and louder the higher Ethan got. Her voice sounded raw and hopeless. Her pained cries made him climb faster. The tower jolted again, and Ethan looked down to see Brady working on the second leg. He reached higher until his fingertips reached the platform. He peeked over the edge and could see Jordan's brown, curly hair spilling over the side of the sacrificial altar. Llao stood with his back to Ethan as he mumbled words Ethan couldn't quite hear. Llao held the hilt of a dagger in his left hand, and then he held out his right hand. Placing the blade in his palm, Llao closed his hand around the blade and grunted in pain. He then pulled the blade through. Blood dripped from his hand as he held it over the altar. Jordan wiggled and fought to keep the blood from dripping on her.

Ethan reached the platform and struggled to pull himself up without detection. He focused on Llao. Every creak in the boards made Ethan's heart stop, and then the tower jolted again. Ethan held tightly and pulled himself up. Climbing onto his knees, he stood slowly. Every deliberate motion rustled the platform, but Llao didn't seem to notice or care. Finally in position, Ethan lowered his shoulder and took four quick steps toward Chief Llao. He dove at the sadistic monster, intent on throwing him from the tower.

But Llao smiled as he turned. With a powerful wave of his arm, Llao brushed away Ethan's attack as though it came from an annoying gnat. Ethan crashed onto the tilted platform and slid to the edge, his fingernails digging into the wood. Then he fell over the edge.

– 50 –

THE IMPOSSIBLE

THE WOOD SPLINTERED INTO THE SOFT TISSUE BENEATH
Ethan's fingernails as he clutched the platform. His mind
told him to remain silent so Llao would ignore him, or better
yet, forget about him. But Ethan couldn't withhold an agoniz-
ing scream as his fingernails bent backward and peeled away
from his skin.

Releasing one hand from the platform, he reached higher
for a better grip and lifted himself up high enough to peer over
the tilted edge of the platform. Llao's moccasin feet were standing in front of him. Llao raised a foot to kick Ethan but stopped
as the tower lurched to the right. A loud crack and a furious jolt
loosened Ethan's grip. Llao staggered, but when he regained his
balance, he planted a foot onto Ethan's right hand and crushed
it into the platform. Ethan screamed again.

With watering eyes, he surveyed the decking beneath the
platform, searching for an escape. It felt like all of Llao's weight
was focused on pulverizing Ethan's hand, and the unbearable
pain caused Ethan to release his grip, but he didn't fall. His
left hand hung at his side, but Llao's weight pinned the fingers
on his right hand to the platform. With his left hand, Ethan
reached for a lower beam but couldn't grab hold. Realizing he
couldn't reach, he instead swung his body and lifted his leg,
wrapping his ankle around the beam. Ethan twisted and pulled

his right hand, trying to free them from Llao's foot. Finally, Llao released Ethan's hand. Ethan fell backward into the open air, but he clamped his legs to the beam underneath the platform.

Ethan moaned but righted himself beneath the platform into a full sitting position. He looked at his fingers, wiped the blood gently against his pants, bit the hanging nail off, and spit it out. Above him, Ethan could hear the boards creak as Llao walked back to the altar—back to Jordan. Her cries resumed, and then she called out, "ETHAN!"

Ethan pushed the pain from his mind and tried to block the emotion caused by Jordan's pathetic scream. He concentrated on the task at hand. Grabbing hold of a crossbeam, he placed one foot on an angled brace that now, with the tilt of the tower, seemed to be nearly horizontal. With his feet turned sideways, Ethan shimmied across the beam like he had in the barn at home. Inching toward the other side of the platform, he formulated a new plan for rescuing Jordan from the tower.

Two legs of the tower had been broken through by Brady's ramming, and only two taut ropes connected to mature trees kept the tower from toppling onto its side and crashing to the ground. Ethan noted the chaos below as Ha-ida's warriors continued to battle Llao's, but then he waved to Brady at the base of the tower. Brady shrugged. Ethan then pointed up and ran a finger across his throat. He hoped Brady would understand the signal—climb the tower and kill Llao. *How could he not understand that?* Ethan wondered. *But it is Brady.*

Ethan wiped an arm across his forehead to remove the perspiration, and then sighed with relief as Brady started to climb—fast. Making his way to the other end of the crossbeam, Ethan listened to the muddled sounds of Llao's mutterings and Jordan's cries above him. He looked down at Brady, who was making quick work of the tower ladder. Then Ethan lifted his injured hand back onto the platform.

"What do you want me to do?" Brady whispered as he approached Ethan on the ladder.

Ethan inhaled two deep but quick breaths and then pointed toward the side edge of the platform. "Hold onto Llao while I cut Jordan loose." Brady nodded. "Oh, and do you have a knife?"

Without hesitation, Brady removed the dagger from his pocket and handed the hilt carefully to Ethan. "Careful with that thing. I want it back."

Placing the hilt into his mouth, Ethan bit down and climbed higher as Brady moved around the side of the platform. Brady gave a curt nod when he was in position, and Ethan pulled the dagger from his mouth and gripped it tightly. He mouthed, "Now."

Pulling himself up easily from beneath the platform, Brady located his target and reached. He wrapped his hand around Llao's left ankle and yanked, causing Llao to crash onto the platform with a thud. Brady dug his fingers into Llao and pulled him toward the edge.

While Brady distracted Llao, Ethan put the dagger hilt back in his mouth, chomped down, and climbed onto the platform. He hurried over to Jordan. Kneeling in front of the altar, Ethan removed the black blade, and with one motion sliced the ropes that bound Jordan to the stone slab. Jordan bolted into a sitting position, thrust her legs over the side of the altar, and wrapped her arms around Ethan's neck. For a moment, the warmth of Jordan's tears against his neck lured Ethan into false sense of accomplishment and safety, but he quickly pulled back to reality when Llao's mumbling words became louder and more determined. Blood trickled down Llao's leg as he pulled himself from Brady's claws and kicked Brady's face. Llao muttered forcefully while pushing and kicking at Brady's attempts to hold him. Ethan could understand the individual words Llao spoke, but they sounded like a jumble of meaningless phrases. The words continued to spew from Llao's mouth. He kicked one last time and sprang to the altar. Llao held his sacrificial knife in his hand as he lunged at Jordan.

Ethan swiped his black blade at Llao and then backed away

toward the ladder. He glanced at the ladder as he positioned himself to go down. Then Llao charged, holding his knife in front of him. Ethan stepped to the side and kicked at Llao, connecting his shoe with Llao's face. Turning back to the ladder, Ethan urged Jordan down, but she sat motionless with her feet dangling from the platform.

"Jordan, hurry! *Go!*" Ethan yelled. He placed the bone hilt of the dagger between his teeth, biting down.

Jordan remained still at the edge of the platform as Llao regained his footing. He stepped slowly toward Ethan and Jordan.

"Hurry!" Ethan nudged Jordan's shoulder, and she nearly toppled over the edge. He pulled her back, and her head flopped over, her eyes open but vacant. Ethan gasped when he noticed a crimson circle of blood seeping through the back of Jordan's coat. His chest heaved, and tears streamed down his cheeks as he looked into the face of his dead sister.

Brady grabbed hold of Llao and resumed his struggle. Glancing back at Llao, Ethan pushed Jordan's body to the side of the ladder and began his descent. When his shoulder was level with the platform, he sat Jordan back up and allowed her body to fall over his shoulder. He checked his footing and began to lower himself. But then he stopped when he heard Brady yell. Ethan watched as Brady fell from the platform. The timbers of the tower toppled Brady end over end as he tumbled to the ground. At the bottom of the tower, Brady quickly stood, stretched his neck, and stared at Ethan. Brady pointed and yelled. Ethan turned around just in time.

Llao stood above Ethan. He grinned and lifted one foot. Ethan grabbed the outside of the ladder and placed the insoles of his shoes against the side. He looked up at Llao and then loosened his grip. With Jordan hanging over his shoulder, Ethan slid down the rough ladder on the side of the angled tower. Above him, Chief Llao followed.

Stopping at the rope supports halfway down the tower,

Ethan squeezed his hands against the side of the ladder. Wooden splinters and shavings dug into his palms, but he gripped tighter until he came to a full stop. He adjusted Jordan on his shoulder and pulled the dagger from his mouth. Ethan sliced through the first rope. The tower wobbled, twisted, and cracked. Ethan looked up to see Chief Llao holding tightly to the tower as it swayed. Then Ethan chomped again on the hilt of the dagger. He grabbed onto the last rope that connected the tower to a nearby tree and swung his head. The black obsidian blade of the dagger sliced through the rope.

Ethan grasped the rope. The tower fell, crashing to the ground, and the rope shredded Ethan's hands. His bloody fingers slid down the rope, so he squeezed tighter, the excruciating pain causing his eyes to well with tears. With Jordan's additional weight, Ethan had to flex his entire body, every muscle fighting to hang on. He swung toward the woods and gained speed as he reached the bottom of the pendulum. As he began swinging back up, Ethan let go of the rope and closed his eyes. He and Jordan sailed through the air before landing in a soft cushion of snow.

Ethan glanced back at the heap of mangled scrap. He noticed Llao's leg sticking out of the rubble, twitching. Brady was already climbing over the pile. Rolling onto his stomach, Ethan stared into Jordan's pale face. He brushed his finger against her cheek, leaving a film of blood. He then waved his hand in front of her eyes, but there was no response. Ethan looked up when he heard Jacob, Allie, and Ha-ida calling for him.

"Jacob, *help!*" Ethan screamed, his voice raw and uneven.

Sprinting forward, Jacob jumped onto the ground beside Jordan with his knees stabbing the snow. He held the back of her hair as he lifted her head and gazed into her empty eyes. He spread his fingers across her face like he had done to Ha-ida. He contorted his face with concentration and closed his eyes.

Ethan sat in the snow, stunned. "Jacob, is she . . . ?"

Jacob didn't answer. He pressed his fingers harder into

Jordan's face, his thumb and pinky on either side of her jaw, his middle finger above her nose, and the other two on her cheek bones. Jacob opened his eyes and looked at the girl. Then he looked at Ethan. His mouth gaped open, and then he swallowed. "I'm sorry, Ethan. I can't—"

"No! It's not possible!" Ethan yelled. "It just can't be! Try again. She can't be gone. This isn't part of the plan. She has to make it."

Allie placed a hand on Ethan's shoulder. "Ethan . . . she's dead."

Ethan shook his head, glaring at Allie. "No! There must be a way. Don't give up, Jacob. Again! Do it again! Save her like you saved Ha-ida. Like you saved the others. Do it *now*!"

Jacob's head lowered. "I can't, Ethan. I'm so sorry."

– 51 –

PLAN B

ETHAN PLACED HIS BARE HANDS INTO THE SNOW AS HE leaned back. The cold stopped the throbbing in his fingers and palms as he stared blankly at Jordan. "I can't believe it," Ethan muttered. "It's not supposed to end this way. I failed all of you . . . and Skell." He shook his head, and a whispered breath seeped from his lips between sobs. "I failed her again. Jordan's dead because of me."

Tears streamed down Allie's face, and an expression of hopelessness was chiseled into Jacob's face. Ha-ida tightened her lips and shared a look of defeat with Jacob and Allie, but Ethan pretended not to notice. Then Allie held the healing bowl close to her mouth and breathed water into it. She sobbed as she held the bowl in front of Ethan. "Here, this will make your hands feel better."

Ethan shrugged away the offer.

Jacob's voice was calm and quiet, as if he was in shock. "You need it, Ethan. Feeling sorry for yourself isn't going to help anything. Drink." Jacob nodded to Allie, so she extended the bowl again. Still Ethan refused to accept it. "Fine, but that's not what Jordan would expect from you. And it's not what Skell needs from you." Jacob scooted beside Ethan and raised his hand as though he were going to pat him on the shoulder. But then he pressed on Ethan's shoulder and pushed him back into the snow.

He hopped on top and straddled Ethan to hold him down. Then he pressed his fingers against Ethan's face.

Ethan felt the healing energy surge through him as his physical pain disappeared. He fought the guilty euphoria of perfect health and energy. Physical pain wasn't what he wanted relief from. "Get off me!" he said, shoving Jacob, who climbed off, stood, and grabbed Ethan's hand, pulling him to his feet.

Jacob wrapped his arms around Ethan's neck and pulled him close. "I'm so sorry, Ethan. I . . . I'm sorry."

Jacob's warm breath soothed Ethan's neck, but Ethan peeled himself away from the condolences and faced the woods, away from the pity of his friends. The group stood in stunned silence until Ethan turned back around and finally accepted a tearful hug from Allie and a pat on the shoulder from Ha-ida. Ethan tried clearing the sadness from his voice and turned to Brady, who knelt on the tower debris while examining Chief Llao's body. "Well, how is he?" Ethan asked.

"Dead." Brady poked at Llao's leg and smiled. "Totally dead."

Jacob placed his hands behind his back as he looked at Ethan. "You did it, Ethan. Llao's dead." The words felt like they deserved a celebratory cheer, but they elicited only a grunt from Ethan.

With Llao dead, crumpled beneath the timbers of the fallen tower, his warriors fled into the woods as Ha-ida's animal warriors gave chase. A sliver of a smile crossed Allie's face as she looked at Brady and the only piece of Llao she could see. "Does this mean we can go home?" The tears flowed more freely. "We don't have to be freaks anymore?" Allie raised her hands over her head to cheer, but she cried instead. She hiccupped, and a blast of fire shot over Ethan's head, catching a nearby tree on fire. Ethan didn't even flinch. Allie clenched her teeth and formed her lips into a frown. "Sorry." She opened her mouth and sprayed water like a fire hose, putting out the small blaze.

From the side of the field, Loha wandered to the tower's

rubble with Che-tan holding her elbow to help her balance. Ethan's blank eyes watched as she bent down and respectfully touched a broken piece of timber near Llao's corpse. Her eyes were solid white, and the necklace hanging at her chest began to strobe, white, red, and blue. Che-tan pressed his lips together, his face firm. But a tear gathered in the corner of his eye as he stood near his dead father. The show of any respect for Llao made Ethan's blood curdle. Llao deserved nothing except loathing and the death that he had received. Ethan hoped it had been painful.

Holding his mother's arm, Che-tan turned toward Ethan. "There is one way to save your sister!" he shouted. "It is not too late."

Ethan glanced at Jacob, who simply shook his head. "How?" Ethan yelled back. "Jacob can't heal her. No one can!"

"You are correct. Jacob cannot heal her. Only Llao can," Che-tan said.

Ethan snarled. "What did you say?"

Che-tan took a slow breath, forming his rebuttal with care. "Lao's sacrificial knife killed her, so only Llao can heal her."

"But Llao's dead," Ethan mumbled. He thought about Che-tan's words. Che-tan had told him to kill Jordan himself if necessary to prevent Llao from doing it. *Why?* Ethan thought. "Because Jacob could bring her back to life," he muttered. But it didn't happen that way. Llao killed her, so only Llao could save her. Ethan's jaw dropped as an idea filled his head. He tried to ignore the thought, but it poked at him like his annoying little sister. It wouldn't leave him alone, but he didn't dare speak it out loud. What would Allie, Brady, and Jacob think? *They'd hate me for even suggesting it.* Ethan looked at his dead sister lying in the snow. He balled his hands into tight fists and closed his eyes. His shoulders tensed. He realized that he didn't care what the others thought. The only thing that mattered was saving his sister.

Ethan fought the urge to voice his idea, but then he

blurted it out. "Jacob needs to heal Llao." The words hovered in the air. Jacob stared at the ground but didn't speak. Allie bit the side of her lip, and Ha-ida's eyebrows knit together as her forehead crinkled with far too many wrinkles for a girl her age.

Ha-ida's usually soft voice pierced the frigid air. *"Are you crazy!"* she yelled from her place near rubble. "It is Llao. He is the devil, and you want to bring him back to life?"

Allie's voice was calm but cracked from the strain of emotion. "Ethan, we won. The battle's over. I love Jordan, but . . . Ethan, it's over."

Brady left the mound of timber and joined Ethan and the others. He crossed his arms and stood beside Ethan.

Jacob leaned close to Ethan's ear. "We can't do it. We'd be giving him another chance to kill us."

"It would give Llao another chance to control everything in the region and destroy everyone who stands in his way," Ha-ida added.

"I don't care!" Ethan shouted back.

Allie stepped close, swallowing. She parted her lips and kissed Ethan on the cheek. "I'm sorry, Ethan, but every evil thing Llao does after being brought back to life will be our fault. Do you get that?"

"We would be responsible for Chief Llao's actions," Ha-ida said. "Can you live with that? I cannot."

Ethan glanced at Brady. His burly friend stood beside him with his arms folded tight. For once, Brady didn't say a word.

Ethan hated to admit it, but Allie made sense. He looked at Jordan's lifeless body lying in the snow, and his shoulders shook with a sob. How could he justify the risk?

"And what if Llao refuses to heal Jordan once I bring him back?" Jacob asked.

Ethan's quivering lips stopped as Jacob's question helped him answer his own question. He grinned and then wiped his red eyes. "Easy—we kill him again."

Allie shook her head. "But what if he escapes and continues with his plans to destroy Skell?" she asked.

"It's true. We can't exactly negotiate with him right now," Jacob added.

"What if Llao kills other people?" Allie gulped and then continued, "I can't be responsible for that. What if he killed one of us? I don't mean this to be insensitive, but is Jordan more important than any of us?"

"Ethan, there are casualties in battle. It is a sad truth," Ha-ida said. "We cannot do it, Ethan."

Brady looked at the others as he raised one hand over his head and broke his silence. "Let's vote on it. Who is in favor of keeping Llao dead? Raise your hand."

Ha-ida, Allie, and Loha raised their hands. Ethan flinched at the response. "Are we going to accept the old lady's vote?" Ethan asked. Allie and Ha-ida nodded. Ethan frowned.

"Who's with Ethan and wants to bring Llao back to life in hopes that he heals Jordan and doesn't keep acting like a maniacal creep?"

Ethan raised his hand, and out of the corner of his eye, he saw Che-tan raise his hand as well. Brady's hand shot up, but Jacob's fingers clenched his pants leg. "It looks like we're three to three," Ethan said.

Ha-ida shook her head with disappointment. "I thought you were a warrior. I thought you understood battle," she said to Brady.

"Brady, are you serious? Think about it. We can't bring Llao back. It's too risky," Allie said.

Brady chuckled. "My vote's final. I'm with Ethan all the way." Then his voice weakened as it filled with emotion. "Jordan was my responsibility. I'm not going to let her suffer because I couldn't protect her. Understand?"

Allie shook her head. "You're making a mistake."

Brady laughed. "Wouldn't be the first time. So we've got boys against girls, three to three, with one non-vote. Which are you, Jacob? Boy or girl? Your vote breaks the tie."

"Guys, this could all be over. Do you understand that? Please. I love Jordan. I'll miss her, but are you going to gamble with all of our lives because you're sad? Besides, are you seriously going to count Che-tan and that old lady in our vote? Who is she, anyway?"

Ha-ida cleared her throat. "She is Loha, Llao's wife and Che-tan's mother." Eyebrows rose among the group, and confused mumbles escalated into jeers, mostly by Brady. "She fears Llao more than most. She knows what he is capable of. We should trust her."

"So Llao's wife wants him dead, but Che-tan wants his father to live. Interesting," Brady said.

"I cannot trust Che-tan. We should not count his vote. He wants to serve alongside his father and rule in tyranny. He wants his father to live so he can gain power," Ha-ida explained.

"Yeah, Che-tan looked pretty cozy with Llao earlier," Allie said.

"Maybe he was staying close to Llao to help Skell," Jacob said.

"Shut up! Everyone, just SHUT UP!" Ethan held his head in his hands and rubbed his temples. "Loha's vote cancels out Che-tan's. Forget them. This is about saving Jordan."

Allie shook her head. "No, Ethan. It's more than that. It's about defeating evil. It's about getting our lives back. It's about being normal again."

Brady uncrossed his arms and pulled the dagger from his pocket. He held it up for all to see. "I will kill Llao if he tries anything funny or refuses to help. I'll slice his head off with this dagger. If he helps, Skell can imprison him again. We can save Jordan and still stay safe.

"Allie, this *is* about Jordan. We'd do the same for you. Don't forget that," Ethan said.

"Would you?"

"No, it is not about saving one girl's life. That is your

mistake. It is about defeating Llao. It is about ending a battle that has waged for centuries." Ha-ida coughed into her hand. "Jordan is sweet, but it is not about her. We should not discount Loha. We can learn from her wisdom. She should be revered."

Ethan frowned. "I know all about the legend of Loha. She's fought Llao for centuries. She was abducted and forced to be his wife. That's what began the whole stinking battle between Skell and Llao in the first place. I don't dismiss her, but I choose to follow Skell. He said that we need Jordan and her gift. Are you willing to ignore that?"

Ha-ida raised her eyebrows, and her lips curled into a scowl. "How do you know these things?"

"I read a lot. Jacob, we're three to three. You haven't voted yet. What do you say?" Ethan asked, his voice taking a sharp edge.

Jacob lowered his head.

"Come on, wolf boy. What's your decision?" Brady pressed.

The group stared at each other uncomfortably in silence as Jacob contemplated his decision. Allie brushed her blonde hair from in front of her eyes. "Jacob—"

"I've been dead . . . twice," Jacob finally said. "It's nothing to be afraid of. It's not even the worst thing that can happen to a person."

"What? Jacob, look at her. What could be worse?" Ethan asked, pointing to his sister. "You can save her by saving Llao. If you do nothing, you might just as well have been the one to stab her in the back."

"Ethan, don't say that." Jacob's voice wavered.

"Skell gave us two missions. Get you the healing bowl and save Jordan. I think they're part of the same mission. Getting you the healing bowl will save Jordan. Skell told you to follow me, right?" Ethan said.

Jacob sighed and then nodded.

"Then vote. Vote to save Jordan and do it!"

"That's just wrong, Ethan," Allie moaned. "You're losing it." Allie shook her head as she glared. Her voice was soft but cutting.

"Shut up. Let's vote. Who's in favor of saving Llao so he can save Jordan?" Ethan asked. The same hands went up, then after a brief hesitation, Jacob raised his hand as well. "Yes." Ethan pumped his hand. "Four to three. Do it, Jacob. Follow Skell and save Jordan's life."

52

DRAWN AND QUARTERED

Llao's warriors retreated deeper into the nearby woods, but Ethan could hear occasional chatter, moans, and heavy breathing. He searched the borders for the remnants of Llao's force, but the men were either well-hidden or still running.

Ha-ida's shoulder bumped against Ethan's as they gathered around the toppled tower that encased Llao's remains. Her fellow animal warriors, who had not been included in the vote, gathered around the rubble and morphed into their human forms. With the aid of the bowl and Jacob's healing work, all of Ha-ida's warriors were alive and accounted for, but they weren't well. With grumbles of distrust and vitriol, they formed in a semicircle around Ethan, Jacob, Allie, Brady, and Ha-ida, and slowly separated just enough to allow Che-tan and Loha to join the group near Llao's mangled corpse.

Ha-ida shook her head frantically, and her army mirrored her agitation. "You cannot restore Chief Llao to life. We have succeeded in defeating him. That was our goal. That is everything." She looked at Ethan, but he pretended not to notice. "Ethan, you cannot do this. It is wrong. It is dangerous." When Ethan still failed to respond, Ha-ida became louder and more defiant. "Ethan—I will not allow you to save Llao. *We* will not allow it," she said, motioning to the army of young Native

Americans. Stan ran his hand through the side of his spiked hair as he glared at Ethan. Then he morphed into a black bear and rose up on his hind legs. With a firm nod from Ha-ida, the rest of the army returned to animal form in preparation for a new battle.

Ethan gulped as Stan bent down and roared at him, his two-inch-long incisors close to Ethan's face. His curly hair fluttered in Stan's breath, and he backed away as he felt Brady pull on his arm. Brady then stepped between Ethan and Stan. Stan roared again, but Brady only smiled.

"Anyone have a mint for my buddy?" Brady asked, holding his nose and pointing his thumb at Stan. "Seriously dude—nasty." Stan lowered onto all fours. He swayed his head and gnashed his teeth as he growled. "I wouldn't do it," Brady warned.

Stan didn't heed the warning. His paws scratched at the snow. Screeching out a final roar, Stan lunged at Brady with his claws extended. Brady shook his head and stepped forward, intercepting Stan's attack. Stan's neck connected with Brady's open hand. Stan fell back into the snow. His legs and arms clawed at Brady, but Brady held him down and placed a hearty punch into Stan's gut.

The black bear version of Stan wheezed, struggling for breath. Brady rose from his knees and stood tall. Ha-ida stepped forward. Her forehead nearly touched Brady's chin, and then she stared up at him. "Why do you help him do something that is wrong?"

Stan morphed back and sat hunched in the snow, coughing and panting for breath. "Yeah. Maybe you're all muscle and no brain. What are you thinking?" Stan took a quick step back and flinched when Brady cocked his fist.

"I'm thinking a few things, really. One—I don't like you. Two—if anyone is going to put Ethan in his place, it's going to be me, not some shlub with stupid hair. And three—like you said, we voted. You lost. We're saving Jordan, and I'll put down anyone who tries to stop us. Understand?"

Ethan could hardly believe what he was hearing. He'd imagined a dozen snarky comments Brady could lob at him because he figured Brady would be his fiercest opponent in saving Jordan. He couldn't have been more wrong. Ethan nodded at Brady with appreciation and took a knee in the snow next to Jacob. "Are you ready for this?"

"Are you?" Jacob responded.

Ethan shrugged. "We'll find out."

Jacob sighed as he looked up at Allie. Then he turned toward Llao and reached between the fallen timbers. He placed his fingers on Llao's face; the middle finger on the bridge of Llao's nose, two fingers on his cheekbones, and two fingers on either side of his jaw. "I'm trusting you, Ethan. This is it." Jacob closed his eyes and furrowed his brow with concentration.

"Wait! Stop!" Che-tan let go of Loha's arm, bent down next to Ethan, and whispered. Ethan nodded. "I agree. We must first bind Llao." Che-tan bowed subtly toward Ha-ida. "We cannot risk Llao's escape. We need to control him once he's revived."

"How do you plan to do that?" Allie asked.

"Easy, give him a taste of his own methods," Brady said. Then he explained how Llao and his men had bound and stretched him on the cliffs above Crater Lake.

"We need five lengths of rope, each at least thirty feet long," Ethan said. "And we need to get Llao out of this mess. Go!" Ethan shouted at Ha-ida's warriors. "We need the rope now. Hurry!" The animal warriors stared until Brady's knuckles cracked as he tightened his hands into fists. "Brady, can you do something about Llao's body?"

Brady pushed against the timbers, rearranging the position of the three largest poles trapping Llao's body. He tugged on Llao's arm and pushed against a timber with his foot until he was able to pull Llao from the wreckage. Meanwhile, the animals separated, searching for rope. Three minutes later, five lengths of rope lay at Ethan's feet, and Llao's mangled body rested in the snow.

Grabbing the first rope, Ethan tied it into a noose and placed the loop around Llao's neck. "I need a powerful warrior." A bear, a cougar, and Stan all stepped forward. Ethan looked at Stan. "No chance. I don't trust you." Stan clenched his teeth. He swore at Ethan and then stepped back next to Ha-ida. Ethan looked at the bear and held him by the chin. "Do exactly what I say. Nothing else. Do you understand?" The bear nodded. Ethan tied the other end of the rope around the bear's shoulders like a harness.

"Ethan, what are you doing?" Allie whispered.

"We need some insurance that Llao will help us. If he doesn't, we'll rip him apart." Ethan repeated the process, tying each of Llao's limbs to an animal. Each animal stepped far enough from Llao that the ropes became taut. "In medieval times, traitors had their limbs tied to horses and were pulled to pieces. I think it will get Llao's attention." Ethan nodded to Brady. "Now we're ready."

Brady raised his eyebrows as he looked at Che-tan. "Now we're ready," he repeated.

"Okay, Jacob. Do it." Ethan placed one hand on Jacob's shoulder. He took a deep breath, and his shoulders shook with nervous anticipation as he tried to exhale. Jacob's fingers pressed against Llao's face, and then his arms started to shake.

"Something's wrong, Ethan. This isn't normal," Jacob yelled.

"Keep going. It's working," Ethan shouted back. Excitement bubbled inside him as he watched the chief's face for any sign of life—a twitch, a breath, a snarl. Anything. Jacob's arm vibrated as he kept his fingers pressed against Llao. Then his hand flew back from Llao's face as if he'd grabbed hold of an electric fence. He fell back onto his rear and stared at his hand in front of his face. Ethan glanced with annoyance at Jacob's distraction. But then his eyes widened with excitement as Llao puckered his lips. Ethan watched more closely as each new sign of life gave him hope for Jordan.

Llao's left pinky bent, and then his eyelashes fluttered. His neck turned, and then his deep brown eyes opened wide. His Adam's apple jumped and he licked his lips. "Water."

Ethan grabbed the stone bowl and held it up for Allie. "Water," he repeated as Allie reluctantly blew a stream of water that barely covered the bottom of the artifact. Ethan frowned at her stinginess.

"What? If he needs more, I'll give him more," Allie said, backing away from the chief and Ethan.

The animals with the ropes took a step forward, causing the ropes to tighten. They pulled tight enough that Llao's wrists and ankles rose from the snow.

Ethan leaned in front of Llao's face. "You're alive for one reason," Ethan said. "Do what we command, and you may live. Try anything foolish, and I'll have you drawn, quartered, and then thrown into Crater Lake for fish food. Understand?"

"I understand," Llao said in his broken English. Then he smiled. "You want your sister back."

Ethan nodded. "Will you do it?"

Llao's neck contorted as he tried looking around the group of assembled teens. Then his eyes rested on Loha. Ethan followed Llao's gaze, staring into Loha's milky white eyes. "You ask the impossible. If the girl lives, the gift will return to her."

"Yeah. So?"

"I cannot betray my wife. She possesses the gift, and I will not take it from her."

"We don't care about the stupid gift. We just want Jordan to live," Ethan spat. "Now tell me: will you do it?"

Llao rested the back of his head into the snow, and he closed his eyes. "No. I will not."

Ethan huffed with anger and nodded to the black bear attached to Llao's noose. The bear slowly backed away, tightening the rope around Llao's neck. "Help me, and I'll help you. Save Jordan, and I'll save you. That's the deal. This is *not* a negotiation." Ethan waited a moment for a response and nodded in turn to each of the animals tied to Llao. Each took the cue, stepping away, stretching Llao.

Chief Llao's body lifted off the ground as he choked and screamed in pain. The animals inched forward, tightening each rope.

Che-tan hugged his mother as Loha turned away. Brady's alarm was obvious on his face. He put his arm around Allie while Llao's tortured body stretched beyond natural capacity and his tormented screams filled the air. Jacob remained still, butt in the snow, his head down, his eyes covered.

"Will you save Jordan?" Ethan repeated as the animals continued to inch apart, tightening the ropes on Llao's arms, legs, and neck. "It's a simple question." Ethan paused as he studied Llao's body. "I doubt it's a question you'll be alive to hear again." Ethan bent down and grabbed hold of the rope around Llao's neck. "We could pop your head right off. Well?"

Llao gasped. A deep rasp escaped from his mouth as he tried to speak.

"I can't hear you."

"I . . . will . . . do . . . it." The words sounded like a whistle in the trees.

Ethan looked at Jordan's body lying in the snow, and then he faced Llao. His chest inflated, feeling the flutter of hope in his stomach. Ethan cocked his head to one side as he studied the chief. Then Ethan's eyes narrowed, and a sliver of a grin creased his face. "Cut him loose."

53

BLINDED

E THAN TRIED TO CALM HIMSELF, BUT HIS HANDS SHOOK with nervous anticipation. He blinked rapidly as he watched Brady kneel next to Llao. Brady sliced the ropes that bound Llao's limbs to the animals. "Maybe another time, boys," Brady said to the animal warriors. He wrapped Llao's neck binding around his hand and pulled Llao forward like he was walking a dog on a short leash. "Good boy," Brady said as he stopped beside Jordan's lifeless body. "Sit." Llao sat in the snow beside Jordan. "Roll over."

"Brady!" Ethan shouted. "Knock it off." Ethan sat in the snow and lifted Jordan's head onto his lap. He brushed back her dark, curly hair with one hand and glared into the eyes of his enemy. "Do it."

Llao pulled at his noose, so Brady yanked back. Llao stretched his neck and bent over Jordan. He placed both hands around Jordan's face as he whispered to Ethan. "This will not solve your problems. She may live, but she will still be cursed."

"I can live with that. Now shut up and get to it."

Llao closed his eyes, pressing his fingers firmly into Jordan's skin. Llao cleared his throat and continued to whisper. "You risk much for this girl."

Ethan ignored Llao, gazing into Jordan's pale face, hoping to see any sign of life. His lips rubbed together in eager anticipation.

"I still live. One day, you will fight for me. We will defeat Skell together."

"Shut up and concentrate."

"The strong one is powerful but arrogant. The fire breather has much to learn. You lack courage to make difficult choices, and the little one—the healer—has lost his gift."

Ethan studied Jordan, but her lifeless body remained still. His head shook as he considered Llao's words. Was Llao right? "Shut up!"

"You cannot change that which you are destined to do. Your lot was set when you chose to help me escape from the Prison of the Lost." Llao chuckled. "You will serve me. It is inevitable."

Ethan wrung his hands together as he searched for the courage to dispute Llao. "I don't believe you, but you should believe me. Bring Jordan back *now*, or I'll let my friends rip you to pieces."

"Very well."

Ethan licked his lips, and his heart leaped when Jordan licked hers. Her eyes fluttered, and the color rushed back into her face. Her chest rose and fell with new breath. "Give her more . . . more life . . . more energy . . . give her more everything," Ethan said.

Llao released his hands from Jordan's head and face. "It is done. Your sister lives. Now we will see if you can live with the consequences."

Jordan's eyelids opened, but her eyes beneath were milky white with no pupil or iris to add any color. Jordan looked up at Ethan's face. "Ethan, is that you? Are you there?"

Ethan gasped with excitement as he pulled Jordan into a sitting position. He wrapped his arms around her and hugged her tight. His cheek rested against hers, and then he held her back to get a good look. "Yeah, it's me." He moved his head from side to side, but Jordan's eyes didn't follow him. "I'm here. Can you see me?"

Jordan whimpered as her head moved from side to side,

searching. "I can't see anything, Ethan. Where are you?" Jordan whimpered again. "Ethan, I can't see. Ethan, can you hear me? What's happening to me?"

Ethan's lips quivered as tears flowed down his cheeks. He looked at his friends standing around him. Allie wiped the tears from her face, but Brady stood there with his mouth hanging open. "I'm here, Jordan. I'm holding you. I won't let anything else happen to you. You're safe now."

Llao leaned close to Ethan. "Do not make promises you cannot keep."

Ethan swung his open hand at Llao but missed. "Heal her. Make her see."

Llao shrugged as he smirked. "She has received the gift. Do not forget, you chose this for your sister. Now, what do you have planned for me?" Llao asked.

A hush fell over the entire crowd as Ethan considered the question. Then Ha-ida spoke. "My people will take him. We will imprison him and watch. He will never escape."

Ethan shook his head as he envisioned a prison cell in the shanty at Skell Village. He chuckled nervously, thinking they were more likely to kill him and be done with it. "No way. I'm not giving him to you," he said, glaring at Stan. Ethan thought for another moment. "Jacob, can you make Jordan see? Use the bowl. Help her."

"Ethan, what shall we do with Llao?" Ha-ida asked.

"We will take him," Che-tan offered. "My people are the Guardians of Crater Lake. We will watch over him."

"No!" Ha-ida's army yelled in unison. "Traitors."

"Jacob, can you help Jordan or not?" Ethan asked again.

"I can't. Something's wrong, Ethan. I feel weak . . . empty. I can try the bowl but . . ."

"But what?" Ethan yelled.

"Don't yell at Jacob," Allie hollered. "It's not his fault."

Ethan held his hands to his head and squeezed as if trying to keep it from exploding. The world seemed to swirl around him. The trees bent down to grab him, and the snow began to fall as the setting sun faded behind the trees. Llao smirked, and Jacob stared back at Ethan. The world spun faster. Ethan saw Brady, then Ha-ida, Stan, Che-tan, Ha-ida's people, Llao, Jordan, Allie, and Loha in a dizzying motion as his body began to sway. His legs wobbled, and then his vision went blank, just like he imagined Jordan's had. He fell backward, and his body melted into the soft, white snow as every sound and image that swirled around him muddled together and then faded into nothingness. At last, peace.

- 54 -

LOVE TRIANGLE

ETHAN FELT LIKE HE WAS LYING IN HIS BED AFTER HIS MOM turned on the lights in the morning. The memory of sleep and the pain of bright light shining from the fixture above him felt serene. He longed for the days when he could sit peacefully at home with his parents without the risk of falling off a wooden tower that looked like a pile of pick-up sticks, or the pressure of leading his friends against a mystical and powerful spirit chief and hordes of bloodthirsty warriors. Ethan wanted his life back, and for a moment, it seemed like he would get it. But the light above his bed grew brighter. It pierced through the flesh of his eyelids, blinding him even more than lying in complete darkness with his eyes closed. He held his arm up and covered his eyes, and then the wet cold of the snow seeped through his clothes and pressed against his skin.

"Ethan, wake up. Are you okay?" The voice was garbled but familiar.

The female voice welcomed him back into consciousness, but he didn't want to open his eyes. "Five more minutes, Mom. Can you please turn off the light?"

"Ethan, wake up. You have to see this." Reluctantly, Ethan peeked through a narrow slit in his eyelids as he stared directly at his own arm. He turned his head and recognized Allie kneeling beside him with one hand on his chest. She faced away from

Ethan and held her other hand over her eyes. "It's beautiful."

Ethan peeled his eyes open as he sat up. He held his palm against his brow and squinted in the same direction as his friends. What had started as a pinprick of light far to the east swayed in the sky as if driving along a winding mountain road. With each passing moment, the light grew brighter, and its speed increased. "What is it?" Looking away from the light, Ethan glanced at Ha-ida on his other side. She knelt in the snow with her head lowered. Her army followed her example.

Still shielding his eyes, Ethan looked back to the light that raced in circles above. Then, in one great flash, Ethan lost all vision, and he felt dizzy. His shoulders swayed back and forth, and he perceived only whiteness, more brilliant than a snowy field bathed in sunshine. Ethan's eyes squeezed shut as tears leaked out. He leaned forward, his shoulders continuing to sway and his head bobbing. He tried to hold himself steady but then gave up, allowing himself to fall back on the snow. But he didn't feel the wet cold of the snow on his head. It felt like he hovered above the ground as the explosion of white light consumed him. Then, eventually, it faded.

"Ethan, can you hear me?"

"Jordan?"

"Open your eyes. Look."

"I can't. It's too bright," Ethan responded. The light faded. He felt his warm tears stream down his face and forced his eyes open. His eyes widened as he recognized the face of Skell leaning over him.

Skell smiled, but Ethan averted his eyes as sudden guilt washed over him. He turned his head but then felt a hand on his chin, pulling his gaze back to Skell.

"Why will you not look at me, Ethan?" Skell asked.

Ethan tried to speak, but his voice caught on emotion and cracked. His eyes watered again as he looked at Skell. Rising to his full stature, Skell extended his right hand and helped Ethan stand. "I . . . I . . . think I failed you," Ethan mumbled. He looked around the crowd of gathered teenagers and saw many nodding heads, especially from Ha-ida's camp. But even Jacob seemed to agree with his failure.

"You *think* you failed me?"

Ethan nodded.

"You accomplished the mission I assigned. You retrieved the bowl—ingenious plan. You also saved Jordan from death at the hands of Llao. It is true—you sacrificed much and accepted severe risks." Skell paused. He looked around the group of disgruntled yet humble teens. His mouth flattened, showing neither approval nor condemnation. "Ethan, you do not understand how critical this accomplishment is. Because of your choice, Loha is saved from the curse, and Llao does not reclaim power over the visions. Jordan's gift is now complete."

"Gift?" Ethan shook his head. "I don't understand. You just called it a curse. And Jordan can't see. Can you help her see again?"

Skell chuckled, but Ethan didn't see any humor in his question. "Jordan sees more than you do," Skell said. "Now that she has received full vision, it will be a gift for her. She has gained power and ability that will help to ensure victory over Llao forever."

"But Llao was already dead. We had won," Ha-ida said, still lowered on one knee. She raised her eyes to meet Skell's gaze.

"Perhaps, but it was not his time. The battle will wage in six months' time on the day of the next summer solstice. Nothing can change that. Then, all powers will be bequeathed to their final recipients. Only then will the final battle commence."

Llao laughed from near the back of the group, but Brady yanked back on his leash, shutting him up.

"But I can't heal anymore," Jacob said. "It took everything I had to save Llao. What good am I without my power?"

"You are faithful, determined, and loyal. That is great power." Skell grinned at Jacob, "And . . . don't be so sure. Stay strong, and you may have a measure of power when it is most critical. Prepare yourself."

Llao chuckled again from the back of the group. "Loyalty will not be enough to save you." He shook his head defiantly. Brady pulled back on the leash, but Llao continued. "This is why you will fail. You are weak!" he screamed.

With an irritated expression on his face, Skell faced Llao, held up his thumb and forefinger, and then zipped it in front of Llao's mouth. Llao's lips melted together, sealing his mouth shut with smooth flesh.

"I've got to get me some of that-there power," Brady said, ending with a "Woo-hoo! Nice!"

Allie rolled her eyes. "Yeah, I can think of a few teachers I'd like to try it on."

Skell's white hair framed his young face. "You see, I could do with Llao anything I please. But that would not be a fair fight. It is not my way. That is not *our* way. Do you understand?" Ethan shook his head to indicate that he did, but he didn't really. "Ethan, your leadership has not been perfect. You have made mistakes."

Ethan heard a grumble of affirmation from the crowd. He lowered his head in shame. "What should I do?"

"Forget the mistakes of the past. Sometimes, intentions are good, but the actions are bad. Sometimes, the intentions are selfish even though things work out in the end. Be pure in your motives and selfless in your leadership. Focus on the needs of many, not on your own."

Ethan nodded. "And what do we do with him?" Ethan asked, pointing to Llao.

"I will imprison him until the time of battle. Then he will be released to unleash his fury."

Skell stepped over to Llao and stared him in the eyes. "If you have a problem with that, speak now." Llao shook his head frantically, and his face contorted. But there was no sound from his sealed lips. Skell grinned. "I thought not."

Then, moving to Che-tan and Loha, Skell bowed gently to Che-tan and faced the old woman. He leaned close to her sagging cheeks and kissed her forehead. Ethan's eyebrows rose, surprised by the tenderness of Skell to the old woman. Then Skell leaned closer and kissed Loha on the lips. Ethan recoiled, and he looked at Allie and Brady. Their eyes were as wide as Ethan's.

"Dude, she's like eight thousand years old," Brady moaned. "Nasty." Ha-ida rose from her knee and squeezed in next to Brady and Allie as she whispered.

"Loha was Skell's first love—his only love."

Brady's chin quivered, and it looked like he might hurl as Skell's kiss on Loha's lips lingered.

"It's sweet," Allie muttered, but she looked constipated. She swallowed hard as she puckered her lips and scrunched her nose. Ethan cleared his throat, turning to Allie. "Well, kind of," Allie corrected.

Ethan's jaw dropped as the old woman began to transform. Her saggy skin turned to a rich brown and tightened against her high cheekbones as her eyes became as rich chocolate. Her white hair blackened as centuries of weather, worry, and pain faded from her face. Loha's posture straightened, and she gained at least four inches in stature and lost fifty pounds of excess weight. Her lips filled out, and her clothes hung from her slimmed figure like burlap sacks.

Ethan had seen a similar transformation when Llao changed into his youthful form in the caverns below Crater Lake. But still, the sight of Loha's makeover took his breath away. The intensity of her beauty rivaled the first moment he stared into the crystal waters of Crater Lake. Skell's lips remained plastered to Loha's until the transformation was complete. Then Skell backed away. His white teeth shone through his broad smile, and Loha returned the gesture. Then they embraced in a firm and long hug while Che-tan squirmed uncomfortably nearby.

Ethan sighed at the tenderness of the reunion as the look of disgust and disapproval vanished from his face. "Absolutely amazing."

THE BEGINNING
OF THE END

Ethan patted Skell on the back, pleased by the reunion of lost love. Skell released Loha from his embrace. Both had broad smiles still lighting their faces. Skell gazed around the crowd at the grinning teens and then reached down to grab Loha's hand. The only person not smiling was Che-tan. He looked like he wanted to but wasn't sure how he should react. Of course, Llao didn't smile either, but that's because he didn't have any lips.

Ha-ida and the other Native American teens gathered closer to their mystical leader, all reaching out for a congratulatory pat or hug from the man they'd only heard of in stories and legends. Then a shriek of pain filled the air as a boy who barely looked old enough to be called a teen fell to the ground. Blood gushed from his chest.

Llao pushed against the gathering throng of teens and raised the black obsidian blade over his head as he swiped at more of the youth who swarmed nearby. Brady patted his pocket to confirm the obvious. The dagger was gone. Brady had kept his enemy close. Too close.

With one slice, Llao cut the short leash that tethered his neck to Brady, and then he stabbed the dagger at Brady's back. Brady screamed in pain as the dagger sank deep into his left shoulder. Llao pushed Brady into Ethan, who fell against Skell.

Llao swiped again through the air with the dagger, and Brady grabbed his bleeding shoulder. He frowned. Then he growled as he regained his balance and lunged toward Llao.

Stepping to the side, Llao avoided Brady's grasp. Then he spun and reached around Loha's neck. He pulled her back, tight against his body, and raised the dagger to her throat. The flesh in front of Llao's mouth wiggled, and then he motioned with his fingers across the place where his lips should be. The signal was clear, and Skell followed his command, raising his hand to unzip Llao's mouth. Lips reappeared on Llao's face. He stretched them from side to side, up and down, as he renewed his grip on Loha.

Skell's jaw tightened. "Let her go." His fingers straightened as if they were ready to claw Llao's face to shreds.

"You speak of a fair fight, but imprisoning me until the battle begins is not just. If you let me go to prepare myself, I will spare Loha, and you will have a chance to reclaim her."

"Reclaim her?" Ethan asked.

Llao laughed and coughed, clearing his throat. He stretched his neck and made a face, rubbing his hand beneath his long hair. "I'm taking her with me."

Skell stepped forward, reaching for Loha, but stopped when Llao pressed the dagger's blade against her neck. Even before contact appeared to be made, a thin line of blood formed below Loha's jawbone where the blade was positioned. "Don't do this again, Llao. Please don't take her again." Llao laughed, and Skell backed away with his hands raised.

"Provide me the power to convey the two of us away. And do not follow, or suffer the consequence."

Skell hesitated as he sucked on his lower lip.

"*Now!*"

Skell raised his hand, muttered a short phrase, and dropped his hand in defeat. Llao held tightly to Loha, giving an evil grin. Llao nodded to Ethan, glared at Brady and Allie, blew a kiss to Ha-ida and her army, and then chuckled as he looked at Jacob.

"Your weakness is my greatest strength." He turned toward Skell and winked. "I will see all of you in six months."

***

Just as the feud began seventy-eight hundred years ago, before the mighty battle that transformed Mount Mazama into Crater Lake, Llao stole Loha from her true love and challenged Skell to stop him. Blackness gathered around Llao, pressing against him until Llao and Loha vanished into a mist of darkness. When the darkness dispersed, Llao and Loha were gone.

The corner of Skell's mouth twitched, and then he screamed. The ground shook in recognition of Llao's pain. Snow fell from the evergreen branches, and brisk wind encircled the group. Gray clouds hid the setting sun as the snowy field fell into dusk.

The group stood in silence. Ethan didn't know what he should say. He raised one hand toward Skell's shoulder, but the chief swatted it away with a wave of his hand. Ethan started to speak but stopped when Skell's eyes darkened and his lips pursed together in warning.

Skell threw his hands to his side, his eyes narrowed, and focused on Ethan. "You have six months. This *will* end once and for all. Prepare well."

A flash of brilliant light blinded Ethan. His eyes watered as he squeezed them shut. When he opened them again, he could see his friends rubbing away the brilliance. Ha-ida and Che-tan glared at him with unified hatred he didn't know was possible, but he understood. Both had lost what they valued most; Ha-ida had lost the opportunity to defeat Llao, and Che-tan had lost his mother. Instead of wanting to destroy each other, they looked ready to take Ethan down instead. Ethan's solemn face surveyed the anxious crowd, and his ears memorized the jeers being flung at him. Some of the sharp words stung, especially those from Allie, Ha-ida, and Che-tan, but most of the blame simply fell to the ground, unable to hurt him.

Ethan stood tall, despite the growing weight of responsibility he felt on his shoulders—the responsibility of saving Loha and serving Skell with honor. But even more daunting was the task of preparing his friends for battle. In one day, he had managed to alienate almost every ally he had. Trust had been broken, and anger had been kindled. Ethan had six months to regain their confidence and rally an army. Ethan firmly set his jaw. "Let's get to work."

ABOUT THE AUTHOR

STEVE GREW UP AND GRADUATED FROM HIGH SCHOOL IN Salem, Oregon. He enjoyed hiking and camping with the scouts in the Oregon mountains, but his least favorite campout was a snow camp on Mt. Hood that is now referred to as "Camp Hypothermia." Instead of building a snow cave like he was taught, Steve and his friends dug a wide ditch and placed their sleeping bags inside, figuring the ditch would protect them from the wind. It did. But it didn't protect him from the rain. His down sleeping bag became a freezing pile of mush, and by 9:00 p.m., he was warming his freezing body next to a small camp stove.

"That camp was the longest night of my life," Steve remembers. When exhaustion set in, Steve gave up the heat of the stove and found a small corner in his Scoutmaster's snow cave where he huddled on the ice in a puddle of water with no blankets or sleeping bag. The Scoutmaster treated Steve for hypothermia, and the entire camp ended early the next morning when the Scouts cross-country skied out of camp and back to warmth.

Steve now lives on a small farm with his wife and four children, chickens, a dog, cats, and a duck. Steve has officially retired from snow camping.